DYING OF THE LIGHT

DYING OF THE LIGHT

Gillian Galbraith

Polygon

This edition published in 2017 by Polygon
an imprint of
Birlinn Limited
West Newington House
10 Newington Road
Edinburgh
EH9 1QS

www.polygonbooks.co.uk

1

ISBN-13: 978 1 84697 401 4

British Library Cataloguing-in-Publication Data
A catalogue record for this book is available from the British
Library.

Set in Italian Garamond BT at Mercat Press

Printed and bound in Great Britain by
Clays Ltd, St Ives plc

ACKNOWLEDGEMENTS

Maureen Addison
Colin Browning
Douglas Edington
Lesmoir Edington
Robert Galbraith
Daisy Galbraith
Diana Griffiths
Tom Johnstone
Johanna Johnston
Jinty Kerr
Dr Uist MacDonald
Dr Elizabeth Lim
Roger Orr
Aidan O'Neill
Dr Garth Utter

Any errors in the text are my own.

DEDICATION

To my sister Diana, with all my love.

I

Annie Wright licked her parched lower lip. At the same time, she touched the packet of cigarettes in her pocket, stroking it slowly, as if to draw the nicotine into her system through her fingertips. A bead of sweat began to trickle down her spine until, deliberately leaning back against her chair, she allowed the material of her blouse to absorb it, bringing relief from its tickling descent. Looking at her shoes she panicked, realising she had made a mistake. They were too red, too shiny and the heels far too high. In a word, cheap. And what had possessed her to combine them with black tights and a skirt that did not even reach the knee? Sweet Jesus! She rose quickly, determined to leave, but before she had taken a step the door opened and a tall fellow, his black gown billowing in the draught, crooked his index finger at her, beckoning her to follow. As if in a trance, she did so.

Pushing the menu card to the side of his notebook in disgust, the Lord Ordinary waited patiently for the witness to arrive and the trial to resume. In the expectant silence a whispered conversation between two jurors became audible to him. Under all that horsehair, was his lordship bald? Casually, as if still absorbed in the business of choosing his lunch from the card, he tipped his wig to one side, revealing copious grey ringlets. Honour had been satisfied.

The sound of Annie Wright's shoes as she clicked across the parquet to the stand transfixed everyone, and all eyes were on her as she teetered up the few steps leading to it. From her elevated vantage point she surveyed the courtroom and then, surreptitiously, stole a glance at the judge. His headgear appeared to be distinctly squint, its front edge at a diagonal rather than parallel to his eyebrows. As she turned to look at the faces of the jurors, an elderly man with food stains on his jacket gave her the slightest nod, but the others, heads bent as if scrutinising something on the floor, pretended not to have noticed her entry.

Suddenly, she became aware of Lord Culcreuch's deep voice and forced herself to concentrate, raising her right hand as requested and repeating the words intoned before her. As she was mouthing them, their meaning sank in. The truth, the whole truth and nothing but the truth. A noble enough sounding phrase, but one uttered only by fools and lawyers. In her experience, the whole truth rarely went down well, and even careful approximations of it cast her as less than human, someone unworthy of respect or sympathy. Scarcely a woman at all.

The first few questions asked by the Advocate-Depute, the prosecution counsel, were easy to answer, and she could hear her own voice becoming louder, more assured, as her confidence began to grow. And as the man continued to probe, turning now to the stuff of her nightmares, the chaotic mass of her recollection began to take on some kind of understandable shape. A proper narrative formed from the shards of memory that had been whirling around her brain for the past few months.

Yes, it had been dark, and yes, rain had been falling heavily. In fact, it had been bucketing down on Seafield

Road as she returned from the corner shop with the night's tea, heading home, soaked to the skin and keen to get out of her wet things. Tam's appearance outside the pub on the Portobello Roundabout had been welcome, he had shared his umbrella with her and his suggestion that they take shelter in his flat on Kings Road until the worst of the downpour was over had seemed a good one. So she had happily chummed him along as he wove his way down the street, joining in his beery rendition of 'Flower Of Scotland'. The wine he had offered her had been welcome too until he had edged up the settee, jamming himself against her and putting his arm around her shoulder, hand dangling uninvited over her left breast. Tam was Thomas McNiece, the accused. The man sitting between the two officers.

The Advocate-Depute continued speaking, questioning her, and she managed to respond, but the description that she heard herself giving seemed to be of someone else's experience, someone else's ordeal. It concerned a woman who had been raped by a man she knew and considered a friend, her bruised body then hustled down the tenement stairs before being bundled out, like a bag of litter, onto the drenched street. A woman who had, somehow, got herself home, only to collapse outside her own front door.

As she spoke she glanced again at the jury box, inadvertently catching the eye of a well-dressed older woman, who was dabbing her eyes discreetly with a little white hankie. Annie Wright had not expected to evoke sympathy in anyone, and the sight of the lady's tears surprised and heartened her. Maybe these people would understand after all. Maybe her own fears would be proved groundless, and the police sergeant's prediction come true.

While she was distracted, gathering her thoughts, the prosecutor cleared his throat, keen to regain her attention, and start the 'new chapter' he had just promised the jury. And she knew exactly what it would be about, and prayed silently that it would be over quickly.

'Now, Ms Wright, it may be put to you by Mr McNiece's Advocate, that on the night in question you were working as, er... a sex worker... eh... a prostitute. What would you say to that?'

'Eh... nah, I wisnae. I wis havin' a nicht in... at hame, ken. I wisnae workin' that nicht, I was spendin' it hame wi' ma lassie.'

'But,' the Advocate-Depute interjected, 'you are a... sex worker? A prostitute?'

'Aye.'

'And you have told us already, I think, that you did not consent to having sex with Mr McNiece?'

'Aye. It wisnae a job. He jist jump't me.'

'Did Thomas McNiece know what your job was, what you worked as?'

'Aye. Tam kent.'

'And on that night, did any money change hands?'

'Fer Christ's sake!' she almost shouted, her voice tinged with despair, 'I wisnae oan the job, ok? I jist telt ye. Tam jump't me. He wis supposed tae be ma friend... ah, wis beggin' him tae stop!'

She looked hard at the jury, defiantly, daring them to disbelieve her. But every face was turned downwards, studying, once more, the floor below their feet. No-one wanted to meet her eye.

Sylvia Longman QC, the Defence Counsel, stood up, hitched her gown onto her shoulders, and strode purposefully towards the witness box. She knew exactly how the moves should go in this particular stage of the game, and had anticipated the Crown's attempt to lessen the impact of the disclosure of the woman's profession. They had raised the matter themselves to rob it of the shock value it might otherwise have had, in her skilful hands. An expected ploy, and one that would not succeed if she had anything to do with it. Conscious of the expectant hush in the courtroom, she began her performance by looking Annie Wright boldly in the face.

'Ms Wright, would you be interested to know that the meteorological report for the night of Friday the fifth of October indicates only the presence of "light drizzle" in the Edinburgh area?'

The witness looked momentarily shaken, but managed to answer.

'Eh? Well, a' I can say wis that oan Seafield Road it wis pourin' doon. Cats n' dogs.'

'Indeed?' – a theatrical pause to let the doubt sink in – 'and I think you have been a prostitute for about ten years or so. Is that correct?'

'Aha.'

'Thomas McNiece would know, of course, that you were a prostitute?'

'Aha. I said he kent.'

'And you also said that the two of you were friends?'

'I thocht so. Aha.'

'In fact, so friendly that I understand that you and he had a drink together before you went for your shopping?'

'Aha.'

'And the night of fifth of October you willingly accompanied…'

'Aye! Accompanied!' Annie Wright cut in, only to be interrupted in her turn by the languid tones of the lawyer.

'If I might finish? You willingly accompanied Mr McNiece up the stairs to his flat?'

'Aha, I said I done that, but I didnae expect him tae attack us!'

'So. You both had a drink together. Then he invited you up to this flat, knowing that you were a prostitute, and you willingly accompanied him there?'

'Aye.'

'Mr McNiece will tell the Court that you, his friend, agreed to have sex with him.'

'I niver done.'

'And that you willingly did have sex with him?'

'How come then I got they twa keekers tryin' to fight him oaf?' Annie Wright interjected angrily.

'I was coming to that, to your "injuries",' the QC replied smoothly, brushing imaginary dirt off her fall. 'Mr McNiece will maintain that after the sexual intercourse had finished you demanded money from him. He declined to pay you, no question of payment ever having been discussed between you beforehand, and you physically attacked him. In the course of defending himself he lashed out, accidentally hitting you on the face.'

'Rubbish! That's rubbish!' The witness shook her head and then said, plaintively, 'Miss, if it wisnae rape then why d'ye think I'm here, eh? Why'd I go along wi' the polis an' all?'

Sylvia Longman smiled. Things were working out better than she could have hoped. 'Mr McNiece's evidence on this matter', she said, 'will be that these proceedings, or at least your part in them, arise as a result of your desire for revenge. Revenge for the "freebie", I think it's called. What would you say to that?'

'Me?' the witness sighed, recognising defeat. She

tugged nervously on a chain around her neck, pressing a small, gold crucifix between the tips of her fingers. 'Me? I'd say nothin' to it. Nothin' at a'. No point. Yous hae got it a' worked oot.'

Only the well-dressed matron noticed the smirk that flickered momentarily across Thomas McNiece's features. But the Judge immediately stopped his note-taking and replaced the cap on his fountain pen.

'Ms Wright,' he began in his sonorous baritone, 'I need to be absolutely clear about this. Are you accepting Counsel's suggestion that you complained about Mr McNiece raping you in order to get revenge on Mr McNiece?'

'Naw, yer Honour. I wisnae the wan who reported it oanyway. It wis ma daughter, Diane. She got the ambulance an' the polis came at the same time.'

Lord Culcreuch nodded his head. 'So your position remains that you never consented to sexual intercourse with the man?'

'Aha.'

'And that no question of payment by him ever arose?'

'Aha.'

'And your explanation for your injuries is what, exactly?'

'Like I said. He belted me when I wis tryin' to get him oaf o' me. He slapped me, ken, richt across ma face.'

The older lady, Mrs Bartholomew, listened intently to the Judge's charge to the jury. Only with such guidance would she be able to discharge her duty properly. Conscientiously. The onus, or burden of proof, it had been explained, was on the Prosecution to establish beyond reasonable doubt, that the accused had engaged in sexual intercourse with the witness and without her consent. And after three whole days of listening, she thought, three utterly exhausting days, they had better get it right. Of course, it was far too late now. She had already missed her own 'surprise' birthday party, not to mention the promised theatre matinee. So, justice had better be damn well done.

Out of the corner of her eye, she caught sight of her closest neighbour doodling on a notepad. Some kind of motorbike or push-bike or other wheeled thing. Well, really! The lad looked too young, too immature, to be on jury service, fulfilling an important civic duty, and now appeared to be wilfully deaf to the guidance issuing from on high. Before she realised what she was doing, she surprised herself by releasing a loud 'Tut, tut,' only to be met with an amused grin and the closing of the pad.

Neither the dry address delivered by the Prosecutor nor the emotional appeal made by the female QC clarified anything for Mrs Bartholomew. And no wonder, she thought. She had, after all, heard all the evidence for herself, already formed her own impressions of the witnesses and knew exactly whom she believed. And, as importantly, whom she did not. But, of course, one could not be sure. How could one be unless one had been in the very room, at the very time, with the two individuals concerned? Had she been in the victim's unhappy predicament she would have tried to fight off the Neanderthal and sustained bruising, abrasions and so on at his hands. A creature, she noticed, now so relaxed, that he appeared to be dozing during his own trial.

On the other hand, and there always was another hand, Mrs Wright was a self-confessed streetwalker. She would not be too choosy, and perhaps there had indeed been a misunderstanding. The accused's version of events, it had to be accepted, was perfectly plausible and could account for everything, including the woman's injuries.

But, she kept returning to it, it was Annie Wright whom she had believed. The prostitute's fear, in the witness box, had been positively contagious. Watching her twisting and turning her poor, blotched hands, she herself had become apprehensive, on edge, afraid in fact. And nothing in the woman's manner had suggested vengeance. It spoke far more eloquently of an unwillingness to participate in the proceedings, a clear reluctance to give evidence. In addition, the policewoman's testimony about the victim's shocked and distressed state immediately after the assault had seemed completely convincing. But again, that could be equally well explained away by the fight that McNiece spoke about. I'd be shocked if I'd been slapped in the face, however it happened, she thought. It was useless. She was going round and round in circles.

The discussion in the jury room was brief, hastened by the unspoken desire on everyone's part to avoid, if at all possible, yet another unpalatable lunch courtesy of the Court Services. Yesterday's macaroni sludge was still vivid in their memories. In any event, most of the jurors considered the case to be unprovable, as it amounted to no more than one person's word against another's.

However, to Mrs Bartholemew's surprise, the scribbler boy argued passionately that the prostitute's evidence should be believed, and tried to convince the others to accept, as he had, her account of her ordeal. In the face of increasingly voluble resistance from the other jurors, he pointed out her ill-concealed reluctance to play any part in the trial. She must have known, he said, that a working girl's version of events would be viewed with scepticism. She appeared intelligent. For her, this would be a poor way of getting revenge. In fact, he said, she had spoken out not in order to get even, but to put a rapist behind bars.

'No,' the man with the food-stained jacket observed laconically, 'she just miscalculated. Plenty of females better than her have done just the same, son.'

At last the longed for Silk Cut. Annie Wright leant against the statue of David Hume, a traffic cone sitting incongruously on his sculpted head and banging against it with each gust of wind. As she slowly inhaled, she felt calmer, almost as if she had, in some intangible way, regained control of her life. Of tomorrow, at least. Well, she thought, I've done what they wanted. Done my sodding duty, for all the good it has done me.

She turned her head towards the courtroom to avoid the glare of headlights dazzling her, as a few homebound commuters processed down the Royal Mile. Suddenly she shivered, her teeth starting to chatter, her body chilled to the bone in the icy air. Hunching her shoulders, she pulled up the collar of her thin coat with her free hand as a noisy rabble, all high fives and raucous laughter, emerged from the High Court, jostling themselves exuberantly onto the pavement. A tin of lager was held aloft, followed by a chorus of cheers and the raising of exultant, clenched fists. One of the stragglers on the margins of the group accidentally backed into her.

'Sorry, hen', he said almost to himself, before, looking at her a second time, he realised he knew her and let out a wild whoop.

'Well, I niver, it's wee Annie hersel'. Hey, Tam the Bam!', he screamed, 'it's her – ken, yer wham bam ma'am!'

From the centre of the excited mob Thomas McNiece elbowed his way towards her, an uneasy grin on his glistening face, and as he did so his followers grew quiet, silent, like hyenas watching for the kill. Just as he reached her, a tall, dark-haired policewoman approached, and the men immediately began to disperse, some shifting themselves towards St Giles and Parliament Square, others heading northwards towards the Castle.

'I'm sorry we never secured a conviction, Annie,' the policewoman said, coming up to the woman, her exhaled breath like white smoke in the wintry air.

'Yeh, right,' Annie Wright replied. 'I stood up and wis counted, eh? So he'd niver be able tae rape anybody again.' She laughed loudly. 'An' he's oot, free! Oh, an' wan ither thing, sergeant, he'll want tae git me fer that an' a', he says as much already. So I'd better watch oot fer masel', eh?'

Detective Sergeant Alice Rice was painfully aware that no words of hers, no truthful words at least, would be adequate. She had no comfort to offer. They both knew that justice had not been done and that a guilty man now walked free. But she could not bring herself to apologise for persuading the woman to complain. It would be altogether too hypocritical, because she would do the same again, tomorrow and the next day. And the day after that, too.

'We'll keep an eye out as well,' she answered, unpleasantly conscious of the hollowness of her reassurance. McNiece had, after all, just routed them all. Made fools of them all.

11

A double-decker drew up at the stop on the North Bridge and the woman clambered in, glad to be back in the warmth and returning to some form of normality. Taking a seat at the back she pressed her face hard against the window pane, conscious of every vibration on her cheekbone as the vehicle juddered over the potholed road, finally squealing to a halt at the Balmoral, ready to cross Waterloo Place. Ignoring an amber light it trundled onwards, stopping and restarting endlessly in the rush-hour traffic, crawling slowly past the brutal architecture marring the west side of Leith Street as if the sight of it was something to savour. Pedestrians streamed endlessly along the pavements, catching the January sales, most weighed down by bulging carrier bags and all wrapped up against the biting cold.

At the first stop at the top of Leith Walk an old man, cap in hand, maundered unsteadily up the central aisle towards her, lurching onto her bench as the bus continued its erratic progress towards Portobello and her destination. Another abrupt halt and he fell against her shoulder, apologising the instant contact was made and righting himself to the best of his ability. And then, hesitantly, he began to talk to her, waiting for a response, nudging her into the usual, inconsequential, companionable banter that can help a journey pass. A daughter in Australia, a doctor no less, he boasted; and a son, fortunately close by in Port Seton. He'd spent Hogmanay there, the little of it he could remember anyway. And once he too had been a bus driver, doing the Haddington run.

The man seemed so kind, fatherly almost, that Annie Wright would have liked to have told him the truth about her day, unburden herself of its painful reality, and in the telling somehow reduce its importance. But she could not bear to watch him recoil. To smash his innocent illusions. After all, she was not, as he probably imagined, just another middle-aged body returning from a day's shopping in the town.

No harm, though, in escaping into make-believe. So, enjoying the sound of his cracked voice and ready laughter, she created a job for herself working as a school cleaner up South Clerk Street, and found that it was easy. She had been one, once, a lifetime ago. Together they exchanged anecdotes about the thoughtlessness of children and the litter trailed by them wherever they went. By the time the bus drew into Baltic Street little flakes of snow were dancing in the beams of its headlights, blown this way and that by the movement of passing vehicles. A few minutes later, smiling fondly, Annie stood up to get off and the old fellow squeezed her hand as she eased herself past his legs.

'Tak' care o' yersel', dearie,' he said, giving her a wink.

The chill air on Seafield Road reminded Annie Wright where she was, and, more importantly, who and what she was. She started to walk, buffeted by blasts of a cutting wind, towards Pipe Street and home. A little figure, head hooded and bowed, stood leaning against the lamppost, bathed in a circle of golden light. Drawing parallel the woman stretched out her hand and felt it grasped by a cold, wet mitt.

'Guess whit, mum?' the high-pitched voice enquired.

'Whit?'

'I've got us a chinky an' it's in the oven, in the hoose!'

'Diane,' the woman replied wearily, 'ye're a star. Ma ain wee star.'

13

He pressed the flat surface of his knife onto the first yolk, noting as he did so that the two eggs had been perfectly fried. An opaque film covered both their yellow suns, and there were no signs of any wobble or slime on the white of either. Slicing the streaky tail off his first rasher of bacon he dipped it in the yolk, then speared a sliver of buttered toast and ate the tasty combination. Perfection. Nothing could beat a good high tea in front of the television on a cold winter's evening. A loud roar drew his attention back to the screen and he watched entranced as Hartson dribbled the ball towards the Hibs goal, nutmegged the final defender and then flicked it effortlessly into the net past the helpless keeper. A goal! He looked at his watch. Only 8.30 and still another twenty minutes of the second half to go. Life was sweet indeed.

Intent on the game, he did not hear the phone ringing until his wife handed the receiver to him, whispering conspiratorially, 'It's Bill'. At the sound of the man's name his heart sank. He knew only too well what the call would mean.

'Where are they?' David Chalmers asked dully.

'Along by the bridge at Ma Aitken's.'

'How many?'

'Four or five.'

'OK. I'll meet you at your gate in ten minutes.'

Thinking only of his wife and twin daughters, he bolted the remainder of his fry-up, no longer savouring the ritual of putting the pieces together, and gulped down his mug of tea. No time for the scones and honey. He'd have them later, when he got back. In the hallway, he picked up his olive green anorak and set off at a brisk pace towards Claremont Park and 'Jordan'.

The night air felt sharp, a strong breeze blowing off the sea from the east, carrying salt in the air and waking him up. In his luminous yellow jacket his neighbour, Bill Keane, was visible a hundred yards away, and David Chalmers waved at him as he approached.

'Forgotten your vest?' Keane asked.

Looking down quickly, Chalmers patted the side of his cheek, cross with himself for being so inefficient. He knew the value of their day-glo wear, distinguishing them from anyone else on the street, drawing attention to any fracas that might ensue and warning all and sundry of their presence. In an attempt to soothe his companion, Keane, his hat nearly wrenched off by the rising wind, lifted his placard from the pavement and handed it to the other man. Chalmers took it eagerly, reading the message emblazoned on it in jet black capitals. 'YOU CAN'T GET NO SATISFACTION IN LEITH'.

'Right enough' he muttered.

———

Together, the pair continued past the Links and headed towards Seafield Place, a few pedestrians eyeing them warily as they marched on, the placard held high, its message lit up by each passing car. Halfway down the street their prey came into view, a woman lurking in the deep shadows cast by the pedestrian bridge, facing seaward and watching the road as if expecting company. The sound of their footsteps on the pavement was drowned by the engine of a huge articulated lorry, its accelerator revving in readiness for the lights to change and filling the air with thick fumes. Keane's tap on the woman's shoulder had her whirling round, the momentary panic on her face quickly replaced by an exasperated sneer.

'Yous again,' she hissed, her hostility undisguised.

'Aye, lassie, us again,' Keane replied calmly. 'So, on your way, eh? Back to where you came from.'

The girl, her face uncomfortably close to the men, unexpectedly flicked the peak of her baseball cap up and shouted in their faces, 'Lena! You up at Boothacre?'

In the distance, from the direction of the cottages, a faint female voice replied, 'Aye. Is it they jokers again?'

'Aha. I'm oaf the now. See you up at Elbe, eh?'

'OK. Over 'n' oot, Belle.'

'Roger,' Belle answered, before, laughing and looking scornfully at the two men, she taunted them. 'Nae rogering for yous though, eh? No the nicht, anyway.'

So saying, she sauntered, hips swaying provocatively, toward Salamander Street and the darkness. In response to a snatch of 'Greensleeves', Keane fumbled in his trouser pocket and pulled out his mobile, his wallet coming with it and falling onto the wet pavement. An urgent voice said, 'Bill, get yourself over here and bring anyone you've got with you. It's the van. They're in Carron Place again, the cheeky bisoms!'

Accidentally dropping the phone from his cold fingers, Keane swore in his frustration and David Chalmers immediately discarded his placard and bent down to pick up his friend's possessions from the ground. Acknowledging his help with a curt nod, Bill finally replied, 'I'll see you there, Raymond. David's going to check the cemetery first. One of them's hanging about the place as usual.'

Lena was neither difficult to find nor troublesome to dislodge. She had found only a token hiding place a few yards up Boothacre Lane. When she saw the man approaching her she did not look knowingly at him, an illicit bargain sealed, but instead raised both hands above her head theatrically to signal her surrender, and then sashayed past the Lodge House, heading back towards Mother Aitken's pub. When, finally, she disappeared past the warehouse corner, David Chalmers began his walk westward towards Carron Place.

By the junction with Claremont he noticed a woman, short-haired and in a calf length skirt, waiting between the tall gateposts of Villa Deodati. As he came closer, she stayed exactly where she was, the defiant hussy, until he was only a few yards distant.

He was familiar with the girls' new techniques – dressing down in an attempt to escape detection. Well, he thought, it won't work with me. I'm not so easily fooled. Anyway, it's the eyes that are the giveaway, the windows of the soul. That adamantine hardness, that inhuman look, cannot easily be disguised.

While he was still openly looking her up and down, a car arrived which, unknown to him, had been shadowing him for the past few minutes. It stopped beside them and a uniformed officer in the car slowly rolled down his window.

'On the prowl, eh, sir? That's illegal now, the new Act... the Prostitutes Act. But maybe that's not enough to put you off? One of the hardliners, I daresay. We'll need to name and shame you, eh?'

David Chalmers heard himself bluster, a string of high-pitched vowels emanating from his mouth, outrage robbing him of the power of coherent speech. Then he remembered that he was not wearing his luminous jacket, and that he had left his placard at the Boothacre Cottages. Well, at least the man was doing his duty, and this certainly was the high visibility enforcement that they had all been promised. While he was still babbling excuses, to his surprise, the woman began to speak. Usually, in his experience, the hussies remained silent, sullen, aware of the need to say nothing in the face of the enemy.

'I'm not exactly sure what you're implying, Constable, but, perhaps I should make my position clear. My name is Sandra Pollock, Sister Sandra usually, and I'm a nun. A Sacred Heart sister if you're any the wiser. I'm based at the convent in Eskbank, but I was seeing a friend. I'm waiting for a lift from Sister Rowena, but she's late, maybe lost for all I know.'

A guffaw could be heard from the passenger side of the car as the driver apologised profusely, his face puce with embarrassment. And as they drew away from the kerb, loud giggles could still be heard from the marked panda car. Flustered and still unable to speak, David Chalmers doffed his cap to the nun, who acknowledged him with the slightest nod. Both felt uncomfortably exposed, left unchaperoned together, some bizarre bond temporarily created between them because of the policeman's mistake. Each felt the need to say something, but neither felt up to the task.

Carron Place is a cul-de-sac, a dead-end leading from Salamander Street to nowhere. The uneven tarmac on its road is flanked by cheap industrial units, each with its own car park, and commercial yards protected by high mesh fencing. During working hours it is a vibrant area, lorries transporting goods to and fro, workmen shouting to each other, and white-collared executives managing things, ensuring that business continues until 5 p.m. But once closing time arrives and the workers have gone, it becomes a desolate, soulless place, a street no longer serving any purpose.

The SPEAR van was parked on a dogleg, facing the docks, ready to move whenever the need arose. Around it were clustered a group of women, some leaning against it smoking, some clutching polystyrene cups, sipping hot tea and chattering to each other. The driver of the van, a plump woman with heavy curtains of hair falling on either side of her face, was handing out leaflets to the working girls. Each bore the photo of a man, together with a short warning of his violent tendencies and a description of the car normally used by him. Annie Wright stood in the open back of the transit clutching a packet of new syringe needles and a plate piled high with chocolate fingers.

'Biscuits, ladies?' she said in a parody of a posh voice.

From her lookout point she was the first in the group to notice the crew of men marching towards the vehicle, and she let out a low whistle of warning. Immediately, the women's chatter ceased and the relaxed, even convivial, atmosphere became tense. As the men approached, Annie, still clutching the plate of biscuits, sloped away, disappearing into the shadows cast by a large warehouse before making a dash for Salamander Street and a safe place from which to make a telephone call. The plump woman came forward with a pained expression to meet the newcomers, halting their progress before they came too near the women who were now bunched together, immobile.

'We are allowed to be here, you know,' she began. 'We have permission. All we are doing, you will appreciate,

19

is trying to protect the sex-workers against blood-borne viruses and…'

Her practised spiel was interrupted by an angry-looking man, wagging his finger as he spoke.

'All you are doing, madam, is attracting these "sex-workers" as you term them, whores to everyone else, to our area. To our homes. With their…', he stopped briefly, his own fury having got the better of him. '…HIV needles, and their used condoms.'

'Aye,' chorused another man, 'their used condoms!'

'And we,' the first speaker continued, 'have had enough.'

So saying he began to bang his fists rhythmically on the side of the van. One by one the other men joined him, until the drumming noise from its metal sides was ear-splitting, loud enough to wake the dead.

———

Detective Sergeant Alice Rice was surprised to get a call from Annie Wright on her mobile, until she remembered that she had, a couple of months earlier, given the woman her number. Listening to her breathless tones, she soon realised that the incident would be no more, in all probability, than a breach of the peace, something easily dealt with by whatever uniforms were in the area. But the concern in Annie's voice, together with the vague disquiet that Alice still felt for persuading her to give evidence in the rape trial, was enough to make the policewoman change her mind. After all, she was already on the Shore, not so far from the main coastal road and the rundown streets around it.

Turning down Bernard Street she put her windscreen wipers on. Urgent flurries of snow were flying down and obscuring her view. Carron Place was one of the roads off to the left, and she peered down each one until, at last, she found it.

She heard the rumpus long before she saw it. Angry men were thumping the panels of the yellow van, the air vibrating, their crashing rhythm drowning the moaning of the wind. Gathered by the bonnet were the prostitutes, resolute. They were asserting simply by their continuing presence on that freezing night their right to come to this meeting point, the only organisation in the whole of the city concerned with them and their welfare.

A stand-off had been reached, and now both camps seemed to consider that they had made their point and were only too glad, on seeing the police car, to leave the chilly site. One group to return to the warmth of their hearths, the welcome of their wives, and the other to disperse into the darkness, searching for trade elsewhere along Coburg Street, Dock Street and their other dank haunts.

Catching sight of a peroxide blonde in the group, Alice waved her over and, reluctantly, the woman left her companions and came to the car.

'Irena,' Alice said ruefully, 'the last time I saw you – well, you've got an ASBO out against you, haven't you? You're not supposed to be here, in this area, I mean.'

The girl shook her head, replying in broken English.

'No madam. I am allowed… allowed… em… to come to van.'

The plump woman, aware of Irena's limited ability to speak any language other than Russian, joined Alice and began to explain that any of the ASBOs served on the girls still allowed them to attend the SPEAR van.

Looking the newcomer squarely in the face, Alice realised that she recognised her straight brow and broad cheekbones. But it could not be the person she was thinking of, surely! All those working for SPEAR were ex-sex workers, she knew that. Everyone knew that. It gave the organisation its strength, distinguished it from all the other charities.

'Is your name Ellen?' Alice asked, tentatively.

'Yes.' The woman looked blank.

'Ellen Barbour?'

'Yes. Why?'

'Well,' Alice began, 'I think we know each other. From school.'

2

Later that same evening, threading their way through the crowded pub, they spotted an empty table in the corner. It had a view of the canal, the lights of Ronaldson Wharf sparkling and dancing on its inky waters.

Alice took a sip of her white wine, and after a short, uneasy silence, Ellen spoke.

'So, Alice, where did it all go wrong? How on earth did you end up walking the streets – as a policewoman?'

'Well,' her companion replied, head bowed in shame, 'after my application to join the order was turned down by Reverend Mother...'

'No!' Ellen gasped, eyes wide with shock. 'You... you wanted to become one of them? A nun?'

Laughing, Alice shook her head, delighted with Ellen's unexpected gullibility and her horror at the very thought of a celibate vocation. After another quick swig from her glass, she described the short path which had led her straight from university into Lothian and Borders Police. She hesitated only when asked the reason for her career choice. The truth would likely sound so po-faced, so self-righteous, that she was reluctant to voice it. She flirted, briefly, with telling an outright lie, before finally, confessing that she had wanted an interesting job, one filled with variety and that allowed her to use such intelligence as she had. For a split-second only she contemplated telling the whole truth. That she also had wanted to do something worthwhile, something that might actually help people. The admission would have sounded unbearably corny, pious even, particularly in present company. She left it unsaid.

'And you, Ellen, the last time I saw you, you were clutching the art prize and swithering between going to art college or straight into business.'

Before answering, Ellen swept the drapes of straight hair back from her face with the tips of her fingers, revealing for the first time her features in their entirety, and took a long draught from her whisky.

'It's a bit of a story,' she began. 'You'll know about S.P.E.A.R., eh? The Scottish Prostitutes Education and Advice Resource. Have you heard of our unusual job qualification?'

Alice nodded. She knew only too well, and was eager for the narrative to continue. And, taking her time, Ellen Barbour told her tale. It had all begun, mundanely enough, with a massive debt following the collapse of her jewellery business in Bruntsfield. She had been determined, she said with emphasis, determined not to let her small suppliers down by being declared bankrupt. She also wanted to avoid the stigma associated with bankruptcy. Nothing to that associated with prostitution, thought Alice, remaining silent, baffled by the strange logic.

Ellen went on to describe how she had agonised for weeks seeking a solution to her predicament, and, ultimately, alighted on prostitution. Her next-door neighbour in Granton, Louise, had worked in a sauna for a couple of years, and that was what had given her the idea. Louise knew about 'escort' work too, a more independent option, which appealed to Ellen's entrepreneurial instincts. It soon became apparent that as an 'escort', easy money, good money, could be made.

As it happened, she turned out to be very talented at her chosen profession. In constant demand, she said with pride. Obviously, she had invested in her new business venture, in fine clothes and other necessary accoutrements, and as a result she had mixed with the best and seen the world. Within less than four years all her creditors had been repaid but, by then, she had become accustomed to a certain lifestyle, to hand-made shoes and fine wines. And she had nothing left to lose by continuing. There was no way back to respectability, even if she had given up the business. Self-respect was all she needed anyway.

'You two lovely ladies lookin' fer company?' enquired a watery-eyed drunk, hovering about their table expectantly and winking indiscriminately at each in turn.

'Be off, grimy chancer!' Ellen said imperiously, and they watched as, undeterred, he turned to face another table of lone females and began to try his luck with them. The same line in use again.

'Go on,' Alice prompted, gripped by the narrative. 'Why and when did you stop?'

'Oh, I carried on for about another eight years. But one day I found that the effort required in being nice, I mean constantly nice, all the time, to every single client, had become too much, even for the money I was making. I simply couldn't listen to any more paeans of praise to Margaret Thatcher and remain silent. So, instead of biting my tongue yet again, I let rip, giving a client the benefit of my actual views on the woman. Well, I knew it was the end then, so I retired from the game, and now devote my not inconsiderable energies to better causes.'

'Weren't you head girl at school?' Alice asked, cautiously, recalling their joint past.

'Yes, indeedy,' Ellen replied, 'first blue ribbon, no less. And a Child of Mary to boot. I'm not sure if the nuns followed my career after that…' she paused for thought, choosing her words with care, '…zenith. Still, you know the Catholic view of womanhood – Madonna or whore. I may not have managed the first, but, by Jesus, I was world-class at the second. A kind of success, surely? Can't boast a Pope, but I did get quite close to a Cardinal once…'

Leaning on the bar, queuing for a refill for them both, Alice tried to impose order on the competing thoughts jostling for space in her mind. She had not often exchanged more than a few words with a prostitute, retired or active, never mind one as assured and articulate as Ellen. She found herself mulling over her story. If the truth be told, she had not imagined that anyone she knew might embark on prostitution or consider such a thing at all. And it certainly would not have occurred to her that it might be chosen by a friend simply as a means of paying off debts, far less as a lucrative career option. Most of the working girls she had come across had ended up on the game as a means of financing their addictions, having by then lost all hope in humanity, no longer valuing anything much, including themselves. Of course, in the massage parlours she had met girls prepared to exploit their assets who were, apparently, capable of remaining unchanged, undamaged, by the transaction. But, naively, she had not expected the same approach from a fellow old girl from the convent.

Looking around now at the pub's customers, a random selection of men, largely elderly, she tried to consider the matter afresh, putting all her prejudices to one side. But, Christ, it would have to be a hell of a lot of money, more

than could be contained in the vaults of a Swiss bank…
So, was it just a question of the right price, then? No.
Money simply did not seem the right currency for such
an exchange. Shared love, certainly; shared lust, for sure,
but not the stuff used to buy pork chops or razor blades.
Her own flesh would be among the last of the commodi-
ties she would choose to sell, and it only when no other
choices remained. But maybe that was it, maybe only
extreme poverty focussed the mind sufficiently, allowing
it to overcome fear of moral opprobrium and to take the
option seriously. Because, whether she liked it or not, the
nuns, with their adoration of the Virgin, had moulded her
and imprinted their inconvenient morality on her. Her
awareness of that fact did not entirely free her from it.
Perhaps only relentless poverty would do so, would add
the necessary dash of reality.

Still, *all* comers. The very thought! And accidentally
catching the eye of a red-faced toper with a grog-blossom
nose, finding herself favoured with a leer, it occurred to
her that whether or not her own moral code would ever
have allowed it, her five senses might have rebelled.

DC Alistair Watt switched the fan heater dial up to four in
the Astra, blasting freezing air onto Alice's face and legs,
making her protest vociferously.

'It'll warm up soon,' he said, unmoved by her entreaties,
and blew into his cupped hands in an attempt to restore
the circulation to his whitened fingers. His long legs were
jammed under the dashboard, and he carefully spread a
newspaper over his knees to act as a blanket. They had
been chatting about the previous night's disturbance in
Carron Place and the revelations Alice had got in the pub.

'I'd solve it all by setting up a designated, state-of-the-art, hoor park,' he said. 'It would have on-site medical facilities, inspectors and whatever. Hoordom has gone on forever and will go on forever, so it might as well be regulated, controlled...'

'And where exactly would this facility be?' Alice asked.

'Well,' he paused, evidently thinking. 'Plenty of derelict industrial units in Leith, eh?'

'So, not beside you, then?'

'No room, sadly. Anyway, they are like homing pigeons, you know. They always return to that area. Or, maybe, more like bees. Buzzing back into Behar.'

'Well, I'm sure you'd know,' Alice replied. 'But in your scheme, what about the freelances, the escorts? They won't want to be penned-up anywhere. They go where the work is.'

'Is that information straight from the whorse's mouth, so to speak?' Alistair asked, laughing unashamedly at his own joke, the newspaper crackling on his rocking knees. But his query remained unanswered. A hesitant female voice, timid and fluctuating in volume, came from the car-radio requesting assistance from all cars in the Leith area, as a body had been reported at Seafield cemetery.

'Maybe a few of them in there, I suppose,' Alistair said drily as he turned the car down Vanburgh Place, only to get caught behind an elderly gritter, meandering along, orange light flashing lethargically, as it dribbled its contents onto the road. Leith Links, under its white covering, glistened in the crisp moonlight, occasional breaths of wind rippling its smooth surface and dusting the highway with snow. When the sound of their siren broke the peace, the leviathan drew sedately to the side of the road, clouds of exhaust fumes in its wake.

They abandoned their vehicle at the end of Claremont Park and ran the last few yards to the rusticated pillars at the cemetery's entrance. Inside, in the distance, the beam of a torch was slicing the air. They headed towards it, eyes getting used to the darkness, feet now wet and aching in the cold. Beside an overgrown flowerbed stood a uniformed constable, his arm around the shoulder of an old lady, the pair huddled together. At their feet lay a fat Labrador, and all three figures were staring intently at an isolated patch of undergrowth, a dark island in a sea of white.

At the approach of the strangers, the dog began to growl and, instantly and as if embarrassed, the constable took his arm away from his companion, flashing his torch-light in their faces. Recognising Alice, he breathed a sigh of relief. He explained that Mrs Craig, the elderly lady, had been taking her dog for its final outing of the evening when she had noticed what appeared to be an arm sticking out from the bushes. As he was speaking, he swept the beam of his torch over the snow-capped greenery, seeking out the supposed limb and eventually stopping on an indistinguishable black object. Naturally, he said, he knew better than to interfere with a crime scene, so he had immediately radioed for help and begun to cordon off the area.

Following Alistair's eyes downwards to a loose strand of tape on the ground, writhing sinuously, snake-like in the wind and attached to nothing, he stammered that Mrs Craig had become tearful and had accidentally released her dog lead. This allowed Sheba to wander off towards the corpse. Unfortunately, her paw prints would be all over the scene. She had returned when called, but he had not felt able to finish the barrier.

Another beam of light on the snow, swinging rhythmically like a metronome, left to right, right to left, advanced towards them, before being raised upwards to scan their heads. Immediately the Labrador began to bark, snapping furiously, pulling and straining on the lead to reach the invisible stranger and almost yanking the old woman off her feet in its enthusiasm. Suddenly it broke loose and jumped, hurling itself upwards at the newcomer, only to be felled by the thrust of a knee, dropping to whimper and yelp in a heap on the ground. Having dealt with the dog, the beefy stranger calmly peeled off his woollen balaclava, exposing his face for the first time.

'I think it's a bloke called Simon – Simon Oakley. A DS with 'C' Division. A benign but lazy bugger, apparently. He must have been nearby, responded to the call-out too,' Alistair whispered to Alice, as she and the dog's distraught owner bent down together to stroke it and check that it was uninjured. Oakley, his head bent against the driving snow, joined them and patted its back.

' Sorry, self-defence, but the d… d… dog will be fine. Anyone called the DCI yet?' he asked.

'No,' Alice said, still caressing the Labrador, 'we've only just arrived. So we'd better check things out first. I don't fancy getting anyone out on a night like this only to discover that we've found an old stick or a comatose tramp.'

As Alistair Watt tried to take a statement from the witness, his fingers so numb that he could scarcely grip the pen, Alice Rice, with DS Oakley following in her footprints, set off towards the patch of undergrowth. Tussocks of dead grass and dried, skeletal weeds tripped them as they worked their way forwards, snaring their hands, catching their calves and entwining their ankles. Cursing, having fallen for a second time, Alice looked down at her feet, only to catch a glimpse of a colourless female face looking back up at her. As the bulb in her torch began to fade she and her companion knelt beside the figure and he touched the woman's neck, feeling for a pulse, his fingers becoming tangled in a necklace of beads. Her arms were crossed on her breast as if to receive a blessing or as laid out by an undertaker. But, below one of her hands and over her heart, a dark stain extended.

Elaine Bell turned over in her bed and lay on her left side but found her breathing no clearer. Her head still felt heavy, her sinuses and left nostril blocked completely. Carefully, she rolled onto her right, conscious, as she did so, that now both nostrils were tightly sealed and she opened her mouth to gasp for breath. Beside her, releasing growling snores, lay her husband, blessedly unaware of her restlessness in his dream-free sleep. Easing back the duvet cover, she slid her legs over the side of the bed and managed to get out without making it creak.

A thorough inspection of the bathroom cabinet revealed only three empty bottles, each with a film of brightly-coloured viscous material the bottom and crystallised sugar making the glass sticky. She turned the one with most in it upside down, but the thin layer of congealed cough mixture remained solid. Her attempt to get some of it with the end of a toothbrush failed, providing only a few small globs of the medicine. Nestling behind a box of sticking plasters she found a discoloured sachet, a fat friar's face beaming from its wrapper, promising 'blessed' relief from chronic catarrh.

In the harsh light of the kitchen she shook out the sachet into a large, enamel jug and added a kettleful of newly-boiled water. The stinging of her eyes told her that the mixture was producing a powerful, irritating vapour, but her nose remained blithely oblivious to everything. Desperate for relief she flung the towel over her head, craning her face into the steam and inhaling deeply as she did so. Despite a burning sensation deep in her lungs she persisted until her cheeks and forehead seemed to be on fire. Only a few more minutes to endure, she thought, and such acute discomfort must be rewarded by results. As her hand fumbled blindly on the table for the egg-timer, the telephone rang. She tore off her towel and ran into the living room to answer it before the din woke her husband.

'Hello, DCI Elaine Bell,' she said, noting angrily to herself that her voice sounded as nasal as it had before she had scalded her face.

'It's Alice, ma'am. I'm at the Seafield Cemetery with DS Watt. We've got a body… er… an unburied, newly dead one. A female, middle-aged. And it could well be a murder.'

Having dressed at speed, Elaine Bell looked in the mirror. Her hair, still wet from the steam, clung to her temples, old mascara had run below one eye and her face was puce. 'The alkie look,' she muttered grimly to herself, feeling her cheeks anxiously and finding them still hot to the touch. 'And on a freezing night like this I'll get bloody Bell's palsy to boot.'

Seeing a strange figure, head crowned in a woolly bobble hat, tartan scarf wound tightly over the mouth and nose, advancing purposefully towards the taped area, Alice ran towards it, intent on blocking the way.

'Sorry,' she said breathlessly, 'only police are allowed here for the moment.'

A muffled voice, but one entirely familiar to her, replied testily, 'Don't be silly, DS Rice, it's me – DCI Bell. Your boss, remember?'

'Sorry, ma'am. But your clothes… it's a bit like a burka, or is it a chador?'

'Never mind that! Has anyone actually succeeded in identifying the body yet?'

Alice handed over a leaflet and waited patiently while her superior read it.

'Is it some kind of "Wanted" poster or something? What is it exactly?'

'It's produced by S.P.E.A.R. ma'am – you know, the prostitutes' charity. It's one of their publications, they hand them out from their van to the working girls to warn them about any particular ne'er-do-wells, batterers and the like.'

'Fine. So where did you find it?'

'It was in the woman's pocket. First thing tomorrow I'll go round to their office in Restalrig with a photo and see if they know her. Find out if they've a name, an address for him, too. He may have left it on her, I suppose, as some kind of calling card.'

Two hours later, the body, its hands, feet and head bagged in clear plastic and secured with brown parcel tape, began its undignified journey to the police mortuary in the Cowgate. So bound, it no longer seemed human, resembling instead a gigantic, grotesque doll or toy. In Edinburgh, despite the city's douce exterior and cultured reputation, the mortuary remained open for business at all hours of the day and night. Even at midnight on Christmas Eve, with carols sweetening the air and kisses landing on cold cheeks, its harsh lights shone brightly, awaiting its next guest. Always room in that inn.

Alice, yawning uncontrollably, tramped up the dusty tenement stair to her flat in Broughton Place. The loud barking, echoing in the stairwell, reached a peak as she stepped onto the landing below her own. As the door opened, her dog, Quill, darted out to greet her, his tail a blur of wagging, claws clattering on the stone as he danced joyfully around her. His temporary custodian, Miss Spinnell, wordlessly handed over his lead before, bowing her head ever so slightly, she retreated into her lair. Her door's multiple locks were being driven home as Alice climbed the final flight to her own front door.

As she turned on the light in the kitchen she saw a note in Ian's characteristic over-large italic hand, lying on the table.

'Back whenever. Don't worry about food for me.'

And without him, the place felt cold and cheerless. With every step she had taken on the journey home she had been thinking about what she would tell him of her evening, luxuriating in the prospect of unburdening herself of its grim sights by sharing them with him. The very act of describing a murder, she found, lessened its impact, focussed her mind and helped her to believe that something could be achieved, that their efforts would, eventually, bear fruit.

Of course, the old order could never be restored. A killing was not like the eruption of a monster's head through the dark waters of a loch, the creature then sinking back into the depths, leaving a ripple-free surface behind it. In some form or other, a murder's repercussions continued forever, extending outwards and permanently altering lives in ways seen and unseen, every bit as profoundly as the flapping of a butterfly's wing in some rainforest somewhere. But Leith might be made safe again, at least.

She longed to tell him what she had seen: the woman's oddly bloodless face, the almost Prussian blue of her lips, the disquieting sight of a bird dropping on her neck and the blackness of the wound. But he was in his studio, oblivious to her need, the time and the freezing temperature, absorbed completely in his work, all his interest centred within the studio's four walls. And, yes, he never complained about her absences or the fact that most of her energies were used up in the station. But, just occasionally, very occasionally, she imagined the reassurance that might come from someone missing her, waiting anxiously for her return. And tonight was just such a night, just such an occasion.

3

Of course, the solution to the problem was easy, as a woman Alice knew that. If you are unable to find the place that you are looking for then you simply ask anyone you meet, particularly those in nearby premises. It stood to reason. Nevertheless, the next morning she found herself wandering past the first row of shops she came to, convincing herself that her destination would be just around the corner. Then again, the nearby office block would, she thought, probably be empty, and the group of young men by the bus stop were too busy talking to each other for her to interrupt them.

Walking past an old biddy, standing motionless as she fished in the depths of her carrier bag, Alice began to ask her for directions, only to find that she spoke only Polish, was lost and appeared to be furious with the world and all its works. Desperate now to find the S.P.E.A.R. office, she peered through the first open door in a row of industrial units and saw a pair of overalled legs projecting from beneath a car.

'Excuse me?' she said, her voice lost against the background of music emanating from a radio resting on the oil-blackened concrete.

'Excuse me!' she repeated loudly, but there was still no answer.

'EXCUSE ME!' she shouted, finally attracting the man's attention as he wheeled himself out from under the chassis, switched off the radio and got up, wiping his hands on a soiled rag as he came towards her.

'I just wondered…' she paused momentarily, trying again to work out the best words for her enquiry, the least damning, which would get her the directions she wanted without having to mention the exact place she was looking for. But it was no use. She could not remember the name of the bloody street. The best she could recall was that it was off Restalrig Drive.

'I'm looking for S.P.E.A.R.'s premises?' she continued brightly.

'Nae Spears round here, hen. There's a shop, Sears, a bed shop at three doors along. Could that be it?'

'Er… no. But thanks, anyway. I'm looking for the er… er… prostitutes' office, their… er… resource centre?'

The man looked at her, brazenly scanning her figure, grinning broadly. 'Like I said, dearie, there's the bed shop. What other resource do yous need?'

In the face of defeat, she had to try again, although her cheeks were now burning and she had begun, foolishly she knew, to devise other questions, ones designed to find the sodding place without conclusions being drawn about her own profession. The next-door building turned out to be a dressmaker's workshop, hand-made clothes displayed on a small crowd of dummies, each with an expensive price tag hanging below the hemline. With a sinking heart she approached a seamstress, head bent as she machined a seam, pins sticking menacingly from her wide mouth.

'Sorry to bother you, but I'm looking for S.P.E.A.R.'s. premises?'

Please God, no further clarification needed. Concentrating on her sewing, and speechless due to her mouthful of pins, the woman jerked her head towards the door. On screwing up her eyes, Alice made out the words on the sign opposite: 'The Scottish Prostitutes Education and Advice Resource'.

—

The squad meeting had been fixed for ten p.m. At five past, Alice edged through the half open door into the murder suite on tiptoe, hoping to slip into a seat at the back without her lateness being noticed. However, to her surprise, she found the room empty, lights off and computers still dormant.

While she was still wondering if she had misheard the appointed time, Eric Manson came into the room, sausage roll in hand, and slumped heavily onto the only seat softened by a cushion. Like the rest of the squad, he looked pale-faced, had only slept for a few hours, and his chin was bleeding from a botched attempt to shave in the poorly lit men's toilet.

Just as she was about to ask him if the meeting had been postponed, three detective constables, Littlewood, McDonald and Galloway, arrived together, their conversation tailing off into a self-conscious mumble as they filed in. DC Ruth Lindsay trailed behind them, yawning and unbuttoning her coat. The remaining vacant chair was beside Alice, and she took it for granted that it would soon be occupied by her friend, Alistair Watt, ideally bearing coffee for them both. Instead, Simon Oakley deposited his heavy frame in it, inclining his head slightly in her direction and smiling in recognition.

Elaine Bell, cheeks strangely flushed and dressed in last night's crumpled clothes, attempted to brief them, racked intermittently by paroxysms of sneezing, her eyes streaming throughout. She fired occasional questions at them with an air of exhausted irritability, becoming more tetchy with every answer.

Listening half-heartedly, Alice's concentration slipped and she began to speculate, wondering idly whether her superior might be the source of all winter infections within the city, the Typhoid Mary of the common cold. She watched as paper hankie after paper hankie, used to dab the woman's dripping nose, was screwed up and flung forcibly into a nearby wastepaper basket. Around it the floor was now littered with her misfires. If Avian flu were, finally, to breach the species barrier through the medium of a single infected human being, then Elaine Bell, surely, would be that one. A morsel of underdone Indonesian chicken entering her flu-ridden system and mankind's nemesis was assured.

Alice's rumination was interrupted when the Chief Inspector's attention suddenly shifted onto her.

'Alice… Alice! if you could just wake up, please? How did you fare at S.P.E.A.R. this morning?'

'Fine,' the sergeant answered, surprising herself by the crispness of her response. 'Ellen Barbour, the manager of the Resource Centre, was able to identify the woman in our photograph. She's an Isobel – known as Belle – Wilson, and I've got an address for her…' She fumbled in her pocket and extracted a torn piece of paper, '…at Fishwives Causeway. it's just off Portobello High Street. Ellen, er… Ms Barbour, says that Wilson's a drug user, and has been for years despite whatever help they've been able to provide. The old chap in the S.P.E.A.R mugshot, he's called Eddie Christie, but they've no address for him. Ms Barbour reckons the best way of tracing him now would be through another prostitute, Lena Stirling. She often worked in a pair with Isobel. And guess who reported Christie to the project, and got his face on the leaflet? Isobel Wilson. A couple of weeks ago he knocked her about in the General George car park when she, allegedly, gave him lip.'

―

Having methodically allocated the day's tasks, Elaine Bell wiggled her toes back into her scuffed shoes and, moving stiffly, rose to her feet, signalling the end of the meeting. And then, finally, noticing the newcomer to St Leonard Street, she introduced him to the squad while she was leaving the room, his presence only noted as an obvious afterthought.

'Oh, and the stranger in our midst, people, is DS Simon Oakley and he'll be with us for the duration of the investigation. Unfortunately, Alistair Watt seems to have contracted some kind of dizzy-making virus. Labyrinthitis... vestibulitis... some kind of itis or other. Anyway, he's off for the foreseeable future, at home, vomiting whenever he stands up. So let's all hope it's not catching.'

―

The old woman stroked the Siamese cat's smooth, dark ears, watching entranced as it closed its blue eyes in ecstasy, webbed toes flexing in and out with pleasure, kneading the eiderdown like dough. Under the bed covers she tried to curl her body around it, resting her head beside its rounded skull, and the passage of time, briefly, stood still with her absorption in a perfect moment. The buzzing of a bluebottle, a few inches above them, started the clock once more. The excited cat sprang up, a long white streak leaping into the air, and landed silently on the quilt with the fly in its mouth, soon crunching it noisily in its delicate jaws. Brushing a single wing off the blanket, Mrs Wilson glanced at her watch. Eleven already. She would need to get up now if she was to make the doctor's surgery by twelve.

Groaning inwardly, she pushed off the bed-clothes and began the long journey to the edge of the bed, grasping the side of an armchair to pull her unwieldy body the last few inches. With a loud bang her swollen feet landed on the bare floor boards. No bloody tea this morning, she thought to herself, wondering whether they had run out of teabags or whether, maybe, the milk was sour. Or, and most likely of all, Isobel had overslept as usual.

Having become breathless trying unsuccessfully to turn on a bath tap, she admitted defeat and gave her face a cursory wipe with an evil-smelling flannel before beginning the troublesome process of getting dressed. Buttons no longer fitted buttonholes; hooks, eyes and even zip fasteners seemed to have become smaller, impossible to grip, fiddly and frustrating. A final yank and her skirt was on, hem crooked but sitting below the line of her knee-length socks. Only the battle with her shoes remained, and she jammed the left one on, whimpering as her big toe hit the leather shoe-end unexpectedly. The right foot was a good size larger than the left, and she looked down at the misshapen flesh, noting the generous curve of a bunion and the clawed, gnarled toes. Hard to believe she had once favoured peep-toes in all weathers, scarlet nail varnish drawing attention to her best features. Time left nothing unchanged, and none of its changes were for the better.

Porridge today, she thought, a hot breakfast to keep out the cold, and fit for a king if topped with a little pinhead oatmeal. And then she remembered the milk crisis, and began to conjure up, instead, a picture of a slice of hot buttered toast awash with raspberry jam. Of course, the pips might get stuck in her dental plate, but by the time she reached the bread-bin she could feel her mouth watering.

When the doorbell rang she shouted, 'Isobel! Get the door fer us, hen. I'm no' dressed yet.' Then she waited, expecting to hear the familiar, angry thuds as her daughter trudged across the floor. But when the ringing continued, and no-one stirred, she dropped the bread into the toaster, shuffled across the hall and undid the bolt, peeping timidly at her visitors.

Jane Wilson took the news of her only child's death unnaturally well, Alice thought. She asked few questions and seemed neither dismayed nor surprised by the answers. It was as if she had been expecting just such news, had already grieved in expectation of it and had no tears left to shed when the moment actually arrived. She was like those wartime wives and mothers, nerves constantly stretched, waiting to read the worst in a telegram from the Front. As Alice spoke, the woman blinked hard and licked the corners of her mouth, shaking her head constantly, as if by disagreeing with what she was being told, she could change it.

While she was leaving the flat in the company of the two sergeants, the little Siamese cat slid through the opening door and strolled across the landing. The first time it happened DS Oakley managed to grab the animal and post it back into the flat, but as it came out again, it skittered past him and tiptoed down the stone stairs towards the open tenement door and the busy street outside. The old woman started to wail, crying out the cat's name and hobbling ineffectually after it. And, miraculously, it stopped and began cleaning itself, licking its immaculate front paws and smoothing its face with them. The overweight policeman waited motionless on the step above it, breathing heavily, and then suddenly pounced, two podgy hands clamping around its waist, lifting it high in triumph. His complexion, usually high, was now ruddy with isolated pale patches around the nose and mouth, sweat shining on his brow. Unperturbed by its capture, the cat continued to groom itself and allowed itself to be deposited in the hallway, wandering off towards the kitchen, its kinked tail waving sinuously behind it.

~

Supported on either side at the elbow, Jane Wilson stumbled across the mortuary floor, her nostrils flaring in the presence of an unfamiliar, chemical odour. In the refrigeration area, the pathologist, Doctor Zenabi, was waiting for them beside a covered trolley and, slowly, the trio made their way towards him. On their arrival, he folded the sheet back, revealing Isobel Wilson's pale, bloodless head. Alice gazed at it. It was a face in complete repose, all muscles relaxed, giving the middle-aged woman the lineless, unwrinkled appearance of a teenager. The kiss the old woman spontaneously bestowed on her daughter's cheek confirmed the corpse's identity, and her white hair remained against the cold flesh until Doctor Zenabi, kindly, eased her away, meeting only the slightest resistance. As if wishing her daughter farewell, she picked up a lifeless hand and stroked it, coming back time after time to a slight indentation on the ring finger.

'What is it?' Alice asked.

43

'Someone's ta'en oaf ma weddin' ring. I gie'd it tae her an' she aye wore it. Still, Belle's at rest the now, eh? Nothin' mair can hurt her.'

The others nodded, as the tears finally began to flow from the old woman's cloudy eyes, rolling off her nose and dripping onto the shrouded form of her daughter.

—

'So, Alice, loose words cost lives!' DI Eric Manson said enigmatically, offering her a chocolate digestive and leaning across from his chair to hand it to her. Being hungry, she was tempted to accept the biscuit but hesitated, knowing that if she did so she would feel bound to take up his word-bait. Of course, even if she did there was every possibility, on past experience, that he would simply fob her off with another sphinx-like statement instead of an explanation. But, seeing the expectant look on his face, and the lack of any signs of curiosity from the rest of the squad, she decided to take pity on him and play the game.

'What are you going on about, sir? Whose "loose words", whose "lives"?', she said, taking the digestive. The inspector pursed his lips, relishing the suspense he had created, and quite incapable of hiding the fact.

'Well, since you ask…' he hesitated for a few seconds, 'our own Chief Inspector's.' Aware that he had not given a satisfactory answer, he then stared intently at his computer screen, knitting his brows theatrically, as if reading important news. No time left for idle chatter.

I could, Alice thought, just leave it at that, he'll crack first on past form. But his ploy had worked, her curiosity was aroused, and she heard herself say, 'Yes, sir, but what words? And to what effect, exactly?'

'Mmmm…' he replied, ponderously. Any delay could only further whet her appetite. 'The words were "Chance would be a fine thing!" uttered by our very own Elaine Bell in response to a Leith resident's query as to how she'd feel if she came across a used condom in her hallway. A rueful reflection on her own inadequate sex life, I suppose. Now, the effect – you'd like to know that too?'

'Yes,' she said evenly.

'The effect is that a complaint, no less, has been lodged against her and is currently under investigation.'

'And how exactly do you know about it all?'

'Sir.'

'And how exactly, do you know about it all, sir?'

'Friends in high places,' he smiled, unwrapping another packet of biscuits and decanting them into a tin.

'Or, as you've just been in the boss's office,' she shot back, 'a dramatic improvement in your already excellent upside-down reading skills, eh?'

'Sir.'

'Eh, sir?'

'No comment,' he answered, crunching another digestive.

Cursing the rain, Lena stepped gingerly towards the very edge of the kerb, unable to see properly through her streaked spectacles and blinded by the passing headlights. The first car to draw up contained three men and she knew better than to attract their attention, someone else can take the risk, she thought to herself, slipping back into the shadows. The second, a Volvo, seemed possible. But it drew close only to speed up in the flooded gutter, deliberately showering her with filthy water. She shook herself like a soaked dog, knowing as she was doing so that it was futile, rain having begun to cascade down, bouncing up off the pavement and splattering her bare legs.

Another vehicle slowed down and she peered, short-sightedly, into it, catching a glimpse of a male and female occupant. No dice. But the man tapped on his window to attract her attention and she sidled over, only to find a police identity card flashed in her face.

With ill grace, she climbed into the back seat, belligerent already, determined to get out as soon as possible. Time in the car was time wasted, and she needed a fix. Life had to go on, murder or no murder.

Shivering uncontrollably in her damp clothes, her impatience on display, she told the police officers the truth. That she and Isobel had been partners, looking out for each other, keeping tabs with their mobiles, ready to raise the alarm should the need arise. But last night, she paused for a second, they had fallen out. Over money, if they must know. So she had not kept watch and, yes, she was well aware that the woman was now dead. Got the *Evening News* like everyone else. The last she had seen of Isobel had been at about seven p.m. on the Tuesday night, the cow had nabbed her pitch at the Leith end of Salamander Street. She nodded her head on being shown the picture of Eddie Christie, swearing at the very sight, and confirming that Isobel had been assaulted by him, just as she had. All she knew was that he worked as a teacher at Talman Secondary. French, *s'il-vous plait.*

Unbidden, the prostitute opened the car door, feeling claustrophobic in its steamed-up interior, just as the sturdy police sergeant was lobbing another question at her. Looking in the mirror at the big blondie, she considered giving him a wink. He seemed vaguely familiar, and anyway, he was just another man, just another policeman, and they were no different under their clothes, plain or otherwise. Actually, there was nothing to pick between the lot of them, from the unemployed to the Members of the Scottish Parliament, except that politicians got a thrill from the risk of getting caught. Unlike those on the dole.

'Lena,' the policewoman said, 'we don't know who murdered Isobel. Whoever it is is still at large, might kill again. May even be on the lookout for prostitutes. Who are you working with tonight?'

'I'm nae workin at a',' the prostitute lied.

'Fine,' Alice replied. 'You're not working, simply enjoying a stroll in the pouring rain where you would be working, if you were working. Anyway, should you consider returning to work, if you must, please don't unless you've got yourself another partner? Ideally, keep off the street altogether until we've caught this nutter.'

'Aye. But a'm nae workin',' see?'

She stepped out of the car, back into the downpour, her mind focussed on one thing and one thing alone. Smack. And until the needle had been plunged into the vein, and released its longed-for load, she could think of nothing else.

Lying contentedly in her bed that night, Alice began to look at the newspaper. The whole of the front page was again taken up with coverage of the abduction of a little boy, a huge colour photograph of the child staring back at her. Inside, three more pages were devoted to him, and the entire editorial. The story was considered from every possible angle: the nature of the police investigations and the particular difficulties encountered by them, profiles of any likely suspects, the precise circumstances leading up to the boy's disappearance and so on. Even the psychological effects of the loss of a brother on a younger sister merited comment by a well-known child psychologist. Alice read it all, appalled, sympathising with the parents' plight, recognising their utter desperation but deliberately choosing not to imagine herself precisely in their shoes. It would be a painful yet completely pointless exercise. Her heartache would assist no-one, remedy nothing. Below the rambling leader, her eyes were caught by a short paragraph headed 'Yangtse River Dolphin Now Extinct'.

'A rare river dolphin, the baiji, is now thought to be extinct. The species was the only remaining member of the *Lipotidae*, an ancient mammal family that separated from other marine mammals, including whales, dolphins and porpoises, about twenty-five million years ago. The baiji's extinction is attributable to unregulated finishing, dam construction and boat collisions. The species' incidental mortality results from massive-scale human environmental impact.'

Reading it, for a second she felt a wave of despair wash over her. The only supposedly rational species on the entire planet, the one with the fate of the rest of the natural world in its epicene hands, thought the matter so unimportant. The possible, not definite, loss of one of the billion upon billion of members of its own species merited four whole pages of newsprint, whereas humanity's unthinking obliteration of an entire class of unique creatures deserved only a tiny footnote. Tomorrow more would be written about the boy's abduction, but nothing further about the end of the baiji. Then again, tomorrow, like everyone else, she would consume the coverage avidly. Possibly she would read it while eating a yellow-fin tuna sandwich from a polythene carrier bag and, certainly, having done nothing for the next species perched precariously on the edge of extinction. Like everyone else, she was too busy living her day-to-day life, her good intentions simply paving on the road to hell.

Sleep was hard to come by, but just as she dropped off the phone rang. Alice woke, and in her dozy state hoped that Ian would answer it before remembering that he was away, visiting his mother. She clamped the receiver to her ear.

'Ali… eh, Alice?' Miss Spinnell, her neighbour, warbled. 'I need your help. Can you come down straight away?'

The World Service was still on the radio. Six pips at two o'clock.

'It's only two, Miss Spinnell. It couldn't possibly wait until the morning?'

'No. It's a drama… an emergy… a crisis. We may even need a doctor.'

Dragging herself out of bed, head still longing for the pillow, Alice shivered in the cold, searching around in the darkness for a jersey to put over her nightie. The recent spell of plain-sailing in her dealings with her elderly neighbour had seemed too good to be true. After all, Alzheimer's did not stop, had no second thoughts about the casual destruction it wrought on its victim's mind and personality. She had watched as, before her eyes, it had transformed a bright independent old lady into a suspicious eccentric, obsessed with the theft of her possessions by unseen intruders. Alice herself was now treated as a suspect, although her dog, Quill, remained the light of the old lady's life.

—

The door had been left ajar by the time Alice reached her neighbour's flat, but Miss Spinnell had returned to her bed and was sitting crouched on it, head down, knees against her chest, whimpering to herself. Alice came and sat on the edge of the bed. Seeing a wizened hand nearby she clasped it in her own, intending to comfort the distressed woman. Instantly the frail fingers were whipped away as if they had, inadvertently, touched lizard skin. The moaning, however, continued unabated.

'What is it, Miss Spinnell?'

In response the crouched figure slowly straightened itself, and Alice was surprised to see that her neighbour was wearing dark glasses.

'Blindness has come upon me! The lights have dipped… er, dimmed.'

Alice edged up the bed, watching Miss Spinnell recoil as she came closer, until she was able to lift the glasses off the ancient nose.

'I think you have accidentally put on the wrong spectacles. You've been wearing dark ones,' Alice said.

Miss Spinnell screwed up her eyes several times, as if accustoming herself once more to light and sight. She looked, briefly, sheepish before an expression of disdain transformed her face.

'Accidentally! Accidentally! Ha! How simper… simplistic can it be. Can't you grasp how they operate? Whilst I've been blind, blind I say, yet more of my artifice… arti… arti… things, will have been purloined. Kindly check the silver, Alice.'

'But, Miss Spinnell, how could they have got in?'

'Through the open door,' the old lady said. 'The door I opened...' she looked hard at her visitor before continuing, 'especially for you.'

To put her neighbour's mind at rest, the tired policewoman opened drawers and dust-laden cupboards, all the while learning more about Miss Spinnell and the havoc the disease had left in its wake. On a high shelf, in among well-thumbed volumes of verse, were little reminders of the person she had once been. A medal dated 1995 from The Poetry Society, a barn owl's wing wrapped carefully in tissue paper, and, most poignant of all, a faded photograph showing a young girl laughing uproariously with a boy in uniform, and an inscription on the back: 'To Morag, the most beautiful of the Spinnell sisters, with all my love, Charlie.' And over the writing in Miss Spinnell's ancient trembling hand had been scrawled 'PLEASE DO NOT TAKE', a pitiful entreaty to a pitiless enemy.

4

As soon as the polythene bag had been removed the corpse resumed its human shape again. A boyish photographer began to prowl around the body, snapping it from every angle, issuing instructions as if at a fashion shoot and smiling ghoulishly at his own joke, until told off by the pathologist. Meanwhile, Alice eased the woman's arms off her breast and down to her sides, lifting one of them up to remove the sleeve before rolling her over to release the material at the back. The final cuff peeled off without difficulty.

'At least she's cold,' Doctor Zenabi said conversationally, while raising the body slightly to allow Alice to pull the coat from under it.

'Does it make a difference?' she replied, all her concentration on the task in hand.

'Certainly does. Give me cold flesh, cold blood, anytime. I don't like it when it's still warm,' he continued, '– the transitional phase. It's horrid cutting them then. Far too close to life. I like my bodies to be... well, thoroughly chilled.'

Conversely, we want the body still warm, Alice thought. No time to have passed and the trail still hot. She felt in one of the woman's coat pockets and pulled out its contents. A mobile phone, a purse and a packet of chewing gum. Putting her hand into the other pocket, she felt a sharp, stabbing pain and withdrew it instantly as if bitten

by a cobra. She inspected her palm, ⸻
puncture mark, immediately below th⸻
finger. Fighting to contain the panic s⸻
within her, and cursing her own stupi⸻
the contents of the pocket onto a near⸻
her heart sink as the rounded cylinder⸻
syringe rolled across its surface. As she pi⸻
plunger, light glinted on the uncapped needle protruding
from the barrel. Things like this were supposed to happen
to other people. Not to her.

'Ahmed,' she said lightly, but he did not hear her, still
busy wrestling an obstinate baseball boot free from a foot
while humming to himself in an eerie falsetto.

'Ahmed, I think I may have been jabbed by something.
A needle-stick injury, or whatever it's called,' she shouted,
holding up the syringe for him to see. Doctor Zenabi
looked up, flung the boot he was holding to a technician
and rushed over to her. He grasped the hand she was
extending towards him and examined it for himself. Blood
had begun to ooze from the pinprick and he hustled her
towards the sink, ran the cold tap and plunged her hand
under its stream. Ten minutes later, her palm and fingers
now white and numb from the icy water, the pathologist
allowed her to remove it, binding the injury for her in
clean paper towelling.

'You need to go to Accident and Emergency right now,
Alice,' he ordered.

Still feeling shocked, her bandaged hand tucked pro-
tectively under her other arm, she asked, 'What may I
have picked up… from the needle, I mean?'

'Probably nothing,' he reassured her.

'Yes, probably nothing,' she repeated. 'But if I were to
be unlucky, what would the something be?'

enabi sighed. 'The main possibilities would
, Hepatitis B, Hepatitis C, I suppose, but you'll be
. A and E will give you prophylactic treatment for the
HIV. Preventative treatment.'

'And for the Hepatitis B and C?'

He shook his head. 'Nothing. Nothing's available. But, don't worry, I'll take some blood from the body and get it cross-matched for infectious diseases. Much speedier than waiting for you to develop something. Which you won't!' he added quickly, his brown eyes fixed on her, no argument to be countenanced. As if the outcome of the risk has anything to do with our discussion, she thought bleakly.

'How long before I'll know… whether the body was clean or not?'

'Two days at most. I'll make sure the hospital gives it priority. And we'll see if the woman's medical records suggest she's clean. And don't forget, even if she isn't clean, it doesn't necessarily mean that you'll have caught anything.'

Returning to Broughton Place from the Royal Infirmary in a taxi, plastic pill containers clinking in her bag, Alice found that she was no longer in control of her thoughts. They ran free, tormenting her, defining and refining her fears, exploring dreadful possibilities or, worse, probabilities, then ruthlessly following the chain of consequences to the most awful conclusions: chronic invalidity ending in premature death. She wondered what she should tell her parents, and Ian, before deciding that nothing should be said. Even if she was now on tenterhooks, there was no reason for them to join her swinging on them.

Examining his passenger's anxious face in the rear-view mirror, the taxi driver said cheerily: 'It may never happen, hen!'

Alice nodded, flashing a weak smile, unable to summon a suitably light-hearted response. It already had.

Back home in the flat, she rifled amongst her CDs for something to raise her spirits, lighten her mood, eventually settling on a collection of songs by Charles Trenet. The laughter smouldering in his voice would surely do the trick, and his French vowels would glide meaninglessly over her, soothing and relaxing as they flowed. Thinking about it coolly, dispassionately, here she was in the middle of a murder enquiry with two days off, and thus far, the threatened side-effects from the prophylactic drugs had not appeared. In fact, it was a perfect opportunity to take Quill for a walk, and in the high, blustery on-shore wind, the waves at Tantallon should be a sight to behold. And what could be more exhilarating, more life-affirming, than the sight of those endless breakers pounding the rocks, crashing skywards in all their bright majesty.

Pleased to have found a distraction, she walked towards the front door, intent on collecting Quill from Miss Spinnell, but found that she was bumping, unexpectedly, against the wall. She straightened herself up and took a few more steps, only to find herself colliding with it again. As she glanced down at the floor it began to incline upwards and then recede, then suddenly reared up once more. She shook her head forcefully, blinking hard, trying to restore normality and her balance with it. But the minute she opened her eyes again, the corridor began to revolve, enclosing her. She fell to her knees, edging on all fours towards the bedroom, stopping every so often to catch her breath, shoulders flat against the wall.

Once in bed, eyes tightly closed, she tried to calm herself, slow her own heartbeat, breathing in and out deeply and deliberately. The spinning sensation continued regardless, its rhythm now becoming disturbed, unpredictable, lurching her with dizzying speed first in one direction and then another. Bile flooded into her mouth and, in seconds, she was violently sick.

———

Eight hours later she was woken by the sound of a key in the lock, accompanied by a series of thuds as Quill pranced exuberantly around Ian, celebrating his release from his eccentric custodian and his return home.

Ian bent over her as if to plant a kiss on her cheek, but hesitated momentarily, taking in her pale face and exhausted eyes. Looking at him she mumbled something about a virulent sick bug at work, remembering to tell him to keep his distance in case he should catch it. At once he recoiled theatrically, taking a few steps back from the bed, and the loss of his presence by her side, fleeting as it had been, brought tears to her eyes. His joke was not funny. If she had caught HIV from the corpse then this might be the pattern for any future that they might share. The thought of losing him, of the closeness, the intimacy that they had so recently found, dismayed her, allowing a sob to escape. Any one of those alphabetical diseases, never mind death, could do that.

'Christ, Alice,' he said, surprised by her reaction. 'What on earth's the matter? I was just joking.'

'Oh, just this sick bug thing…' she replied, unable to say more. But however hard she tried, she could not halt the tears which continued to stream down her face, wetting the pillow and her hair on it.

'Darling, it can't just be that.'

Hearing the tenderness in his voice and the unfamiliar endearment, she sobbed again. He had never called her 'darling' before, and now joined the precious few she knew who meant the word. His concern undid her, crumbling her resolve so that when he repeated his question she told him the truth, managing a fairly clinical account of what had happened.

He listened, nodding occasionally, and then applied his mind to the problem. Doctor Zenabi had said he thought it improbable that she would catch anything, and he was the medical expert. He was the man they should trust and believe in. So she would not catch anything. But suppose, at the very worst, she had contracted HIV. Drugs were now available making the disease treatable, and its presence need make little difference to their lives. Couples all over the world lived with it. Also, he knew a few people with Hepatitis C and they appeared to lead completely normal lives too. He seemed so confident, so unperturbed, by her news that she began to wonder if it was, after all, so very serious. Perhaps she had been melodramatic, had overreacted. All might indeed, as he had predicted, be well; and they had faced the worst together and he had not run away.

With the subtlety of a practised butler, present but unobtrusive, he caused freshly laundered night clothes to appear, her jug of water was filled regularly and innocent enquiries from her parents were fended off. However, the lure of the studio proved as irresistible as ever, and once he returned from it clutching in his icy hands a sketch of Quill, done from memory, to appease her for his day-long absence. But when, early on Monday morning, the phone rang and Ahmed Zenabi broke the news that the victim's blood had shown nothing, Ian jumped onto their bed and hugged her, laughing out loud and, she noted, every bit as relieved as she was herself.

———

With the car idling at a red light, Simon Oakley peeled the silver paper from around his packet of Polos, rested the now unstable column of sweets on the dashboard and put four of them into his mouth.

Alice did not like mints, but she watched with interest as he chewed them up methodically, then helped himself to another three, never offering one. And it seemed to her that some fundamental rule of hospitality or, perhaps, comradeship was being broken. After all, he did not know that she would have refused one had it been offered. He appeared, in his confectionary-crunching, simply unaware of her presence. Or, and worse yet, careless of it despite their proximity, like a stranger in a railway carriage. Alistair would not have done that, he would have offered her his last crisp, but then, they were friends. Unless it was cheese and onion, of course, or salt and vinegar or… She must try to get to know her new colleague.

'Simon,' she began, 'who d'you think killed Isobel Wilson?'

'Er…' he swallowed his mouthful, 'like a p… p… polo, Alice?' Then he corrected himself, 'No, no, of course, you don't like mints.'

'Quite right, but how on earth do you know that?' she asked, disconcerted by his remark, blushing at the thought of her hasty judgement.

'I don't, really, but you did turn down the pepper-mints that Ruth was distributing in the office after the meeting.'

'Well, thanks for the offer. Anyway, what do you think?' An unusually observant colleague.

'A disgruntled punter, maybe?'

'Why?'

'I don't know. Perhaps, someone who needed her serv-ices but was r... r... revolted by his own need? Well, that it should be met in such a way? It would f... fit with the likely time of death Doctor Zenabi gave us. Some time between about 9.00 p.m. and 11.00 p.m. That would be office hours for her.'

'And a punter who just happened to be carrying a knife?'

'Possibly. A gangland type? Or maybe a married man lured of the s... s... straight and narrow by one of them?'

'Like a hungry, obese person is lured off the straight and narrow by a chocolate gateau, cake-slice at the ready, you mean?'

They turned right onto a short drive, leading from Clare-mont Park to 'Jordan', a grand villa built of red sandstone and with an immaculate Jaguar parked on its gravel sweep. Bill Keane led them into his drawing-room, cof-fee already laid out on a tray for visitors, and stood with his back to a flame-effect gas fire, warming his mustard-coloured corduroys on the faint heat it provided. If the Wilson killing did not focus police attention on the resi-dents' clean-up campaign, then nothing would. That was surely the silver lining from that particular cloud.

'Yes,' he said, handing back the photograph of Isobel Wilson to Alice, 'I've come across her. I know most of them by sight, although not by name, you'll appreciate. She always wears a baseball cap, usually hangs about with another girl.'

'Did you see her on Tuesday night?' Alice asked.

'No. We went out, straight after work, and had an early supper in the Grassmarket and then walked on to a concert at the Festival Theatre.'

'What time did you get home?'

'I can't be sure, I'd guess maybe half eleven or later. After the performance we went on to the Dome for a drink.'

The door opened and a solid, middle-aged woman, spectacles suspended on a chain and bouncing off her pneumatic bosom as she walked, marched into the room bearing a large plate covered in shortbread pieces. Don't take one, Alice willed Simon, looking at her own empty coffee cup and watching him drain the dregs from his own. She knew a trap when she saw one.

'Yes, do take more than one, constable,' Audrey Keane said acidly, watching with a fixed smile as the sergeant removed the two largest slabs, resting one on his saucer and starting to eat the other immediately, releasing showers of sugar to fall onto the deep pile of the beige carpet.

'Since I have you here, officers,' Mrs Keane said, 'I'll just take advantage of your visit to fill you in with what we have to put up with,' and she smiled at her husband, who blinked at her on cue.

'Yesterday, once more, I found two used condoms on our own little lawn, and I heard that Mrs Keir, at number thirteen, had the unpleasant experience of interrupting a fornicating couple at the bottom of her stair. Two days ago

60

I myself, believe it or not, was accosted by a kerb-crawler who was abusive, obscene actually, when I put him right. Oh yes, and when I went onto the West Links on Thursday with my grand-daughter, Katie, I stopped her, in the very nick of time I might add, from picking up a used hypodermic syringe. I am, I have to admit, almost at the stage of thinking that one less – one less streetwalker, I mean – would be a good thing!'

DS Oakley, mouth still filled with shortbread, nodded as if sympathetically, and Mrs Keane, spurred on, continued to address her captive audience.

'As for S.P.E.A.R., don't get me started! The van attracts them, you know, like flies to… well, waste. If it parked somewhere else I'd bet my bottom dollar they would follow it and go somewhere else too. And we'll have no more "tolerance" zones, thank you very much. All very well to impose them when it involves other people's toleration rather than your own. Perhaps, they could be "tolerated" in the vicinity of Holyrood, somewhere by the new Parliament building. Save the MSPs a journey!'

'Audrey!' Bill Keane said, in a shocked tone.

'Well,' his wife continued, unabashed, 'despite your valiant efforts, sweetheart, and I mean that, valiant efforts, the "problem" has not been solved. And for as long as it continues, Katie, and all the other small children we know, are at risk of jabbing themselves with needles, catching Aids and so on. And these constables need to understand how we feel…'

I understand only too well, Alice thought, unconsciously stroking the miniscule scab on her palm. And Ellen Barbour's account of her career, with its high-living and free choices, seemed a million miles from the grubby world of prostitution on display in the dark, unsavoury crevices of the City. Places where the meter ran not by the hour but by the minute, and warm flesh could be bought for the price of a Chinese meal for two.

'To get the full picture of what we have to bear, they should really speak to Guy, shouldn't they, darling?' Audrey Keane said, belatedly offering the shortbread to her husband.

'Guy?' Alice asked.

'Guy Bayley, the head of our group. Our founder, in fact,' Bill Keane replied, ignoring his wife's outstretched arm and smoothing both his winged eyebrows with his fingertips, checking his reflection in the mirror above the mantelpiece as he did so.

—

Talman Secondary gave the impression that it had been formed by the occurrence of an earthquake at a trailer park. Portakabins had been attached to each other at unexpected angles, creating asymmetrical E or T shapes, some ornamented by tired graffiti, and the tarmac on which they rested had wide fissures, like the edges of tectonic plates They had an unsettled, temporary appearance as if their unfortunate inhabitants might be awaiting the clearance of the site followed by the construction of permanent school buildings.

The headmistress, a flustered Asian lady with ebony hollows below her tired eyes, directed them briskly towards the staff room, assuring them that Mr Christie would be in there and that they would not be disturbed before three o'clock. Knocking on the flimsy door, they entered to find an elderly man sitting gazing at a couple of lethargic goldfish in an aquarium, a rolled-up newspaper sticking out from his jacket pocket.

When he stood up, Alice was surprised to see how small he was, such height as he had being in his spine rather than his legs. From her own six-foot vantage point she found that she towered over him, overlooking the extensive bald patch on the crown of his head which was in a perfect pear-shape.

Until he was shown the photograph in the S.P.E.A.R. leaflet, Eddie Christie played dumb, firmly refuting any suggestion that he might have used prostitutes in Edinburgh or anywhere else. When confronted by his own picture, he stared hard at it as if in disbelief, and then a faint smile flitted across his lined features and was gone.

'OK, sergeants, how can I help you?'

'Our enquiry,' Alice said, 'is concerned with the death of Isobel Wilson, a prostitute working in the Leith area'.

'And?'

'We understand that you knew her?'

'No, no, not... I don't think so...'

'It may s... s... save time,' Simon Oakley interrupted, 'for all of us, if we tell you that S.P.E.A.R., who produced the leaflet, informed us that the photo you are looking at was taken on Ms Wilson's phone, and that she reported you to the centre shortly after you had b... b... beaten her up.' He rested his heavy buttocks on the edge of a table and crossed his arms, glaring at the man, an expression of impatience on his face.

'Well, I don't accept any of that, obviously, but now you mention it she does seem familiar.'

'You knew her?' Alice asked.

'"Know" might be putting it a bit strongly, other than in the bibli –'

'Fine. You were acq... acq... acq... ac...' Simon Oakley stammered uncontrollably, then shook his head in frustration and tried again. 'You had m… m… met her before the occasion on which you hit her?'

'Yes.'

'Can you tell us where you were between, say, 5.00 p.m. and 10.00 p.m. on Tuesday night?' he continued.

'Last Tuesday?'

The policeman nodded.

'Easy. With my wife at home, marking homework.'

'And your wife's name, and address?'

'Rona Christie. We live at number five Rintoul Drive.'

'We've got Isobel Wilson's phone. The one she took the photo of you with. We'll get the date off it. Why did you h… h… hit her on that occasion?'

'You really want to know?'

Simon and Alice looked at each other in disbelief before answering 'yes', simultaneously.

'Because she called me "Crocker".'

'So?' Alice asked.

'It's part of a school chant, chanted by my pupils. Or, in this case, ex-pupil. "Who's oaf his rocker, Crocker, Crocker…Crocker Christie!"'

'She was an ex-pupil of yours?'

'So I discovered.'

5

DI Eric Manson handed Alice the pathologist's report and she leafed through it quickly, learning a few facts of which she would rather have remained in ignorance, including that the woman had been five months pregnant when she died. The stab wound to her chest had damaged the left ventricle, completely severing the left anterior descending coronary artery and perforating her left lung. The cause of death was given as a stab wound, haemothorax, external blood loss and haemopericardium.

'Has the knife turned up yet?' she asked Manson, folding the pages and filing them temporarily under a coffee mug.

'Nope. The dogs have been all over the place and uniforms have hoovered the entire area, but nothing's shown up so far, doll.'

'Simon told me yesterday that an approximate time of death's been given?'

'Yeah, well… Professor McConnachie's never prepared to commit himself, obviously, but the boss kept on pressurising him, and sometime between about 9.00 p.m. and 11.00 p.m. Tuesday ninth is the best they can do.'

'And no sign, from the swab or anything else, of recent sexual activity?'

'Condoms, dear. One of the tools of her trade, I hear.'

'I was thinking more of the combings and so on. Anything else happen while I've been away, sir?'

He opened his eyes unnaturally wide, and nodded his head vigorously. 'I thought you'd never ask', he sighed.

The usual game to be endured. And the quicker it was begun the quicker it would end.

'Well, I'm asking now, sir.'

'We've got a match from a bloodstain, with the DNA, I mean. And the shit may well soon hit the fan so I'd duck if I was –'.

On Elaine Bell's unheralded entry into the murder suite he fell silent, watching his superior like everyone else as she patrolled the room, eyes raking the place, clearly in search of something. Approaching Alice's desk she swept up the blue-and-white-striped mug, breathing a sigh of annoyance as she did so.

'Bloody cleaners! Rearranging everything,' she said through gritted teeth. Alice smiled an answer, uncomfortably aware that she was now in close proximity to a hornet, its angry buzz warning that it was liable to sting at any moment. Keep still. Say nothing and it will fly past, she thought, trying to maintain her now fixed smile.

'And don't let it happen again, Alice!' the Chief Inspector spat.

Perhaps she should just shake her head in apparent remorse and remain silent, play safe and avoid any more unwelcome attention, thought Alice. On the other hand, she had no idea what it was that she was not to let happen again, so it might. At any moment. Was she an accessory to mug theft, perhaps?

'Or you, Simon!'

The DCI's attention, though not her physical presence, had shifted on to her other sergeant. Unfortunately for him, he was not familiar with the finer points of the Elaine Bell's body language and blundered in, a sweet still in his mouth.

'Sorry, ma'am. I'm not sure what you are t... t... talking about?' he asked nervously, cheek swollen with his humbug.

Instantly, she whirled round to face him.

'Contamination, DS Oakley, that's what I'm talking about. It's thoroughly unprofessional, I'm sure you'd agree. The single hair from DS Rice was bad enough, but your blood... God save us all! Fortunately, being present when the body was found, seeing the scene myself, I got the lab to check the elimination database and, fortunately once more, you're both on it, but we would have looked complete arses otherwise!'

'It must have been the b... b... brambles,' DS Oakley stuttered 'I was c... c... cut to shreds.' He looked to Alice for support, and glancing up momentarily at their superior, she nodded her head in agreement.

'Brambles, alopecia... I don't care what caused it, but it is not, I repeat not, to happen again. Is that understood?'

The two reprimanded officers nodded again and the Chief Inspector, venom now drawn, bustled out of the room, blue-and-white mug quite forgotten.

'If only you'd listened, Alice...' Eric Manson said, with phoney regret.

'Was that all? The only traces being mine and Simon's?' Best ignore his jibes.

'No, there's another two, one from blood and the other semen, both less good than those of Simon the Pieman and his dancing bear, but they managed to get a match for one of them at least. The blood. You and I are off to see Mr Francis McPhail of Jerez Street this very evening.

They got his DNA in 2005 for drink-driving, and he's the match.'

When she did not immediately rise from her chair to follow him, he said, 'Come on, Bruno. Time to perform!'

A woman was on her knees scrubbing the stone landing outside McPhail's flat, her ample rump waggling slowly in the doorway, following the rhythm of her outstretched arms. Her bucket blocked their way up the stairs.

'We're looking for Mr McPhail?' the Inspector said loudly, ensuring that he could be heard above the din of the cleaning.

'He's away at the church,' she replied, hardly looking up.

'Which church?' Alice asked.

'St Aloysius, further down the road. Obviously.'

'Obviously,' whispered the Inspector as they retraced their steps down the stone stairway to the street below.

The exterior of the church was vast but completely plain. No more than a rectangular, red-brick box with shallow slits for windows, each one positioned a few feet below the stark horizontal created by the flat roof. A structure so simplified and bereft of ornamentation as to fill any onlooker not with awe or wonder but instead with a kind of desperate depression; that humanity could waste time, money and energy in constructing anything so dull and mundane. Ambitionless. A piece of architecture either consciously subverting centuries of tradition, churches built to uplift the faithful and glorify God, or dictated by the excessive penny-pinching of a dying faith.

Passing through flimsy, oak-effect doors, they entered a well-lit nave, its white-painted surfaces bedecked with brightly coloured tapestries, each embroidered with a fish, a lamb or a lily, as if depicted by a child. Facing them, behind the altar, a massive stone crucifix was attached to the wall, a relief of the crucified Christ carved on it and the whole sculpture lit by a raft of concealed spotlights. A circlet of barbed wire adorned Christ's head and his eyes looked upwards seeking deliverance.

As Alice and her companion processed towards the only occupied pews, those next to the altar step, the Inspector whispered, 'What's the awful pong, Yogi?'

But he had misjudged how his voice would carry, and his last words echoed around the space – 'Yogi… Yogi… Yogi…'

'Stale incense, sir,' Alice replied, her voice hardly audible, fearful that her words, too, would be magnified as his had been. Arriving at the step, they automatically separated, taking a side each as if they had discussed the matter beforehand. Alice's gentle tap on the white-haired man's shoulder made him start with surprise, dropping the rosary he had been fingering to clatter onto the floor below.

'Very sorry to disturb you, sir,' Alice began, 'but you're not Mr McPhail, I suppose?'

'No.' The impropriety of the question, in such a place, was communicated forcefully to her by his stern expression. The next man along, eyes clamped shut in prayer, shook his head impatiently in answer to her query, and the third one in the row did the same, her voice having carried to him. Defeated, she manoeuvred her way back through the empty pew to find the Inspector waiting for her.

'Any luck?' he mumbled under his breath.

'No.'

'Me neither. The bastard must have gone.'

While they were still engaged in a whispered discussion, an elderly woman joined them and asked in a broad Irish accent, 'Would it be Father McPhail, now, that you're after?'

'It might well be,' the Inspector replied, smiling politely, and unconsciously adopting her brogue. 'And where would we find him?'

'Well, you'll have to wait your turn like everyone else… he's taking confessions at the minute. I'm number eight, so you'll be numbers nine and ten. Keep your eyes skinned, mind, or other bodies after you in the queue will nip in before you and take your place.'

Sitting on the hard bench, Alice watched as Eric Manson, passing the time in between bouts of fidgeting, methodically hunted down any smut available in the *Good News Bible*, from Susanna and the Elders to Onan and his seed. Each one was discovered in seconds, a testament to the boredom of his own churchgoing years and a retentive memory. She knew them all, of course, and a few more besides; too many masses, benedictions and complines to fill and too little reading material.

After over an hour had limped by, the elderly woman emerged from the side-chapel followed by the priest in his white surplice and purple robe. He beckoned Alice, as if to signal that her turn had arrived, and she rose together with the Inspector.

'Father McPhail… Father Francis McPhail?' she asked.

'Yes.'

The dumpy figure seemed untroubled by their approach, as if used to dealing with pairs, handling inseparable couples. Despite his small stature, he had a magisterial air; they were in Christ's house perhaps, but he was their earthly host. His strange, deep-set eyes looked out at them with an enquiring expression from beneath arched eyebrows. The eyeballs seemed to have no white, vast brown pupils taking up all the space, more like a chimpanzee's than a man's.

'I am DI Manson of Lothian and Borders Police,' the inspector began, and then hesitated, grimacing on hearing his last words returning to him, before continuing softly, 'and I'd be grateful if you would be good enough to help us with our enquiries at the station, at St. Leonards Street.'

Francis McPhail looked astonished at the request, disbelief gradually becoming apparent on his face, but he quickly recovered his composure and said sternly, 'Of course I'll help you, officer, but first of all I must finish taking confession. Two of my parishioners have still to be seen, and if it's all right with you, I'd like to see to them before accompanying you to the police office.' So, for another forty minutes, the police officers waited in the unheated church, their breaths becoming visible, legs and arms crossed in an attempt to maintain their body heat until, to their relief, the priest emerged from the sacristy, clad now in black jacket and trousers.

—

The removal of the suspect from his own surroundings had been DCI Elaine Bell's idea, but he remained ostensibly at ease, comfortable in himself and with the world around him, despite the alien environment. Alice glanced at her watch. Nine p.m. already.

'Good of you to assist us, sir… er… Reverend, sorry… Father,' Elaine Bell began, unusually courteous, seemingly thrown by the man's dog-collar. In reply, he nodded affably, looking straight at her, his dark eyes shining, unashamedly curious to discover why he had been summoned.

'Well, can you tell me where you were on Tuesday the ninth of January, between the hours of, say, 8.00 p.m. and 11.00 p.m.?'

'Can I look at my diary?' he asked, removing a slim leather-bound pocket book from inside his jacket, and holding it unopened in his hands.

'Yes.'

He flicked the diary open and examined an entry, before meticulously inserting the ribbon marker and closing it once more.

'I helped Mrs Donnelly clear my study in the early evening and then, as far as I recollect, I went to church.' He blinked at his interrogator.

'Mrs Donnelly?' the DCI enquired.

'My housekeeper.'

'And at about what time did you leave to go to the church?'

'I can't be exactly sure. It would probably be at about 8.30 p.m. or so.'

'Was there anyone there with you at the same time?'

'To begin with there was a boy. I didn't recognise him though. He's not one of mine.'

Now, apparently completely relaxed, the priest rested his face on his elbow, stroking his ear-lobe, his eyes never leaving the DCI's face.

'When did he leave?' She asked, clearing a stray curl from her forehead.

'Maybe about nine or thereabouts.'

'And when did you leave?'

'Well after him. I'd say at about 11.00 p.m.'

'What were you doing in the place between 8.30 and 11.00 p.m.?'

'Praying.'

'Praying! For two and a half solid hours?' Elaine Bell said, amused scepticism written on her face.

'I am a priest, Chief Inspector. Most evenings I'm out and about visiting – the sick, the bereaved, anyone who needs me, really. I have to take my chances when I can.' His unblinking, simian gaze did not leave hers until, put in her place, she flinched, lowering her eyes as if to check her script. Something about his presence disquieted her.

'Mmm.' The DCI cleared her throat, and Alice became aware of an uncharacteristic hesitancy in her questioning. The priest now stared expectantly at the Chief Inspector, but she remained silent. Perhaps she was unused to dealing with the clergy or, at least, had not met one quite like this.

'Now, about Isobel Wilson,' she started again, an anxious look on her face, 'I assume you knew the woman?'

'Should I?' the priest replied instantly. 'Who is she?'

It was a foolish error in the DCI's approach, and one of which she was immediately conscious, the hint of a blush beginning to rise upwards from her neck to her already flushed cheeks.

'Erm… she was a prostitute working in Leith, Seafield.'

Francis McPhail sat up straight, an amazed look on his face.

'Why on earth would you assume that I would know her? Seafield's not even within my parish boundary.'

'No,' the Chief Inspector said, trying to recover her lost momentum, 'but you still might know her. To be clear on this matter, er… Father… are you telling us that you did not know her?'

'I certainly am. I've never even heard the name.'

'Well, they don't always use their real names. So, do you know, or ever use, any of the working girls down there?' Outrage, followed by anger, transformed the man's features, and when he spoke his tone was emphatic, impressing upon all that no quibbling with his answer would be tolerated.

'Let's be clear about this, shall we? I do not "use" anyone. I have never "used" anyone or needed to. As far as I am aware I do not know, am not even acquainted with, any of the "working girls" in Leith or anywhere else. Perhaps you would now have the courtesy to tell me what this is all about?'

Having watched her superior conduct many interviews, Alice expected a terse response to the implied reprimand. After all, the man was being questioned because DNA from his blood had been found on the body. And the Chief Inspector's mild-mannered reply, surprised her.

'Of course,' Elaine Bell began almost apologetically, 'our enquiry is concerned with the murder of Isobel Wilson. A prostitute killed on the ninth of January. We are asking everyone, everyone we can think of anyway, to assist us to that end.'

'And me,' the priest said evenly, his anger now controlled if not yet expended, 'what precisely makes you think that I could assist you "to that end"?'

But the tables were not to be turned this time, the interrogated becoming the interrogator. He had gone too far. Nothing would be allowed to compromise the investigation, not even the normal requirements of good manners.

'I'd rather not answer that question at present, Father,' the DCI said firmly, re-asserting her control over him, and this time he took it meekly, simply nodding his head.

The interview over, Elaine Bell returned to her room, closing the door slowly behind her. She leant against it and breathed out. The creep had fancied her! Clearly fancied her! And the way he had looked at her had temporarily unsettled her, making her lose the place, flustering her. Hopefully, no one else in the room would have noticed.

Then she shook her head as if shaking the very notion out of it, deciding that it was a ludicrous one anyway. She was a middle-aged woman in a crumpled suit with more grey than brown in her hair, unfanciable by anyone, including her own husband. And no doubt that fact, more than any other, accounted for her delusion, which was all it must have been. The man was a priest, for Heaven's sake! Unlikely to be eyeing up anyone, far less a dowdy policewoman firing impertinent questions at him, in the course of a murder investigation. An investigation with him as the suspect.

'Quite a delicate operation ahead, eh, sir?'

'In what way, teddy?'

Alice and Eric Manson were travelling together in the Astra to number five Rintoul Place in order to check out Eddie Christie's alibi, and the Inspector was at the wheel. Periodically, he lifted one hand off it to flex his fingers in and out in his immaculate leather driving gloves, like a cat extending and retracting its claws.

'Smart, eh? A Christmas gift from the wife,' he said, waving an arm in her direction.

'Very lovely, sir. As I was saying though, a delicate operation, this morning's task.'

'As you said, but I have no idea what you are on about, Boo Boo.'

'Could we stop this bloody bear nonsense, sir?' she replied, annoyance surfacing at his prolonged joke.

'Can't "bear" it any longer, eh?' he smirked. 'Bit grizzly now, bi-polar even?' He laughed uproariously at his own wit, and Alice could not help smiling, amused at his amusement.

'OK, OK, so what exactly is the problem, dear, Bambi... Rudolph... Dum...' his voice tailed off, unable to think of any other names to sustain the gag.

'Well, asking Mrs Christie about her husband's whereabouts. She'll surely want to know why we're interested in them?'

'No problem. I'll handle it, just leave it all to me. Man o' the world stuff.'

Subtlety, Alice knew, did not form part of Eric Manson's social repertoire, and as she walked behind him past a car with a disabled sticker towards a front door with a cement ramp, she stopped, a thought having crossed her mind. Meanwhile, the Inspector peered through the open front door, and when Alice caught up with him, it was to be greeted by a woman, past middle age, seated in a wheelchair.

In her sitting room Manson attempted to begin his interview but, being well acquainted with his ways, Alice could tell that he was feeling uneasy, and thus likely to flounder and cause needless offence.

'Mrs Christie...' he paused. 'We simply need to ask you a few questions about your husband's whereabouts on the ninth of January.'

'Really!' the woman said, surprised. 'Well, I'll help you if I can.'

'Now, can you tell me where he was on the ninth of January between about 8.00 p.m. and 11.00 p.m.'

'That would be a Tuesday, eh?'

'Aha, yes.'

'He'd be here with me. He has three sets of double French on Mondays, so Tuesday evenings are always devoted to marking. He does it in here, beside me. Nice to have company, as he's out all day, you see.'

'Sure about that, that he was here with you all evening?'

'Yes. He made us our tea at six, he brings home salmon on Tuesdays, then he did the homework. He always does on Tuesdays. I'd have noticed if he hadn't. Why do you need to know where he was then anyway?'

'Er…' Eric Manson hesitated, 'to help us with our enquiries – a murder enquiry.'

'A murder!' the woman repeated, excitement enlivening her voice. 'Whose?'

Instead of stopping the conversation and redirecting it, Manson seemed to feel compelled to answer.

'Em… an Isobel Wilson. Just… eh… a woman in Edinburgh.'

'The prostitute! You mean the prostitute! I read all about it in the *Evening News*. What's Eddie to do with her, exactly?'

The Inspector swallowed, now looking rather pale, clearly in difficulty with the line of questioning but, apparently, unable to extricate himself from it. He threw Alice a pleading look.

'Nothing,' she cut in, 'he's nothing whatsoever to do with her – with it. He was here with you, after all. But, you see, we have to check up on the movements of anyone living nearby. Proximity, in itself, to the scene… we have to exclude neighbours and so on. Get assistance from anyone, really.'

'But why do you need to know where he was, then?'

'Routine enquiry,' she lied, stonewalling the woman for her own sake. 'Purely routine, Mrs Christie.'

6

Miss Spinnell peeped timidly from behind her half-opened door, loosened the final chain and came out onto the landing. Quill, attached to an over-long lead, trailed behind her, wagging his tail slowly in appreciation of Alice's arrival. The old lady's head was down, her shoulders drooped, and, in some mysterious way, the dog seemed to have absorbed her desolate mood, showing little of the characteristic elation he normally displayed at the handover. A fleshless hand was extended and Alice took the lead from it, looking into Miss Spinnell's face and noticing that the huge orbs of her eyes were now red-rimmed, swollen with recent tears. She seemed so pathetic, so small and dejected that the policewoman longed to put an arm around her shoulders to comfort her, but resisted the impulse. She knew that physical contact, never mind the familiarity it implied, was considered unwelcome and, in all probability, unpleasant. Any kind of human touch was anathema to the old woman, something to be endured and, in itself, a test of her good manners.

Miss Spinnell handling a dog, however, was quite different. On countless occasions Alice had surprised her neighbour cuddling the animal, kissing his soft muzzle or cradling his head in her lap. Even now, she was absent-mindedly squeezing Quill's ear, easing it through her fingers. Between caresses she spoke: 'Today... Ali... Alice, is my birthday.' But her leaden tone suggested that the occasion was not one of celebration but of mourning instead, just another milestone on the way to dusty death.

'How splendid... I must get you something. Is there anything that you would particularly like, Miss Spinnell?'

'Yes,' her neighbour replied forlornly, 'A new self.'

'What's wrong with the old one?' Alice asked brightly, unsure where the conversation was leading.

'I don't know... and that may, possibly, be part of the problem.'

Sodding, sodding Alzheimer's, Alice thought. A fiend so skilled in cruelty as to leave odd, disturbing flashes of insight, but enough only to compound the anxiety it brought with it.

'How about...' she racked her brain for inspiration, 'some... chocolates?' A favourite treat, she knew, remembering the time her assistance had been required to catch imagined pilferers, supposedly bloated on Milk Tray and Black Magic. In fact, Quill himself had been the culprit, canine teeth shredding the cardboard packaging, but the marks attributed, by his devoted admirer, to the long nails of the criminal classes.

'No.'

'What about a book then, poetry if you like?' She could still see, in her mind's eye, the Poetry Society Medal collecting cobwebs on the shelf.

'I do not like poetry any more. Stop guessing. I can tell you exactly what I want.'

'Yes?'

'My sister. I would like my sister.'

Alice discovered that Miss Spinnell had lost touch with her sibling well over fifty years earlier. She asked for any details that might assist with the search, and was surprised to find herself escorted into the old lady's drawing room. A visit to the Holy of Holies was an unexpected privilege. On the floor by the bow window lay an assortment of unwashed soup plates, packets of cornflakes, half-empty tins of beans, Oxo cubes and a heap of dog biscuits. Evidently, the area was Quill's kitchen-cum-dining room. The carpet was strewn with single, unmatched pop socks and, crossing it, Alice inadvertently stood on a wet sponge.

Once she was seated on the sofa, Miss Spinnell returned from a search in a chest of drawers, weighed down by an old photograph album. Inadvertently, she flopped down next to Alice, their thighs momentarily touching. Springing up instantly, she removed herself to the far end of the sofa and placed the open book between them. After much fumbling, a crooked finger was pointed at a black and white image.

'Annabelle,' she said, 'my older sister... em... eight years older than me.'

'And on this birthday, Miss Spinnell, if you don't mind me asking, how old are you?' Alice asked gently. A suitably oblique enquiry, surely.

'Eighty... ninety, that sort of figure or thereabouts,' the old lady said, before, seeing what Alice was getting at, she added crossly, 'She is alive, you know. If not kicking.'

'Excellent,' Alice replied, 'you've been in some sort of contact recently?'

'Of course not! If I had I wouldn't need you. No. But she is here, on this earth. I've been along to the Scarlet Lodge, you appreciate.'

'The Scarlet Lodge?' Alice enquired, bemused.

'Our spiritualist meeting place, dear. I attempted to

make contact and failed. So she cannot be in their world…
the spirit world, I mean.'

'Spiritualism?' Alice exclaimed in wonderment. A new
facet of her neighbour.

'Yes, spiritualism,' the impatient reply shot back, 'Spiritualism! Good enough for Sir Arthur Conan Doyle, no
less, so good enough – nay, too good – for you. Now, were
I to entrust him with the case of the missing sister he'd
be sure to come up with the goods! A real detective that
one… unlike you, dear.'

Leaving the flat with the scant information she had
been able to glean, Alice smiled to herself. Dealing with
her neighbour was like trying to tame an ancient and confused stoat, an unlikely pet, and one which even in its
dotage required to be treated with the utmost respect.

—

'Four rolls. A Twix and a soup, if they've t… t… tomato.'

'Four rolls!' Alice repeated, astonished.

'Yes. FOUR rolls, a Twix and a soup. Any kind of roll,
by the way, ham, t… t… tomato, cheese, tuna. I'm not
fussy and I'm still building up my strength after the accident,' Simon answered, unabashed.

Chewing the dry pastry of her Scotch pie and feeling,
for once, strangely virtuous in her comparative restraint,
Alice decided to continue with her plan to get to know the
new DS. If she said nothing the silence in the car would
remain unbroken. Either he was shy or else conversation
was not his forte.

'In the accident, what happened?'

'A car crash in 2007, on the bypass. I was in hospital for over three months… emergency transfusion
after emergency transfusion. They didn't think I'd pull

through, actually. But here I am, and twice as large as life.' He patted his ample belly, chuckling to himself.

'Must have frightened your family?'

'No. I never knew my dad, and my mum was d... d... dead by then.'

'Sorry...' An unexpected impasse.

'Oh, don't be. She and I never hit it off. But,' he grinned, 'the last laugh was mine!'

'Oh?'

'Well, the c... c... cussed old duck chose to die on my birthday! But I got my own back on her. In her w... w... will she directed that she was to be buried so I took her off to be burnt in the Mortonhall Crematorium. Ashes to ashes, dust to dust and... flames to flames for her.' He laughed loudly, glancing at Alice's face to see if she was shocked or, perhaps, shared his black sense of humour.

'Where did you sprinkle her remains? A car park, perhaps, or maybe, a sewage farm?'

'I didn't. I never collected her ashes at all, so she'll either have been scooped up with someone else or be residing permanently in the incinerator..'

If he was serious, pursuing revenge beyond the grave did seem a tad extreme, Alice thought. But since the topic (like Simon's mother) seemed to have died a natural death, the only sound in the vehicle now that of the passing traffic, she racked her brain for something new to prolong their chat. With a lewd wink, Eric Manson had murmured to her that Simon was not married and was available, but otherwise nobody in the squad seemed to know anything much about him. If he had a girlfriend, then no doubt that would be disclosed by him in his own good time and she had no intention of attempting to winkle out any such information out of him. She had suffered enough enquiries into her own love life to ensure that she did not inflict that particular indignity on anyone else. Maybe, with his fondness for food, he liked cooking? Rick Stein, perhaps, or maybe Gordon? But before she had time to work out any other conversational openings, the car drew up outside Father McPhail's tenement building.

On closer inspection, no-one would have mistaken his housekeeper, Mrs Donnelly, for a cleaner. Or for the priest's floozy, as had been suggested by DCs Littlewood and Gallagher the previous evening. Celibacy, they argued, was a state proclaimed for public consumption but never, in fact, privately maintained. It was an unnatural condition abhorred by man and woman alike, and surely, by their creator too. And, indisputably, it was impossible to achieve.

In convents nuns seemed to manage it, Alice observed. These 'Brides of Christ', DC Littlewood shot back, rarely had any choice in the matter, being too fat, bearded or plug-ugly to attract any earthly suitors. And when eventually he conceded that his own experience of convent life might be inferior to her own, he had expressed frank disbelief when told that a few of her teaching order had been stunners. Recovering quickly, he had thrown a sly glance at DC Ruth Lindsay, and added that it was culpable, sinful, of the beautiful not to reproduce. The young policewoman raised her eyes from her nails only to reply, *sotto voce*, 'In your dreams, Tom. And you'll be the last in your line, for sure.'

Eric Manson, adopting the authoritative tone of an *eminence gris*, proclaimed that for the ordinary person, the 'normal' person, complete excess would invariably be preferable to complete abstinence. But, Alice, picturing the sad souls she had seen flitting in and out of the shadows at Seafield, selling sex indiscriminately to feed their habits, then the ancient and venerable virgins who had taught her, trilling innocently, joyfully in their choir stalls in the side chapel, shook her head.

The housekeeper, a grey plait coiled around the crown of her head like a torpid snake, led them into the kitchen and pulled out chairs for them. Her face remained unsmiling, intimidating even, and despite the steam billowing from the kettle she offered them neither tea nor coffee. In a voice which implied the impertinence of the question, she confirmed that she and Father McPhail had spent the early evening hours of the ninth of January giving his study a good spring clean. Sounding even more affronted, she told them that the priest had, indeed, gone to St Aloysius afterwards, but she was unable to say when he returned. However, she emphasised, he must have gone there; that was, after all, where he had said he was going. As she had gone to bed before his return from the church she was unable to 'vouch', as they put it, for the time of his arrival, other than to say that it must have been after 9.00 p.m. No doubt they would appreciate, she added reprovingly, that Father McPhail was an ordained Catholic priest, and thus a Man of his Word.

As they were tramping back to the car, their eyes smarting in the bitter wind, Alice telephoned the DCI to break the news that their suspect had no witness to support his alibi. In turn, she was told, between unpleasantly amplified bouts of liquid coughing, that they should bring him in, on a voluntary basis, if at all possible. He was currently to be found in Jerez Street, under surveillance by a constable borrowed temporarily from the drugs squad. There followed an explosive, mannish sneeze, and then, suddenly, the line went dead.

No sooner had Alice settled into the passenger seat than her phone rang and she picked it up, battling with her seatbelt while trying to listen. Everything had changed. They must go this very minute, pronto, to Cargill's scrapyard on Seafield Road, Elaine Bell ordered, her voice periodically muffled as she continued to issue instructions to someone beside her in the office. The foreman of the yard had just reported the presence of a body in one of the wrecked cars. She would join them, if she could get away, within the next half hour or so.

The pale winter sun hung low in the sky and heavy clouds began to encircle it, gradually obscuring it, stealing precious daylight and imposing a premature dusk on the chill city. From nowhere, large flakes of snow appeared, an endless, hostile stream of them, choking the windscreen wipers and smothering the icy road.

At the scrapyard, a man waited for them, ill-dressed for the sudden blizzard, stamping his hob-nailed boots on the ground, trying to preserve any feeling in his feet. Seeing them he hurriedly pushed the heavy double gates open, gesticulating towards the north side of the yard, then jogged behind them to their parking place. As DS Oakley slammed the passenger door shut, he lost his balance on the snow-covered cement, falling forwards heavily and striking his right hand on a length of rusted, exhaust piping.

'Oh, fuck!' he bellowed on impact, kicking the tube as he lay, still spread-eagled on the ground like an over-turned turtle. His thumb had a huge gash on it, running from the pulp down the front of the joint to the knuckle, and blood jetted from it, reddening his cuff as he held his bloody hand upwards, attempting to stem the flow. Taking Alice's outstretched arm, he pulled himself up and examined his wound for a few seconds, then, grasping his injured hand in the other one, he smiled widely as if to signal that he was now all right. The two sergeants trailed behind their guide towards an untidy mound of skeletal, scrapped cars, smithereens of shattered windscreen glass crunching beneath their feet.

'It's in there,' the foreman said, waving vaguely in the direction of a doorless Renault Clio which rested precari-ously on the burnt chassis of another vehicle.

'I seen it when I wis liftin' the car up wi' the crane… so I jist dumped it oan the other wan, and called yous.'

'You're sure it's a b… b… body?' Simon Oakley asked, his thumb pressed hard against his mouth. Thin strands of his fair hair were being blown by the wind into his eyes, making them water.

'No. But it looked like wan… less Andy's up tae his games again.'

'What do you mean?' Alice asked.

'A couple o' months ago he got wan o' they naked dummies, ken, and put it in a Jag. I nearly wet masel wi' fright.'

From their viewpoint on the ground, nothing could be seen inside the Renault, so, exchanging nervous glances, they simultaneously began to climb up to it, Alice clam-bering onto the bonnet of the burnt hulk and Oakley stepping up onto its boot. He got up there first, bent his weighty torso through the gap on the driver's side, and craned in.

'It's a body alr... r... right, Alice,' he shouted, wobbling slightly on his makeshift platform, snowflakes starting to lie on his broad back as he continued looking inside. Half a minute later, as he remained motionless, gazing into the space, Alice said, 'Come on, Simon! We'd better get going, eh? Start taping off the area. I'll get the stuff from the car. The boss may be here any minute, and she'll expect us at least to have made a start by the time she arrives.'

Immediately Oakley's head re-emerged from the interior, and like a great lumbering bear he began slowly and carefully to descend, stepping warily along the curved surfaces until, in an undignified rush, he slid to the ground, bumping his buttocks and landing feet first, his balance saved only by Alice grabbing his arms.

'Thanks, pal,' he said, looking anxiously into her eyes.

'Well?' she asked, still holding onto him as if they were engaged in some kind of strange dance.

'Well, what?' he replied, bemused, blood from his injured thumb dripping on to the ground.

'A man? A woman? The body. What was it?'

'Female,' he said wearily, 'maybe thirty-five or forty. Arms across her chest like the other one. She had a gold chain around her neck and it looks as if she's been s... s... stabbed, too.'

Sets of stepladders were produced for the Scenes of Crime officers and the photographers, together with halogen lamps from the garage. Throughout all their measured, meticulous activity, the snow continued to fall, thick and fast, coating everyone and everything. It laid a spurious mantle of innocence over the scene, disguising its real character beneath a spotless veneer.

Recognising one of the cameramen as he shook his head free of its white thatch, Alice asked to see the images that he had taken of the victim's face. In the biting cold, he showed her, shivering theatrically to hurry her along. But it was academic. She knew, in her heart of hearts, before seeing a single picture, that the dead woman would be Annie Wright. And, sure enough, her pale features had been captured by the camera. Her soul, lost.

'Seen enough?' the man asked gently, brushing the snow from Alice's shoulders as she continued to gaze at the face, deep in thought.

—

Walking down a corridor formed by parallel rows of rusting gas cylinders, the dismembered entrails of a digger littering her route, she spotted the DCI, tucked behind a skip, hugging herself, trying to keep warm in the raw wind. She was in conversation with someone, and every time she spoke a cloud of pale vapour billowed from her mouth like smoke from a small dragon, followed immediately by an answering puff from the other person. Suddenly catching sight of her sergeant, she hollered across, 'What news?'

'We can identify the victim, Ma'am,' Alice called back, finding that even forming the words was an effort in the biting cold, her mouth numb, lips curiously inflexible. 'It's Annie Wright, the prostitute who was raped a couple of months ago. I told you about her, remember – the trial that went ahead not so long ago and we lost? I've just seen a photograph and it's her.'

Elaine Bell closed her eyes. 'Christ Almighty! All hell

will be let loose now. They'll think it's another bloody Ipswich. And it can't be the sodding priest this time, either, we've had him babysat ever since we let him go.'

'Not necessarily,' Dr Zenabi began, stepping away from the skip and finding himself interrupted instantly.

'What d'you mean, Ahmed, 'not necessarily?' the inspector demanded.

Taken aback by her intensity, and with an uneasy smile on his face, he mumbled, 'Nothing. Well, we'll see at the PM, eh?'

———

The kitchen was tiny, lit by a single, bare light bulb, and smelt faintly of stale gas. Diane led her into it, puzzled that a policewoman should call on them at such an hour. But she showed no signs of concern, her fingers travelling deftly on her play station as she walked.

'It's about your mum,' Alice said, already feeling sick to her stomach.

The girl looked up from the flashing screen and replied, in a matter-of-fact tone, 'She's oot the noo. I've been away at Aviemore on a school trip the last three days, got back at tea-time. She'll no' be hame till later, but I can phone her if it's important, like.'

No, she won't. No, you can't, Alice thought, still saying nothing but preparing herself for her role as the bearer of bad news, the destroyer of happiness. And the task became no easier for her however many times it had been done, and practice did not seem to make perfect. Over her ten years in the force she had been chosen as the herald of death nineteen times, and remembered every single occasion. Each differed from the others, but they were all, without exception, horrible. Parents weeping over the loss of a child, husbands over wives, sisters over brothers. And most other combinations, too. All of them, when linked with the word 'death', bringing about the collapse of small worlds, the ending of any pure, unmingled joy.

Old Mrs Wilson had been no exception, her grief as real as all the rest. But this was the first time Alice had had to break the news to a ten-year-old, fatherless girl that her mother had been killed. Hearing her own voice, she felt that in telling the child she was, in some way, complicit, as if her hand, too, had been on the knife.

Paper crumples, she thought, not people, yet it was the word which came to mind on seeing the child's reaction to the awful news. Looking at Diane's tearful face, she wrapped her arms around the slight body, feeling her quivering like a frightened bird, aware that the protection she could give was illusory, shielded her from nothing. Tomorrow Diane would have to face the world alone, having lost the most precious person known to her; and her childish love had not yet curdled, become judgemental, still remained open and unashamed.

By the time the family liaison officer arrived, the girl had stopped crying and was drinking from a mug of hot chocolate, sniffing to herself between sips. Alice waved goodbye to her and then crept out, feeling drained and inadequate, worried now that her replacement had seemed so cool, detached, in her dealings with the child. Should the possibility of 'care' even have been mentioned, when there might be a relation somewhere or other, a grandparent unaware of the existence of a grandchild, or an uncle or aunt prepared to give her a home? Preoccupied, she almost walked past the mail she had seen stacked neatly on the hall table, remembering before crossing the threshold to check the most recent postmark on the letters. And the neighbours must be seen too, questioned as soon as possible while anything of any significance remained fresh in their memories.

Finding that all the flats in the tenement bar one were boarded up, she knocked on its scratched front door, getting no response. Then, noticing a gap in it where a spy hole once had been, she put her eye to it and found herself eyeball to eyeball with the occupant.

'Ye're lucky I didnae poke a sharp pencil right through it,' an old voice croaked, and the door was opened a foot or two to reveal an unshaven little fellow, his pyjama top visible below his knitted jersey. Concluding that his visitor posed no threat, he said cheerily, 'C'mon, hen, c'mon in.'

The sound of dozens of budgies cheeping and chirruping greeted her as they entered the kitchenette, making any conversation impossible until the old man turned on a tap, soothing or intriguing them into silence. Nonetheless, many of them continued to fly free, swooping from cage to cage, some now sitting on the mixer tap, heads bent to one side. Moving a soiled newspaper from a chair, their owner sat down and began to speak, cutting an apple into budgie-size bites as he did so.

'The last time I seen Annie wid be oan the Friday night, eh... the twelfth, that'd be,' he said, running his fingers up and down over the stubble on his cheek. 'No since then, mind. Mebbe she's been away or somethin'.'

'Does she go away often?'

'Naw. She's nivver away. I seen her oan the stair, aboot the back o' eight. She wis oan her way tae her work.'

'Her work?' Did he know that she was a prostitute?

'Aha. She's a cleaner, ken. Cleans nights at schools up the toon. Sleep a' day, practically. Looks aifter the wee yin perfect, though,' he added quickly, anxious not to create official suspicion about her child-care arrangements or anything else. She was much more than a neighbour to him, she was his friend.

'So, sir, you've not seen her since the back of eight on Friday night. But have you maybe heard her? Coming up the stairs or in the flat or anywhere? Even the sound of a radio or TV?'

'Naw. Not a cheep, darlin'.'

'Get the fucking result and get it now!'

Elaine Bell banged down the phone and looked up at Alice from her desk.

'Bloody lab,' she said, by way of explanation. 'We'll see about that. I'll have it in a couple of days or they'll feel the Chief Constable's hot breath on their collars. What do you want, Alice?'

'Er...' stammered the sergeant, confused, 'DI Manson said you wanted me, had something in mind that I am to do – now.'

'Right,' the DCI said, trying to gather her thoughts as she spoke. 'Quite right. I need you to go down to the Cowgate for 9.00 a.m. tomorrow. Professor McConachie's going to do the PM and, if I can make it, I'm coming too. First, though, go back to S.P.E.A.R. and see who we should speak to about Annie Wright. Find out who'll know her movements and so on.'

'But it's eight o'clock at night, ma'am. The office will be empty.'

'Yes, the office will be empty but, for Christ's sake, use your initiative! The van will likely be out and about. Check Carron Place and then any of its other stopping places. You said the Barbour woman usually mans it, so go and find them. Now!'

And, as was so often the case, DCI Bell turned out to be correct. The yellow van was parked on the cobbles in Salamander Street, beside a vacant lot. On the high mesh fencing surrounding the waste ground a sign swung creaking in the wind, bearing the words 'Scheduled for Re-development'. Plumes of grey smoke curled from a few slush-dampened bonfires dotted about the site, their embers casting a tangerine glow on the snow surrounding them. Soon that area, too, of the ancient, venerable Burgh of Leith, with its winding streets and decayed grandeur, would be no more. Its place would be taken by comfortable and characterless flats interspersed with retail parks, the place's independent status already no more than a fading memory.

Despite the harsh weather, a woman leant against the vehicle chatting to the driver. Snatches of their conversation reached Alice's ears as she walked towards the van. Something about polis cars, lights, and the scrappy's yard. Not surprising that the prostitutes know, she thought – another killing in the heart of their territory, they should be among the first to hear.

Sensing the approach of a stranger, and keen to avoid any confrontation, the woman slunk into the darkness, padding silently away on the compacted snow. Alice tapped on the window on the other side and watched a sleeve wipe away the condensation, to reveal the face of its owner. A jerk of the head was all that needed to communicate where the policewoman was to go and Alice climbed into the van, relieved to be out of the cold and heartened by the smell of coffee.

'So, it's true?' Ellen Barbour said immediately.

'What?' Best give no information away yet.

'Another murder!' Barbour said crossly, aware that some sort of fencing was taking place and having no truck with it.

'How do you know about it?'

'Bush telegraph, so to speak. How d' you think?'

'We need your help, Ellen. It's Annie Wright this time. She was found, as you've probably heard, in Cargill's yard. Who would be able to tell me about her movements this evening and in general?'

'Easy. She always works with Christine, they're pretty inseparable. She'd be able to help.'

'Christine?'

'Christine Hunter.'

'And where would I find her?'

'Well, usually they work just up from the junction with Seafield Place, by General George's car park. If I were you, that's the place I'd try first.'

As the policewoman opened the car door to leave, Ellen Barbour added, angrily, ' And that Guy Bayley, Alice, see him too – check him out.'

The name sounded familiar. 'Why? Where would I find him?'

'You'll find him under 'B' for bastard in the phone book, or try the offices of Scrimegour and Woodward WS in Queen Street. That's where he works, I gather.'

'And why should I see him?'

'Because he's a fanatic, he started everything. He's always on the phone, complaining to us, to the council. And he hates prostitutes, truly hates them – all of them. Sometimes I wonder if it's because... well, maybe his mother was one or something.'

7

A man was walking along the pavement towards her: waterproof jacket, starched blue jeans and a cloth cap pulled down low over his face. Christine Hunter knew the type. A prim wife at home fondly imagining hubby to be at the Rotary, the Residents' Association or some other worthy gathering, waiting patiently for his return, blink-ered to the real nature of his hotly anticipated meetings. And a punter on foot meant no cosy car despite weather cold enough to kill a cat.

To her surprise, as the stranger drew near, he unfurled a striped golf umbrella and thrust it aloft, high above his head, like a tourist guide. She gazed at his face expecting the usual expression of fear mingled with excitement, but found instead something rather different. Unadulterated loathing.

'Filthy bitch!' he mouthed.

She turned away from him to face the traffic, but to her amazement he lined himself up beside her so that their shoulders and elbows were in contact, and they were side by side like figures in a paper chain.

'The others are on their way. So, best get back to your kennel, eh?' he added, beginning to shuffle sideways, pushing her along with him until, annoyed, she jutted out her hip, temporarily stopping him in his tracks. As if on cue, two other men, one wearing an orange day-glo jacket, emerged from a parked car and silently joined the strange chorus line, starting to move in unison with their leader. The prostitute was forced along again until, suddenly, she stepped backwards and the men came to an unscheduled halt, bumping into each other like railway carriages colliding. Immediately, the shufflers reformed, feet together, aligning themselves beside her to restart their sideways progress along the pavement. A few more seconds of pressure and Christine Hunter felt her legs going from beneath her; she slipped on sheet ice and fell backwards onto the unyielding ground.

Lying there, panting from the effort of resisting their combined pressure, she glared up at her tormentors as they stood speechless, exhaling their warm breaths into the cold air, more like dumb beasts than fellow human beings.

'OK, OK, big men, yous win,' the woman said in her nasal, sing song voice, her ribs aching, bruised from the heavy landing. The buggers would not see her cry though. She would not give them that satisfaction.

To her surprise a gloved hand was stretched towards her and she took it, wondering, as she did so, if it was some kind of sick joke and she would find her grip unexpectedly released. But it did not happen, and two cloth caps were tipped at her as she turned northwards heading for Salamander Street, blinking hard as snow flakes landed in her watering eyes. A tap on her shoulder did not make her halt or turn around, it would only be the vigilantes making sure that she did not retrace her steps, shepherding her as if she was an old ewe. But when the figure drew level and she saw a woman's face, she stopped at last.

Back in Fishwives Causeway, the prostitute stretched upwards for the coffee jar on the wall unit and felt, as she did so, a stab of pain in her left chest, savage enough to make her wince, and instantly she retracted her arm as if she had received an electric shock. Unasked, the police sergeant reached it for her, and took over the preparation of their drinks, searching in the fridge for the milk and unhooking the mugs from their place below the shelf.

Christine Hunter was still trying to take in the meaning of what she had been told. Annie Wright. Annie of all people! On the other hand, why not Annie? Why not her, for that matter? Leaves in the wind mattered more to most people, were less of a nuisance than the so-called underclass. Her class. Maybe the time had finally come to quit? But she rejected the idea immediately. It could not be afforded, best not even contemplate such a thing. Maybe, when she was clean, but she had failed often enough at that. Drumming the warm coffee spoon on her palm, she turned her attention to the questions being fired at her and began to speak.

'Last time I seen Annie wid be oan the Friday. I've no' been back oot since then, as Marvin's been ill in his bed an' I stayed hame wi' him.' Hearing the name, Alice wondered, idly, whether the man was the girl's pimp, present somewhere in the house but hidden. She said nothing, letting the woman continue.

'She'd hae been at the warehouse though. She gaes even if I'm off. Annie needs the money, like, aye works there... unless the bastards are out 'n aboot. Like the nicht.' The prostitute stirred another spoonful of sugar absentmindedly into her half cup. 'No-wan showed on the Friday, mebbe the weather, mebbe the new law, whitever. By ten we ca'ed it a day. Nivver seen her aifter that.'

'So the last time you saw your friend alive was at about 10.00 p.m. last Friday?'

'Aye.'

The kitchen door creaked open and a small boy, clad in oversized pyjamas, peered round it until his mother beckoned him and he skipped across the floor, his hems dusting the lino, then jumped delightedly onto her lap.

'Your son?' Alice asked.

'Aha. Ma wee boy, Marvin.'

'Did you have a bad dream?' Alice enquired, beaming at the child as he traced the shape of a stain on the kitchen table with his finger. She got no reply.

'Did you have a bad dream, Marvin?' she tried again.

'He'll nae hear ye, hen. He has tae see yer mooth tae ken whit ye're sayin'. He's stane deaf, like me. We're gaen tae get implants wan day an' join the human race.'

—

A gleaming hearse with its engine idling was waiting at the vehicular entrance to the Police Mortuary in the Cowgate. The driver, his black topper resting on the dashboard, was having a smoke while listening for an answer at the entry phone.

Inside the building, Alice looked at the naked, bruised female corpse lying on the table, exposed to the gaze of all as she had been when first born. The circle completed. She looked over the record of items removed from the corpse, her gaze flitting down it until she found the jewellery section. An eternity ring, a pair of stud earrings but, oddly, no gold crucifix listed with the chain.

Jock Brady, one of the technicians, nudged her out of the way, fussing about the place like an old hen, compulsively arranging and then re-arranging the tools and equipment, ensuring that they were all in their proper order in readiness for the arrival of the principal *dramatis personae*.

'Heard about the Prof?' he asked cheerily, buffing up an oversized metal ladle on his sleeve.

'No.' Alice shook her head, tense in anticipation of what she would soon have to witness. What in Heaven's name would the ladle be used for?

'He's fine, but the poor auld bugger lost a lot o' blood, I've heard. His gastric ulcer blew up early this morning, and he was rushed – blue light an' all – into the Royal Infirmary.'

Maybe the post mortem would be postponed, then, Alice thought, feeling her spirits soar at the prospect. If so, someone else might find themselves assigned to it instead of her. Surely, luck was on her side.

'So, is this thing going to go ahead then?'

'Obviously. We're all here. Doctor Zenabi's going to do it wi' some bint drafted in for the occasion frae Dundee. Eh… a Doctor… Doctor… Doctor bloody Who for all I can remember. She's reputed to be a real glamour pu…' His voice tailed off as Doctor Zenabi, with the female pathologist in tow, approached the table. Jock smiled ingratiatingly at both of them.

'Doctor Todrick,' the woman volunteered, introducing herself in a business-like fashion. She was, Alice noticed, strikingly attractive despite her unflattering garb and scraped-back hair, and had the upright carriage of an empress. On the other side of the body the technician raised an eyebrow and winked conspiratorially as if to say 'I told you so'.

And as the minutes ticked slowly by, Alice noticed that Ahmed Zenabi could not take his eyes off his new colleague. Due to his infatuation, his movements, usually so precise and assured, had become subject to a marked delay, out of synchronisation with everyone else. He was only a few seconds behind, but enough to cause a degree of irritation to Jock if no-one else. The usual practised choreography of the mortuary was being upset.

Now the technician stood with the saw in his hand, eyes rolling upwards, waiting impatiently, and in vain, for the signal to apply it to the skull. Several times he mimed the anticipated action, making loud brooming noises as if he were about to wield a chainsaw, but neither of his superiors paid any attention to him. One was busy taking scrapings from beneath the dead woman's fingernails, and the other was busy too, transfixed by the sight of his colleague performing her duties. He might as well not have been there.

'Lovesick puppy!' Jock murmured under his breath to Alice, before deliberately knocking an empty metal collecting jug off the table with his elbow, causing it to bounce noisily on the tiles below. Doctor Zenabi looked up, glaring angrily, only to find the saw thrust unceremoniously towards him, an indignant expression on his colleague's face rather than the expected contrition.

Gently placing a limp white hand back onto the table, Dr Todrick turned her attention to the ragged flesh around the chest wound. Oblivious to the fracas, she said quietly, 'Some bites... rat bites, by the look of things. She must have been outside for quite a little while.'

Elaine Bell, handkerchief hastily clamped over her nose as if she might sneeze at any moment, moved closer to the body, craning forward to get a better view. In her eagerness she jostled a photographer. Her irritated snarl elicited a speedy apology from her victim.

'Doctor Todrick, you said she'd been outside for a fair bit. How long exactly?' she asked.

'Quite a few days, judging by the rodent damage – and the faeces,' the pathologist replied, extracting a black pellet from the centre of the wound and examining it carefully in her tweezers.

'Fine… dead for quite a few days,' Elaine Bell repeated, gagging and swallowing her voice, '…but how many days exactly? When was she killed?'

Adjusting her goggles, and re-focussing on the dropping, Dr Todrick replied 'I can't say with any real precision. My best estimate would be three or four days. Something like that. The cold's certainly retarded the decomposition process. '

'Four days, ma'am, would accord with the last known sighting of the woman alive and the date of the earliest letter unopened by her. It was postmarked the twelfth, a Friday, second class…' Alice began.

'OK, OK,' the Detective Chief Inspector said, impatiently cutting her off, determined to extract maximum information from the pathologists while she still had the chance to do so in person.

'And the wound, Ahmed, is it the same sort of shape, size or whatever as the one on Isobel Wilson?'

His gloved hand now around a human heart, the man nodded. 'Looks like it. I can't be sure without measurements and so on, but yes, it appears that way. Single-sided blade, un-serrated. If the vaginal swabs and other stuff are all negative, then it may well be the same perpetrator. Same M.O. at least. Isobel Wilson wasn't touched was she?'

'Mmmm,' Elaine Bell assented unthinkingly, momentarily taken aback by the sight of the object in the pathologist's hand. Meanwhile Doctor Todrick folded her arms for a few seconds respite, and her colleague immediately put down his handful to do the same, unconsciously mimicking her movements once more and allowing his gaze to return to her face. Briefly, their eyes met. Doctor Todrick quickly lowered hers, only to raise them again to meet his a few seconds later. And despite the smell of the butcher's shop in the air and the presence of a dead body between them, Alice recognised what she was witnessing. She marvelled at the strangeness of life; that love should blossom, in a mortuary.

⟶

That evening, Eric Manson parted his lips, allowing the cigar he was smoking to fall to the ground, trod on the butt, exhaled heavily and pulled open the side door to the church hall. Religion in its place, he mused, was all very well, but like homosexuality should not be flaunted. Its trappings should be kept to a minimum, with no bells, smells or catwalk costumes. Full grown men nancying around in purple silk 'vestments'. Frocks, more like! Had they no pride? The Church of Scotland, of course, seemed to have pitched it about right, allowing little more than a fur trim on the minister's hood, but otherwise leaving out the disco tinsel so cherished by the rest of them. Would the fur be stoat, weasel, ferret or what? Badger, even? And then there were the Kirk's good works; the Boys Brigade and Africa.

Traipsing through the vestibule, he entered a well-lit hall and saw, directly in front of him, a troupe of twenty little boys and girls, sitting cross-legged and arranged in a semi-circle at the feet of the seated priest. As the door slammed unexpectedly behind him, some of the children spun round on the floor to look at the intruder and he attempted a warm, reassuring smile in return, striding purposefully towards the back of the room where there were rows of chairs and, thankfully, other adults sitting in them. Only one free. He lowered himself on to it and peered around. Nothing but couples everywhere. The woman on his right whispered enthusiastically, 'Which one's yours?'

Suddenly panicking at the thought that he might be taken for a paedophile on a reconnaissance trip, he pointed dumbly at a freckled, red-haired youngster sitting slightly apart from the other first communicants in the class, then asked, 'How much longer have we got to go?'

The woman glanced at her watch and whispered in reply, 'It's nearly half seven. Four more minutes to the break and then, maybe, another fifteen after that.'

The break! Heavens above, that was when his 'daughter' would surely expose him as a fraud or worse. Then things really would get sticky. Elaine Bell, entrusting him with the job of persuading McPhail to attend the station voluntarily once more, had impressed upon him that he would have to use all his tact in order for them to get this second bite of the cherry. Thinking quickly, he began to cross and uncross his legs, shifting this way and that on his hard seat until he was sure he had created the intended impression.

'So sorry to bother you again,' he said, an expression of desperation on his face, 'but is there by any chance a toilet in the hall?'

'Vandalised, I'm afraid.'

No matter. The thought had been planted in her brain. As the children rose for their orange juice and biscuits he stood up, staying slightly bent as if his bladder might explode at any minute, and, smiling politely at his fellow parents, left the hall. In the street, a few wet snow flakes were idling down and he shivered, opening his packet of Hamlets and hurriedly lighting up. Another father slunk out of the hall and joined him, looking longingly at Manson's face as he exhaled his cigar smoke.

'Like one?' Manson asked, feeling generous, his spirit buoyant, his cover still intact..

'Thanks. The wife thinks I've given up but… well, you never do really, eh?'

'Aye,' his companion replied, offering a match and taking a deep, satisfying drag.

'Lovely sight, eh, all the wee yins gettin' prepared an' everythin'.'

'Lovely.' And the last one in the packet. Damn it!

'And what's yours going to be called on confirmation? My wife's set on Philomena, so there'll likely be a battle ahead.'

'Eh?' What was the man going on about?

'You know, the name that she'll choose on confirmation?'

Bloody hell, bloody, bloody hell. More mumbo jumbo. He racked his brain. 'Mmm… Judy.'

'Judy's no a saint's name!'

So, another fucking trap, but a show of knowledge ought to win the day.

'Oh, very much so. Er… St Judy's comet. St Jude's sister, you know.'

Back at his original seat in the church hall he gave a familiar nod to his female neighbour and mumbled something designed to cover the next eventuality. 'Fortunately, er… Philomena's auntie and uncle are here tonight too,' but she appeared to have drawn no adverse conclusions from his long absence and, presumably, the child's greeting of others.

Eventually, the priest got up and the children scampered to their parents. Careless now of any impression he might make on his neighbours, he marched over to Father McPhail.

'We have a few more questions, Father.'

'At the station?' His voice sounded tired.

'Aye. At the station.'

'Very well.'

The DCI removed her supper from a Boots bag. One Mars bar, one packet of Nurofen, one bottle of Covonia and a fever scan strip. She unwrapped the Mars bar, sniffed it, found it unappetising and quickly shoved it in a desk drawer. A couple of fast acting caplets washed down with a swig of glucose-filled cough mixture would do nicely.

Having wiped the sugary moustache from her upper lip with her hand, she held the strip over her forehead for half a minute and then removed it. A green square appeared, no doubt indicating a high temperature, but the instruction sheet would clarify that. Before she had time to consult it, the phone interrupted her. It was the Chief Constable, Laurence Body, and he sounded cross. Regardless of what he was actually saying, his tone communicated that he was expecting a catastrophe, and that he wanted to pounce on the likely culprit and if possible avert it.

'I assure you I fully appreciate the extent of the public's interest in this matter, sir...' The tirade was unstoppable. 'Steady progress has been – correction – is being made.

The priest's coming in again very shortly, on a voluntary basis... Indeed, just as well... and the lab should be reporting to me first thing.'

The rant continued, unappeased by any of her answers. It was punctuated by veiled threats including the imposition of unnamed officers onto the case, some of a disturbingly high rank. The swine! It was hardly her fault that the entire round of door to doors had proved fruitless, the witness appeals had fallen on deaf ears and, for that matter, the 'girls' had not come up trumps. The telephone went again, doubtless some further threat he had forgotten to mention in the heat of the moment.

'And one more thing, Chief Inspector. The plan's changed, so you'll be fronting the press conference. Is that understood? Charlie says it'll be packed out, they all think this may turn out to be another Ipswich. It's been fixed for 4.00 p.m. on Thursday, but I dare say, by then, you'll have found some titbits to feed to the hounds. By the way, I've arranged for McPherson to speak to your squad.'

'I thought he'd retired, sir. He must be eighty at least.'

'Sixty-four and still accredited, actually. We needed someone to show we are doing everything we can, and the other basta... candidates declined to become involved on a variety of pretexts. Some man from England may come up later, but we'll try our own home-grown talent first.'

8

Elaine Bell awoke the next morning with a neck so stiff that she cursed out loud in frustration. Three nights in the office with only an undersized settee to sleep on had taken their toll. Another of the trials of middle-age, she thought bitterly, folding the rug she had used for makeshift bedding and plumping up the cushion that had served as a pillow. Huge feathers of snow floating lazily past her window attracted her attention, and she walked towards the curtains, gazing at the scene that now met her eyes and found herself unexpectedly moved by it.

The grey slate of the nearby tenement roofs was hidden under meticulously tailored white blankets, and the cobbled streets and wynds looked flawless, immaculate in their new clothes. She felt a sudden overpowering desire to feel the snow herself, under her own feet, before it was robbed of its pristine allure by the city's traffic and churned into mud-coloured slush. It was only five o'clock; time enough for a short expedition, time enough to enjoy the fragile scene before it was destroyed. Hurriedly putting on her coat and boots, she set off up St Leonard's lane, exhilarated by the crisp air, experimenting as she walked with different footprints, leaving first a flat-footed trail and then a pigeon-toed one. Reflections from the yellow streetlights glinted in the high tenement windows and, for a second, the blanket of thick cloud parted, revealing the stars above. Seeing them, she began to feel revitalised, almost elated. Glad to be alive.

The slope leading to St Leonard's Bank was deceptively steep and she puffed her way up it, stopping to catch her breath at the summit and marvelling at the small grove of trees she found there, the exposed side now covered in snow and the sheltered side black as soot. She continued along the narrow roadway, determined to reach the waste ground at the end of the street and enjoy the promised view of Salisbury Crags and Arthur's Seat in all its mid-winter glory. And she was not disappointed. Queens Drive had disappeared, becoming, with the Galloping Glen, a continuous white field lapping the base of the crags. And the cliffs themselves had been transformed, in their new apparel appearing rugged and untamed, like the foothills of some remote range at the edge of the Cairngorms or Glencoe. They bore little resemblance to the tired, city-encircled landmark found on countless cheap postcards, the sad spectacle of nature domesticated and subdued.

Snow feathers were still cascading endlessly from the pale sky, gliding silently downwards and coating every-thing, including her head and shoulders. So she turned back down the cobbles and was amused to see a cat padding blindly towards her, lifting its paws unnaturally high and occasionally shaking them with a perplexed look on its face. However, the second it became aware of the stranger in its path it gave a frightened yowl and dashed across the street, seeking cover behind a couple of parked cars.

Unthinkingly, Elaine Bell turned her head to follow its swift departure and instantly suffered agony, her neck rigid with pain, immobile, reminding her that she was no longer young or fit, and that she carried the weight of the world on her shoulders. A murderer was running free in this Winter Wonderland! What the hell had she been thinking of? She should have been preparing for the squad meeting, re-reading witness statements, polishing her armour for the press conference; she had a hundred things to do. Instead, here she was gallivanting outside like a bloody teenager. It was ridiculous. She was ridiculous! And this depth of snow would impede the investigation, help the killer and cause chaos with the city's traffic. Sod the stars. Her feet were cold.

———

By the time the last of the squad arrived for the nine o'clock meeting the DCI knew exactly what she intended to say, had rehearsed it several times and now looked forward to the press conference, like a prize fighter sure of his purse. Having been up for hours she was also unnaturally alert, impatient to get her information across and press on with her other tasks. No concessions would be made to any bleary eyes, sleep-befuddled thinking or attempts at humour.

'I'm going to recap, ladies and gentlemen, for your benefit to ensure that we are all familiar with events so far. Furthermore, I want no interruptions until I have finished speaking. Is that understood?'

Silence and a chorus of nods greeted her question.

'As you will recall, Isobel Wilson, a prostitute working the Seafield area, was found dead on the night of ninth January in amongst a patch of undergrowth at the north east corner of Seafield Cemetery. She was a known drug user, aged thirty-seven. The body had been concealed in its ultimate location, hidden below vegetation. Forensic evidence has established that she was killed within the cemetery, a few yards from her final resting place –'

'What forensic evidence, ma'am?'

The DCI glared at the speaker, DC Littlewood. He had been warned.

'No bloody interruptions, I said. The forensic evidence amounted to a few droplets of blood and fibres from the woman's clothing on some blades of grass. Is it all coming back to you, Constable? The murder weapon has still not been found, despite an exhaustive search of the location. Conclusion, anyone?'

But not a soul dared answer, given her forceful earlier instruction.

'Conclusion, obviously,' she shook her head as if appalled by the slowness of her team, 'either the weapon remains undiscovered, possibly somewhere beyond the location, or, and more likely, the murderer took it with him or her, when he left. The pathologists are of the opinion that it was probably a knife, single-bladed and unserrated. Its minimum length has been estimated at three inches. No eye-witnesses have come forward about the attack. Post-mortem examination revealed that the death was somewhere between about nine and eleven on the ninth. She was last seen alive by a fellow prostitute, Lena Stirling, at about 7.00 p.m. at the Leith end of Salamander Street on that date. DNA from the deceased's clothing has been matched with one Francis McPhail, a Catholic priest living in Jerez Street. He denies all knowledge of the victim and maintains that at the time she was killed he was in his church on the same street. But no witnesses to his attendance there then have been found. The victim, who had not been recently sexually interfered with, was found with her arms across her breast –'

'As if in p… p… prayer,' DS Oakley added out loud.

'I beg your pardon?' the DCI said, sounding as if she had just been publicly insulted.

'Er... the victim's position, m... m... ma'am, it was if she was in prayer.'

'Thank you for your entirely unsolicited interpretation of the facts, Simon. The next time I require such a service I will request it from you. Is that quite clear?' A chastened nod sufficed for an answer, all the other occupants of the room now stunned into an unnatural silence by the fierceness of her expression.

'Our only other suspect in the Wilson case is Eddie Christie, but he, to all intents and purposes, has been excluded. He has an alibi, albeit provided by his wife, for the relevant time, and no forensic evidence to link him with the crime has been forthcoming.

Turning now to the second victim, Annie Wright. On Monday fifteenth her body was found in a wrecked car at Cargill's scrapyard. She was aged thirty-five, a prostitute and a known drug user. From traces of blood found a couple of yards to the east of the car it seems that she was killed on the site and then concealed within the vehicle. She, too, was found with her arms crossed on her breast...'

'As if in p... p...' Eric Manson said, unable to resist the temptation, his voice becoming inaudible following the basilisk stare the Chief Inspector gave him. '...prayer,' he mouthed.

'Shut up, Eric!' Elaine Bell snapped, continuing in the same breath, '...she, too, had not been recently sexually interfered with. Post-mortem examination suggests that she was killed on the Friday, approximately three days before her body was found. That estimate for her time of death accords with two other pieces of information. First, the earliest date for her unopened mail. Second, the last sighting of her. On the evening of the twelfth at about eight p.m., her neighbour, a Mr Holroyd, saw her on the landing of her flat, probably as she was leaving the building for the street. Unfortunately, the prostitute with whom she teamed up as a pair was herself absent from their beat from ten p.m. onwards on the Friday. So she didn't notice or report her pal's absence.'

'Ma'am?' Alice asked timidly.

'DS Rice?'

'I've asked to see various members of the Leith Vigilante Group, CLAP or whatever their acronym is, from twelve onwards today. One or other of them may be able to help with the final time for a sighting of…'

'CLRAP,' Elaine Bell corrected.

'Sorry?'

'Their acronym. CLRAP. Central Leith Residents Against Prostitution.'

'LRAP, surely,' DC Lindsay said. 'Just Leith Residents –'

'Never mind what the hell they're called!' the DCI interjected, 'you're going to see them, Alice, so that's fine. If you get anything worthwhile from them, then let me know as soon as possible. Where was I? Oh yes – over much of the likely period that she was killed, Francis McPhail has no alibi. I spoke to him last night in the station and he told us that on the night in question he was, surprise, surprise, alone in the church. So, Eric, I want you to check on his whereabouts with his housekeeper and then go and see that guy, Thomas McNiece. McNiece stood trial for rape, Annie Wright was his accuser, and he was acquitted. He threatened to "get her", so away and check him out, eh? He lives on Kings Road, off Portobello Street.'

Eric Manson nodded, mute, his cheeks bulging with his breakfast roll.

'The weapon used on Annie Wright hasn't been found, but the pathologist believes that it may well be the same one as was used on Isobel. The MO in both cases, you will be aware, appears to be identical. Accordingly, we may, God save us all, be dealing with some kind of serial killer. I want you three constables –' and she stared each one in the eye in turn, 'to re-do the door to doors. Something may have been missed. Re-do around both the cemetery area, the scrappie's yard and the prostitutes' known beats. S.P.E.A.R. could give you information on their territories. The newspaper appeals, as you may have guessed, have produced precisely nothing. The area's insalubrious reputation, of course, does not help us.

Finally, there are two other things you should know. Firstly, the Chief Constable intends to expand our squad and is, I understand, currently involved in doing that, and secondly, he has decreed that Professor McPherson is to address us. This morning, immediately after I finish in fact.'

A groan went round the room.

'Has Methuselah not been put out to grass yet?' Eric Manson asked.

'No, but he is coming from the Meadows especially to speak to us.'

Professor McPherson touched the material within his pocket, a hand in it would look more assured. Stop the brute shaking and giving him away, too. His hidden fingers encountered three pills and he realised that he had not taken his morning blood pressure or water tablets. But neither the nervousness he initially felt nor the panic that replaced it were evident on his face. It had an inexpressive, mask-like quality, impervious to everything, and easily explained, although not in the terms of the temperamental coldness or permanent boredom guessed by many.

The explanation, the Professor would have said, lay in the works of the great Mr James Parkinson of Hoxton Square. The man after whom the disease, his disease, was christened, or perhaps, more accurately, re-christened, changing from the Shaking Palsy to Parkinson's Disease. And of course, as a result of it, his voice had become a monotone and he, in short, monotonous. But there it was, and it could not be helped. He tried to clear his throat, thinking that once he had begun to speak he would feel the old enthusiasm which had carried him through his final days as a lecturer.

'The personality profile of a serial killer...' he heard himself say in a dull drone, 'can only be an uncertain business. Nonetheless, of the various theories I continue to favour the disorganised/organised theory of offenders' characteristics.' He looked at his listeners, hoping that some of them might be familiar with his subject, but saw no evidence of it on their faces.

'Mrs Bell has, kindly, described to me the crime scene of both the murders currently under investigation. The relevant aspects, as far as I am concerned are, of course, in each case the absence of the murder weapon at the locus, or around about it, and the movement of the body after the act to a place of hiding. There could be added to this list, I would suggest, the fact that the killer appears to have left relatively little forensic or other traces of himself. These factors all indicate to me that the killer will display the profile characteristics of the organised offender. He, or she, may well be a first-born or an only child, and is likely to have an above-average IQ. Despite such intellectual ability, the offender's work history may be sporadic and he probably had a poor relationship with his parents or, more likely, parent. His killing "spree", if I may call it that, has probably been triggered by...' His voice faded away, his mouth suddenly dry, and he grasped the glass of water that had been provided for him.

The minute his fingers gripped its curved surface he felt his hand beginning to shake, the tremor taking control. And the more he concentrated on lifting it up to his mouth, the worse the shaking became, until by the time it reached his lips water was beginning to splash out of it. Taking a hurried sip he quickly put it down, misjudging the distance to the table and allowing it to land with a loud thud.

'...Some form of precipitating stress,' he continued, noteless but unerringly exact in what he wanted to say. 'You may wonder what I mean by that?'

He studied his audience, but in the absence of a reply or a raised hand he carried on. 'What I mean is something like a breakdown in a marital relationship, the loss of a job, that sort of thing.'

He paused again, evidently thinking. 'Perhaps I should say something about classification. I could tell you about Jenkins and the unpredictable and respectable types but –' He stopped again, looking quizzically at Elaine Bell. 'Maybe I should just plump for the revived Holmes and De Burger classification. Let me see, of their retained five types I only need to trouble you with, I believe, the missionary serial killer – the man or woman who appears to believe that they have responsibility or a special mission to cleanse the world of a certain category of human being, for example, whores or clergymen. Then again, perhaps, you should know too of the visionary serial killer – the person, usually psychotic or schizophrenic, who hears voices instructing them to kill other human beings. But maybe,' he paused, 'we are getting unnecessarily complicated. What I can say is that almost all serial killers are Caucasian males between the ages of twenty-five and thirty-five. Some take "mementoes" or "trophies" from their victims, hanks of hair, pieces of jewellery, that kind of thing. Fred West, for example, retained body parts from all…'

'Sorry, sir, but just to understand the essentials – we should really concentrate on the organised/disorganised… umm… division?' Tom Littlewood asked, bemused.

'Certainly, but exercise caution. Douglas et al, in 1992 I think, introduced a third category into the taxonomy, the "mixed" offender. The introduction of this additional, intermediate category does, obviously, highlight a fundamental question, i.e. whether any empirical support for the basic dichotomy can be found. Does it not?'

Embarrassed silence greeted this enquiry, broken eventually by a question posed by Alice Rice.

'Professor, do you think that human beings fall into distinct types? Because unless they do, templates for defining the characteristics of any distinct type won't be of any use?'

'Indeed I do. However, in Canter's paper "The Organised/Disorganised Typology of Serial Murder: Myth or Model?" The learned author casts doubt upon the utility of –'

'Thank you, Professor,' Elaine Bell said, smiling broadly, raising her hands and beginning to clap loudly, 'for a most helpful talk.'

The frail academic managed a stiff bow and then walked out of the room, his body bent forwards and taking little hurried steps as if to catch up with himself. Once the door had closed, Elaine Bell turned to face the small gathering. 'Any questions?'

'Yes. What are we supposed to make of that? Apart from anything else, the priest left his blood on the first victim, didn't he? That's a "forensic trace" of himself, surely?' It was DC Ruth Lindsay, looking genuinely puzzled.

'Yes, but that was all. Much more could have been left... is often left. All you need to remember, I think, is that the killer may, and I emphasise may, as he may well not, be an elder or only child who loathes his parents or parent, and may, despite his cleverness, have a sporadic work history. What else? Er...'

'A Caucasian male between the ages of twenty-five and thirty-five,' Tom Littlewood prompted.

'Aha,' Elaine Bell replied, stroking the end of her inflamed nose. 'And he may have just lost his job or had his marriage crash or whatever.'

'That's ok then,' Eric Manson said, leaning back on his chair with his hands behind his head. 'We'll have reduced it to a mere tenth or so of the population. In this room, for example, only Tom, Jimmy and Simon are left.'

'I'm off the hook, sir,' DC Littlewood said smugly. 'I'm the youngest in my family.'

'Me, too, I'm innocent. I love my mum and dad,' Jimmy Galloway said.

'Simon?' Eric Manson demanded. 'That only leaves you!'

'Well... I am an only child and I didn't like my mum much, but – well, I'm a woman, sir.'

'Enough of this drivel,' Elaine Bell ordered, her mind already on the cup of coffee she intended to brew in the privacy of her room.

Google. There could be nothing to lose and something to gain. Alice typed in 'Francis McPhail' and waited for the entries to appear. And there were a surprising number of them, centring around three obscure publications – *Sacred Spy*, *The True Path* and *Catholic Light*, all editions produced in 2006. The first one, she noted, seemed to be little more than a collection of articles gleaned from other sources, all discreditable to the Catholic Church. They had titles such as 'Celibacy: The Quick Route to Sexual Abuse', 'Bishop Gorged on Kiddie Porn Feast' and 'Sex and the Soutane'. McPhail's name was only included as he had produced a commentary on a matter described by the rag as 'One of the False Doctrines of Rome'. *The True Path* consisted of an extended diatribe against the evils of the modern world and any priests foolish enough to keep in touch with it. Such men were excoriated as 'heretics, apostates, closet homosexuals, stunted adolescents and wrong heads'. McPhail had managed to draw the author's ire by blessing a homosexual couple celebrating their twenty-fifth year together. For such an act he was labelled as 'a Promoter of Sodomites and a Destroyer of the Family.'

A longer article about him, however, was unearthed in *Catholic Light*, a publication that made Alice feel queasy even as she ploughed through it. It was evidently no more than a semi-literate scandal sheet, peddling rumour and innuendo as news. Its creators had adopted the cheery language of the tabloids, and gave every impression of enjoying their self-appointed task. It, too, seemed to specialise in lurid headlines, such as 'Priest's Pants Off' and 'The Laity's Love Machine'. The first half of this particular issue was given over to a justification of their current witch-pricking activity, a crusade to root out the 'Evils of Homosexuality' from within the Catholic Church. However, on page three, Father McPhail had been accorded a paragraph to himself entitled 'Can of Worms':

'The insatiable Parish Priest of St Benedicts, Father Francis Xavier McPhail, has, we hear from reliable sources, become very close to yet another of his lady parishioners, this time a married mother of one. He used his position as her Parish Priest to "befriend" her, regularly "counselling" her on his own. Well, Father McPhail, lay your hands off ------- right now, or we'll use our organ to expose you much more fully!!'

No other mention of McPhail appeared in the online version of the magazine, its last few pages being devoted to another chosen cause, this time the exposure of any Parish Priests who had expressed concern over the church's teaching on contraception, with guarantees of anonymity expressly provided for informers. Reading *Catholic Light*, Alice was reminded of her schooldays and a rare breed of adherent she had then encountered, one she had thought extinct and whose passing she had not mourned. This was the passionate believer who knew the name of every Saint and Blessed from Aaron to Zita and the dates of their feast days; who lunched on haddock on Fridays, but saw no place in their lives for Christ's teachings in the New Testament – love, forgiveness and other such peripheral matters – content that they were constantly in tune with the Magisterium of the church.

Eric Manson's loud knocking on Mrs Donnelly's door got no reply. So he went instead in search of Thomas McNiece. He discovered him sitting alone in The Severed Head, a pub off Portobello High Street. He was at a table by himself, hunched over his pint, eyes shut, and his head swaying to some internal tune. An untouched bowl of soup was by his elbow, puckered skin covering the thick, green liquid. When the policeman sat down next to him, McNiece moved down the bench seat, unconcerned who his neighbour might be, head still swaying in time to his own music.

'You Thomas McNiece?' Eric Manson asked.

'Aha, have a' won the pools or somethin'?' the man replied jocularly, eyes still closed.

'No, and I need to speak to you.'

'Do yous now.' A slight note of menace crept into the reply, as if to convey that the favour of an interview might not be forthcoming.

'Yes, I do. In connection with an ongoing investigation that we are conducting, we need –'

'Why didn't you say you were a polisman?' McNiece interrupted him, his eyes now wide open, mouth shaping itself into a cold smile. 'Jist tell us whit you want, son.'

'Son! Chief Inspector to you, McNiece.'

'Oh, aye, Chief Inspector, sir, Your Holiness… didnae take you long tae show yer teeth, eh, tiger? So, whit d'you want?'

'What were you doing on Friday last, from, say, ten p.m. onwards?'

'The twelfth?'

'Aye. The twelfth.'

'Do you mind if a' ask why, your honour?'

'Yes.'

'So that's how it's tae be. Fine, an' it's easy peasy an a'. I wis at hame havin' a wee pairty, a birthday pairty. Ma birthday pairty.'

'How long did it go on for?'

'A' nicht.'

'So your guests, if we speak to them, will presumably be able to confirm that you were there all night? Eh?'

'Aha. Ma pals, as I cry 'em. No probs there… sir. You'd no' hae a pairty, eh? No pals tae come!'

'After the party, what did you do?'

'Ye'll nivver even hae been to a pairty, eh? Whit d'ye think I done? I lay doon in ma bed a' day wi' a sair heid.'

'On your own?'

'Ma flat wis fu' of folk, sleeping a' o'er the place. Some oan the settee, oan the lounge flair… an' Jessie wis in bed wi' me.'

'Jessie who?'

'Jessie May McNiece.'

'Your wife?'

'Naw. That's where we're alike eh son ? Both sleepin' wi' dogs. But a'm the lucky wan, ken. Mine's got French blood. She's a poodle.'

Getting up to leave and sticking a finger in the congealed soup, then sucking it and re-inserting it, Eric Manson growled, 'I'll not be taking your word for any of this, McNiece, I'll be checking up on it all.'

'Aye, right,' the man replied, supping his pint. 'Ye just do that, yer worship.'

9

The lawyer did not smile when Alice entered his office. Her appointment with him had been fitted into his already packed diary by his secretary, who was shortly off on maternity leave and now careless of whether he approved. Guy Bayley made no attempt to conceal his annoyance at the re-arrangement of his timetable. Instead, he waved towards a hard chair opposite his own, then pushed all the papers on his desk to one side as if to clear a space for whatever matter she might raise with him. It seemed a slightly petulant, almost hostile reception, and all the while his expression remained unchanged, his mouth set tight as a trap and his brows furrowed. He had thin blond curls which fell in every direction on his scalp and a complexion as pale as ivory, but extending just below his hairline was an angry, red margin of psoriasis, framing his forehead like a wreath of blood. Despite remaining silent he managed to convey an impression of extreme exhaustion, a tiredness with life and terminal ennui.

Just as Alice took her seat the door opened and a heavily pregnant young woman came in bearing a tray with two cups of tea on it. She threw Alice a shy smile as she lowered the tray onto the desk, but before she had a chance to take the cups off, her boss said wearily, 'Not now, Susannah. I'll have mine later.'

As the door closed again he turned his attention to the policewoman.

'I'm afraid I don't have long, Ms Rice, and although I did set up the group I don't think I'll have much information – or at least much information likely to be of any use to you. I co-ordinate our activities, orchestrate our campaigns, act as a spokesperson and so forth. I see it as a type of social work really. No-one, I think, could suggest that the "sex-workers" are anything other than a public nuisance.'

He waited a few seconds for her assent, which did not come, and then continued in the same dull tone, 'and finally, despite our best efforts, they have now achieved the double – sex and murder, no less.'

Sounding slightly more interested in the subject, he told Alice that on the nights of both crimes he had been on duty, scouring the streets for prostitutes, ready to winkle them out of Salamander Street, Boothacre or any other of their shady cracks and crevices. By the time his vigil had ended he had encountered one whore only, a Russian creature whose accent seemed tailor-made for the foul insults she flung at him.

Talking to the man in his sedate, New Town premises, Alice saw no signs of the hate-filled fanatic described by Ellen Barbour, and wondered, momentarily, if her friend had confused him with someone else. His office, with its black-and-white Kay prints, vapid watercolours and thick carpet, seemed so far removed from the front-line in Leith that it was hard to see how the two worlds might meet, far less collide. And had he not lived in Disraeli Place, their two orbits would have remained fixed, distant and discrete, each unaware of the other spinning past.

'Well, sir, those two unfortunate women…' she began, but immediately he cut in, now emphasising his point by rapping his fountain pen on his desk.

'They are not, sergeant, "unfortunate women",' he intoned, a humourless smile of correction on his face.

'Sorry, sir?' she replied, puzzled.

'They are not "unfortunate women" as you described them,' he answered, repeating himself but making no attempt to explain his statement.

'No? Then what are they, sir?'

'Dead whores,' he said, brushing a shower of thick scurf off his right shoulder.

'Murdered women are surely unfortunate women?'

He rolled his eyes, eloquently expressing his exasperation at her apparent sentimentality.

'No, sergeant, my point is that they are not women, not real women, at least. No real woman would do what they do, I'm sure you'd agree.'

Finding herself annoyed by his response, she said coolly, 'Again, I'm not sure what you mean, sir. Every second all around the world women are doing what they do – not for money, perhaps, and out of choice, but many of the prostitutes have no choice.'

'Firstly, many but not all. And secondly, and more importantly, there is always a choice,' the man said, as if addressing a particularly slow child.

'If they are not women, then what exactly are they, sir?'

'Society's flotsam and jetsam, obviously. Society's, let's not mince our words, rubbish, detritus, garbage.'

'And such rubbish should be cleaned up, eh, sir?' She wondered how far he would go.

'Well, I don't know where you live, sergeant,' he said, looking hard at her, 'but perhaps you and your neighbours would welcome with open arms those "unfortunate women"? Welcome their used needles, their discarded condoms, their pimps and punters, them and all their revolting paraphernalia, to your leafy suburb. If not, then you too might find that if they arrived, uninvited, you also would want them cleaned up and got rid of, from your own area at least.'

'And how should they be cleaned up?'

'With a BIG BROOM,' he said, opening his eyes unnaturally wide to express his sarcasm, 'anything to move them on… but killing's a bit extreme, don't you think?'

'Are there any witnesses to your movements on –' she began, but before she had completed her question he returned to the fray.

'No. I live alone. But think about it, detective – all that they could corroborate would be that I was in the vicinity of the murders on the night on which they were committed.'

'At what time did your tour of duty begin on each of the nights?'

'Oh, I don't know. Seven-thirty maybe. I never go out much before then, it's not worth it.'

'And on neither evening did you see anything on your rounds, any punters, any prostitutes other than the Russian?'

'No. But the women do hide, you know. Anyway, it's now twenty-five past nine and I really do need to do some preparation before my next client. She will be paying for… er…' He hesitated for a moment, having lost his drift.

'Your services,' Alice said, rising to go.

Holding the door open for her, the pale man stood erect, and as their eyes met, he closed his as if to shield his soul from scrutiny.

There was nothing much in the fridge, so it would be a relief not to have to cook the dinner today, Mrs Donnelly thought, looking in the cutlery drawer and wondering what she should put on the table. Not, of course, that Father would like the stuff produced by Iris Pease. Far too highly spiced, and she would insist on dropping chillies into everything, even, Christ have mercy on us all, in the mince. And it was not as if she had not been told, forcefully on at least one occasion, that he preferred food without a 'bite' or 'kick' or whatever it was called.

She had a touch of the black fever that one, eyeing Father up, simpering, volunteering before volunteers had been asked for. Imposing more like! Of course, all the women on the rota were dangerous, but that one, 'Ms' Pease, would have to be watched, for sure, prowling around like a lioness seeking someone to devour. She knew the signs.

At least there would be time to do the crossword before she arrived, pans clanging like cymbals. And the policewoman would surely now wait until after lunch before wasting any more of their time. Mrs Donnelly searched unsuccessfully for a pen, and then sank into the chair. Opening the kitchen drawer to continue the hunt, she pushed her hand into it past envelopes, string and polythene bags, suddenly releasing a little gasp as her fingers landed in a cold pool of spilt glue. While gingerly extracting her hand, trying not to get the glue on the envelopes and other contents of the drawer, she heard the doorbell go. Distracted, she yanked her hand out, bits of wool still sticking to it, and rushed to the tap. Vigorously shaking the water off, she hurried to the front door. 'Ms' Pease did not like to be kept waiting.

As she talked to the housekeeper, Alice became aware that whenever she mentioned the priest, the subject of their conversation, the woman bristled, as if giving a warning against some form of intimate trespass. It was as though his name should not pass the policewoman's lips, for fear of it being soiled in some way when spoken by her. Watching the housekeeper's increasing annoyance, she persevered. Her reaction revealed an obsession, a fixation with the man. He was her exclusive property; his business was her business, and if she did not know what he was doing, then whatever it was could be of no real importance. By definition.

'So, Mrs Donnelly, you said before that you couldn't confirm that Father McPhail was present in the church on the ninth of January between about 8 p.m. and 11 p.m. Is that still so?'

'That's right, I can't.' She smiled as if breaking good news, her inability to provide the priest with an alibi not troubling her. She was busily laying the table as she spoke.

'You are aware,' Alice said slowly, 'of the seriousness of the charges that Father McPhail could face?'

'Och, it'll not come to that sergeant. You'll get the fellow and then we'll all get on with the rest of our lives.' She beamed again.

'But we think that Father McPhail may be the fellow.'

'Do you really?' Laying a knife and fork at the end of the table, the woman threw a patronising glance at the policewoman.

'I'm not here on a social call, Mrs Donnelly. We do think Father McPhail may be the fellow.'

'You've got to be joking! That's a very far-fetched suggestion indeed.'

'Well, someone killed those two women, and so far he hasn't been able to explain away –'

'What are you going on about, those two women! Father McPhail is no more involved than I am myself!' She gave a brittle little laugh, dismissing the suggestion, her head cocked to the side as if to ridicule the very idea.

'You, on the other hand, have not been tied by forensic evidence to Seafield, to the crime –' Alice stopped herself in mid-sentence, afraid that in her frustration she had already disclosed too much, but the effect on the house-keeper was immediate.

'Evidence!' she said excitedly, 'forensic evidence? Inspector, you have my word that Father has been nowhere near Seafield – or any of those kind of women.'

Mrs Donnelly was looking Alice straight in the eye, blinking hard, but never moving her gaze.

'How do you know?' Alice asked calmly, hiding the disquiet she felt at her earlier slip.

'I know.' The woman nodded hard. 'I know.'

'Well then, tell me how you know?' Please God, tell me.

'I can't, no. I'm afraid I can't. You'll just have to find out yourselves.'

'I suppose that woman from the parish is involved…' Nothing to lose now. The time for a gamble had definitely arrived.

Mrs Donnelly's jaw dropped open in surprise. 'What do you know of any such woman, sergeant?'

Nothing. 'Enough.'

Returning to her table-laying duties, the housekeeper began speaking quietly, almost as if she did not want to be heard. 'The Sharpe woman will be somewhere in all of this, no doubt, offering the apple again. That's what she does, you know, tempt him. Otherwise, he'd be fine. In all our years together he's never so much as laid a finger on me!'

'That Sharpe woman?'

'June Sharpe.'

'Where would I find her?'

'I can't tell you... I shouldn't say.'

'Not much help to me then,' Alice said, closing her notebook. 'Not much help to him, either.'

'St Benedict's. St Benedict's church. That's the place to start.'

The doorbell rang once more and the housekeeper turned slowly, disturbed and annoyed, and shuffled towards the landing in her tattered sandals. And as Alice let herself out, Iris Pease strode into the kitchen as if it were her own, chic as a Parisian, and as unexpected in the drab tenement flat as a phoenix in a hen-run.

———

A trace of matched DNA on the body. That was all she had to offer them. Elaine Bell stretched, pulled her chair out and rose, putting her hands on her hips and pushing her chin out. She cleared her throat several times and began striding about her room, preparing to speak. To make a speech, in fact.

'Ladies and gentlemen...' No more than a hoarse whisper emerged, and she clamped her mouth shut instantly. That simply would not do. She needed to appear confident and authoritative, not on the edge of collapse, weaving unsteadily towards a nervous breakdown. With a deep cough, and inadvertently triggering a spasm of spluttering, she began speaking again: 'Ladies and Gentlemen...' It was no good – the same weak tone, breathless, bodiless. A sodding Strepsil would have to be sucked, that would clear the passages, restore the natural timbre of her voice. In the meantime, she would continue her dress rehearsal for the press conference, but this time silently, in her head, playing all the parts.

'The trace of DNA,' she asked herself, in a suitably aggressive tone, 'have you got a match for it?'

'Certainly,' she replied to herself, as herself. 'And we have several leads that should produce results very shortly. I am confident –'

'So,' she interrupted herself ruthlessly, in a male voice this time. 'Since you have a match, I assume you have a suspect. Is anyone in custody?'

'Not at present,' Elaine Bell mouthed, then repeated the words in a more optimistic tone. 'Not at present, sir, but we are very confident that, possibly within the next few days, we will be in a position –'

'Had either of the prostitutes been raped?' she interrupted herself again, using the characteristic squawk of the giantess from the *Evening News*. Time for a standard but anodyne answer, one unobjectionable to any reporter with the slightest grasp of the constraints imposed by a continuing investigation. 'I'm sorry, madam, I'm not in a position to disclose such details at this stage in our enquiries.' A fine, pompous ring to it too.

'If you have a match and the match is your suspect, why has he not been apprehended?'

The questions she was posing herself seemed to be becoming increasingly difficult.

'Well, there are often…' A poor start. It sounded too tentative, almost timid. She tried again. 'DNA can be found on a body, or whatever, for entirely innocent, even serendipitous reasons. Rarely is its presence alone sufficient to –'

'I see,' she broke in again in the male voice. 'The DNA match is not your suspect. Do you have any real suspect at all?'

If that one was actually to be asked by the press, in such bald terms, a number of possible strategies opened up. Her favourite one, sadly a fantasy, was a dead faint. The lesser alternative, knocking over a glass of water, would create no more than a temporary diversion. Any reporter worth his salt, having scented blood, would return for the kill the second the tumbler had been righted. No. If the need arose a faint would be the answer. Considering it, she wondered whether she should practise now, let her legs buckle and see where she ended up. Hitting her head on the table as she collapsed would be most unfortunate, even if it did add authenticity to the performance. As she was daydreaming, wondering whether to faint to the left or the right, the telephone rang. It made her strained nerves jangle, returning her to reality and her lack of any adequate response at the press conference.

'Yes.'

'Elaine, is that you? It's Frank at the lab.'

'Frank! Frank! Great to hear your voice. Have you got any news for me?'

'Yep. Summer is a-coming in, loudly sing cuckoo. We've got a match... Francis McPhail again. Not perfect, but good enough. Fucking contamination – sorry, Elaine, excuse my French – contamination again, blood from that DS Simon Wanker of yours. But no worries, McPhail's DNA was in the stain again.'

A single phone call and the sun had emerged from behind the clouds. At last, they had a proper suspect, a bloody good one at that. One trace could, perhaps, be explained away, but not two! No, siree. And now she could stride into the press conference with her head held high, no blustering needed, and not just withstand the slings and arrows but thwack them back at the pack. With gusto! If the Chief Constable had been given the same news then by now he would be falling over himself in his haste to shed his alternative commitment – if it had ever existed. She spat out her cough sweet, tore up her notes and left the office, headed for the murder suite with 'Nessun Dorma' playing in her head.

An 'A. Foscetti' was listed in the Perth and Kinross directory at 'Barleybrae', Milnathort. Alice looked at her watch. 5.30 p.m. She could go home, the press conference was over and their suspect out of circulation. Still, Ian would not be there yet. His working day never ended before 7.00 p.m., and on recent form he was unlikely to be home before 9.00. So, she had an abundance of time, even if there were rush-hour queues at Barnton or raging blizzards at Kelty.

Best try the number first, she thought. No answer. Perhaps she should wait until tomorrow and phone again, save a wasted journey. On the other hand, if she succeeded there would be rejoicing in Miss Spinnell's bosom. Spurred on by the thought, she grabbed her bag and set off for the car.

'Barleybrae' turned out to be an austere villa on the Burleigh Road. The house had once been a doctor's surgery, and high hedges, now unclipped, continued to ensure its genteel privacy. Alice knocked and stood waiting, arms crossed tightly for warmth, willing the front door to open. Not a sound within. She knocked again, more forcefully this time, rapping the solid wood as if on urgent police business. Nothing. One final hammering before setting off back across the Bridge, she decided, bruising her knuckles in her enthusiasm. She listened intently, and made out a shuffling sound, coming closer, stopping, and then the sound of a Yale snib being released. One half of an aged little face squinted through the crack that had opened.

'Mrs Foscetti?' Alice began, 'I've come about your sister. I'm a neighbour of hers, a friend. Actually, I've lived in the same tenement as her for the last ten years'

The front door opened fully, and to her amazement Alice saw Miss Spinnell standing before her. Dumbfounded, she stared until the old lady broke the silence.

'Well, dear, what do you want? What about my sister?'

'Miss Spinnell!' Alice exclaimed.

'Yes, I know her name, thank you.' A characteristically tart reply.

'No, no…' Alice began. 'How did you get here?'

'Oh, I see.' The old lady spoke again, a wide smile lighting up her features. 'You think I'm Morag, don't you? Morag Spinnell.'

'Yes,' Alice answered, disconcerted.

'No, dear. She's my sister. I'm Annabel Foscetti, nee Spinnell. We're identical twins, in fact.' Now, looking at the woman intently, Alice began to notice differences. The white hair seemed thicker, less tousled, and her protruding eyes were more co-ordinated, moving together in unison, working as a pair.

'Oh… I'm sorry.'

'She is alright, my sister?' the old lady asked anxiously, touching Alice's hand for a second.

'She's fine. She wants to see you.'

'Oh, I don't think so, dear,' the old lady replied firmly, 'we had a falling out.'

'Yes,' Alice insisted, 'Yes, she does. She "lost" you, so to speak, couldn't trace you. It was her birthday a few days ago, and now she wants to see you.'

'OUR birthday,' Mrs Foscetti said, in an irritated tone. 'Our birthday, dear. She always tells people that I'm older than her, although I'm actually the younger, by a full eight minutes. We haven't seen each other for, oh, must be... well... years and years. We fell out.' Having had her say, the old lady waved the policewoman into her house.

—

Seated in her snug, well-ordered sitting room, Mrs Foscetti explained the origin of the rift between the twins. Pouring out of tea for her guest with a steady hand, she confided that it had been over a man. Charlie Foscetti, in fact. Morag had considered him her "property". She had "found" him first, after all, and had never forgiven either of them when Charlie transferred his affection from one twin to the other. To the younger of the two, as it happened.

'Well, she wants to see you now,' Alice said, warming her hands on the bone china cup clasped between her hands.

'How is she?' Mrs Foscetti asked, looking concerned.

'A bit forgetful, muddled sometimes, but physically in pretty good shape.' Should she mention the Alzheimer's, Alice wondered. What if, given their identical genetic make-up, the disease had Mrs Foscetti in its sights too? Better say nothing. 'Muddled' covered a wide spectrum of possible complaints.

'In that case, I'm going to give her a ring!' Mrs Foscetti said, plainly delighted at the idea, replacing her cup on its saucer.

'Her phone's off, I'm afraid.' Knocked to the floor by Quill once too often.

'I know, then,' the old lady said, excitedly, 'I'll give her a big, big surprise. On Saturday, I'll catch the bus and go and see her. Where is she living now?'

'Edinburgh. And I've a better idea,' Alice said. 'I'm supposed to be off on Saturday the twenty-eighth. If you like, I could come and pick you up then and take you to Broughton Place myself. How would that be?'

Spontaneously touching Alice's wrist again, Mrs Foscetti nodded enthusiastically 'Why not? I'll wear my smartest outfit, and knock the spots off her!'

10

The young man straightened his striped tie. His first proper assignment as a qualified solicitor and it would have to be advising on an interview under caution. Oh, and not any old interview under caution, just one involving a suspected double murderer. Christ on a bike! Here he was, monkey masquerading as organ-grinder, and all because that fat git McFadden was taking a sickie to go ski-ing.

He glanced warily around the interview room, nauseous with apprehension and increasingly aware that his bladder needed emptying. But all the police personnel seemed eager to start, quivering like dogs in their traps, desperate to catch the passing hare. And even the hare, his so-called client, seemed ready to go. And if this had been for some trivial charge, say, a peeing up a close or a minor assault, then he too might be happily placing his toes on the start line. Presumably, they all imagined that he knew what he was doing. No-one could say that he did not look the part, at least.

On cue, and as soon as requested by the Chief Inspector, he left the room, feeling in some incongruous way as if he had been demoted, now a stage-hand rather than a performer. Thank goodness he had listened to the office secretary again, she knew her onions. Otherwise he would be vainly protesting his right to stay beside his client until he was forcibly ejected, his inexperience exposed for all to see, for all to laugh at. The humiliation just did not bear thinking about.

Obviously, the warnings he had remembered to give his client provided a sort of comfort, justified his initial attendance at public expense. Any difficult or dangerous questions were to be responded to with 'no comment', or 'I'd rather not answer that', and the consequences of such apparent lack of frankness could be sorted out later. But now, watching the priest through the internal glass window of the interview room, and, worse yet, hearing him, the holy fool appeared to be busy shooting himself in both feet, ignoring all the earlier whispered advice as if it had been imparted in Pushtu. In fact, for all the difference he had made, he might as well give up, enjoy himself instead, relax and take in his surroundings. Plainly, he lacked the requisite gravitas to influence a man of the cloth.

The young policewoman sitting opposite the priest caught his eye. DS Rice, he recalled, from their brief pre-interview conversation. Very tall indeed. And what was the polite word for thin too? 'Willowy'. Pussy willow. He looked at her face, became absorbed in his study of it, heedless now of anything the priest was saying, or anyone else for that matter. Strange. Pussy Willow's face was registering concern, distress even, the sort of expression to be expected from an onlooker at an inevitable crash. Unexpectedly, she threw a hostile glance at him, or was it aimed at someone near the door? Either way, he took no notice and carried on, whenever the opportunity presented itself, of studying her.

Unknown to him she was only too well aware of his presence, his grimacing face occasionally pressed to the glass, nose and chin flattened and yellowed. The mouth opening and shutting like a goldfish in a bowl.

'Truly, I've never met Isobel Wilson,' the priest said imploringly, and Alice Rice watched him intently as he spoke. 'Nor Annie Wright either. On the ninth I was, as I told you the first time, helping Mrs Donnelly clean my study in the early evening, then I went to my church. I got back home at about eleven, I think. On the evening of the twelfth I was…' he hesitated briefly, 'in my church again. I spent the night there.'

'Anybody else there with you?' Elaine Bell enquired.

'No-one.'

'Sure about that? No-one in the church throughout the entire period that you were there? The entire night?'

'No-one. I'm sure.'

'And when did you go there, and when did you leave the place?'

'I went there at… maybe seven o' clock, and I left there… about six or so.'

'Eleven hours on your knees!' Elaine Bell spluttered in disbelief.

'I sat some of the time, officer,' the priest said coolly.

'Your housekeeper saw you return?'

'In the morning? Yes, she saw me.'

'So, Father, if traces of blood, with your DNA, have been found on the bodies of Isobel Wilson and Annie Wright, what exactly would your explanation for that be?'

The priest stared at the DCI. 'What did you say?' he asked, incredulous. Elaine Bell repeated every word she had said, and looked expectantly at him.

'I'd say…' he paused, meeting the eyes of his interrogators. 'I'd say… it's impossible, because I've never come across either of those poor souls.'

Alice looked towards the door, spotting the young solicitor framed outside in his usual window, entertaining himself by misting the glass with his breath and then rubbing a clear circle in it with his nose.

As Father McPhail was being taken down to the cell, Alice picked up a list recording the possessions taken from his pockets at the charge bar. His diary, a lottery ticket and a wallet containing a £5 note, a debit card, the photograph of a baby and a biro. While she was reading the diary, Elaine Bell was busy on the phone to one of the turnkeys, becoming increasingly frustrated as the conversation went on. 'No – I said NOT to put him in the pink cell. I don't care if all the others are occupied, just shift them around, eh? Why? Why? How about because the priest doesn't need pacifying in there, or to see "FUCK THE POPE" scrawled on its walls. That's why!'

At 10.30 a.m. the double doors of St Benedict's opened, and a sad trickle of silver-haired people emerged, chattering among themselves in a subdued fashion, preparing to brave the snow-glazed church steps that led to the pavement. The celebrant was nowhere to be seen, so Alice buttonholed a stooped old lady, who stood motionless and staring hard down the street as if in search of her lift, to enquire whether June Sharpe was among the congregation. In clipped tones she was directed towards the parish secretary, a dowdy woman in a headscarf, busy cramming her missal into her handbag.

Like an inquisitive jackdaw, the secretary's head bobbed to the left and right as she scrutinised her fellow attendees, eventually declaring that Mrs Sharpe must have dodged Mass on this occasion. Fortunately, she was able to produce her address, smiling triumphantly at her effortless recall, careless to whom she was divulging the information or for what purpose. Still cupping Alice's elbow and with reflected sunlight cruelly illuminating a clutch of white whiskers on her chin, she pointed down the road to the junction of West Pilton Gardens and West Pilton View, indicating the woman's house.

June Sharp turned out to be a fragile, doll-like creature with enormous blue eyes, straw-blonde hair and a wide upturned mouth. When Alice showed her identification, she seemed both excited and apprehensive, guiding the policewoman to her narrow galley-kitchen, while cooing loudly to the baby that was perched on her hip. In the kitchen she immediately bent down to stroke the head of an old dachshund, curled up in its basket, its black lips rippling as it snored contentedly in its sleep. Suddenly the washing machine began to whirr noisily on reaching spin-cycle, and she switched it off, looking first crossly at the machine and then anxiously at the dog to see if the racket had disturbed its rest. But it slept on, an occasional wag of its tail betraying its dreams.

'Pixie's being put down today – at two o'clock,' the woman said, her large eyes brimming with tears, giving a graceful wave in the direction of the basket, 'and I have to collect Nathan from nursery at twelve o'clock, I'm afraid. So I'll have to go then, Sergeant Price.'

'Rice,' Alice corrected gently, 'Sergeant Rice.'

'Mmm… Sergeant Price,' the woman nodded, 'that's what I said.'

'It's about Father McPhail,' Alice continued, disregarding what she was being called. 'I've a few questions about him. If you could help us, it might help him too.'

'Oh. Yes?' Her voice was childish, unnaturally high-pitched.

'Can you tell me, did you see him on the night of

Tuesday the ninth of January?' The woman hesitated, searching the policewoman's face as if to read the desired answer, before tentatively committing herself.

'Yes.'

'What time did you see him?'

'He came here,' she paused again, looking enquiringly at Alice, 'he came here at about… seven o'clock in the evening?' It sounded more like a question than an answer.

'And at what time did he leave?'

'I didn't leave.' Mrs Sharp looked puzzled.

'No, I'm sorry, I can't have made myself clear. When did *he* leave?'

The woman sucked in her cheeks, apparently thinking, before replying in her strange treble, 'Maybe one, two o'clock? That sort of time…'

'And on Friday the twelfth of January, did you see him at any point on that date?'

'No,' she shook her head like a petulant child 'I haven't seen him since he left the parish.'

Confused, Alice asked, 'but… I thought you just said that you saw him on the ninth?'

'Oh… yes,' the woman replied, unperturbed by her illogicality, if aware of it at all.

'So you did see him on the ninth, then?'

'I did, yes.' Mrs Sharp smiled broadly, as if pleased that she had provided the correct answer.

'And what about the twelfth?'

'What about it?' She seemed bemused.

'Did you see him on that date?'

'Eh…' she looked into Alice's eyes, as if to find the solution there. 'No. No, I don't think so… then, again…'

'Mrs Sharp, I really do need to know!'

142

'Then yes… yes, I did see him on the…' she paused, '…whatever date you said.'

'I simply need to know, Mrs Sharpe. Did you, or did you not, see Father McPhail on –'

The query remained incomplete as the phone rang, Mrs Sharpe starting at the sound. She picked the receiver up as if it might be dangerous, and placed it warily to her ear.

'Oh, George, it's you… Yes, I am going to do it… I'll get it all done before lunch, honestly… Well, I can't go at the minute – I've got someone with me…' She faltered, looking Alice in the eye. 'I've someone with me… No, just a salesperson. A woman. Mmm… I'll get rid… honestly, everything will be ready in good time.'

'My husband. We're having a party this evening,' she offered, apologetically, before continuing. 'Frankie, er… Father… was here on the ninth because, well… he wanted to see me. George was away on business. We just talked, of course, that's what we do. Talk and talk for hour after hour.'

'That's fine,' Alice replied. 'We'll need, obviously, to take a statement from you – you know, for the trial.'

'Trial? You never said anything about a trial!'

'No. Sorry. It's simply that we'll need a statement from you confirming when he was with you – and then you may be called as –'

'I'm very sorry,' Mrs Sharpe said, 'but I can't give a statement. I can't do that. I don't mind telling you here, between the two of us, right, but nothing more than that. I can't say anything that might get back to George.'

'Why not? Your statement will be needed, you know. Without your testimony he might be wrongly convicted.'

'Look, I'm saying nothing to no-one, I'm afraid. I'm not supposed to see Frankie, you know! If my husband

143

thought I had, he'd kill me. Honestly. Last time he threatened me, threatened to divorce me, said he'd get custody of Nathan…'

'I'm sorry too, Mrs Sharpe, but we really do need your help. If necessary, we can compel –'

'Compel! What are you talking about? You can…' she hesitated, exasperated, racking her brain to think of a suitable torture, 'pull my toenails out, if you like, but I'm saying nothing. I'll deny I said anything to you. It wasn't true what I said, anyway, I haven't seen him since he left St Benedict's. That is the truth if you want it. I'm telling you the real truth now!'

—

'I've told you, Alice, the man who did it is inside, banged up in Saughton,' Elaine Bell said testily, holding down a piece of shortbread in her tea as if to drown it.

'Yep,' Simon Oakley added, 'give it a rest, eh? The woman may well be competent, compellable, blah, blah, blah, but she's also a waste of space, so what's the point?'

'The point is…' Alice tried again, aware that the rest of the squad did not share her view, 'that she can provide an alibi for McPhail for the likely time of the first murder.'

'Alibi my arse!' Eric Manson said forcefully. 'Provide an alibi, my sainted arse! They had it off together, OK? Forbidden love, like that holy mag implied – then it ended. But she thought she could help him, so she blabbed away, and it sounds as if she said whatever came into her head.'

'No, I don't think so,' Alice replied. 'She couldn't know, then, I mean, what would help him. It might have helped him to say she hadn't seen him on the ninth. Anyway, if she was only helping him with that kind of lie, why didn't she begin by saying that he was with her on the second occasion too?'

'Doesn't know which way's up or lost her bloody nerve, I guess,' DC Littlewood replied, never lifting his eyes from the computer screen.

'Look, sergeant,' Eric Manson said with a weary sigh, 'let's get real, eh? They had a fling, it all went pear-shaped…'

'Yes,' Alice interrupted. 'But why did she tell me that he was with her if he wasn't?'

'Because,' Elaine Bell said, rolling her eyes, 'she thought it might HELP him! You asked about a particular time. Obviously, that suggested that an alibi for that time might be needed. Without too much thought she fabricated one… and when things finally sank in, or she got muddled or whatever, she lost her nerve. Anyway, Alice, the question you should be asking yourself – if you don't believe she was lying,' and she pointed at her sergeant, 'is why she's not prepared to assist us, even with her lies? Why she's gone back on everything she said!'

'But I told you, ma'am,' Alice said, exasperated in her turn, 'she told me her husband would divorce her, beat her up, take the kids…'

'Nope,' Elaine Bell shook her head, 'from what you said she's just not very bright. To begin with, she thought she could help him, the priest I mean, get her oar in, say whatever. Then realisation dawned and she didn't fancy lying on oath *and* losing her children and so on. Remember, she openly admitted to you they were lies!'

'Well,' Alice said, sounding more confident than she felt 'I still think we should follow it up…'

'Jesus H. Christ!' Eric Manson bellowed. 'We've got our man in the pokey! What more do you want? Have

145

you not noticed or something? Everything fits together. The man's a priest, eh? The poor cows are left in a position of p... p... prayer. Geddit? He doesn't screw them, being celibate, just arranges them into a praying pose. And then – get over this if you can – he leaves his DNA on them. And it's not an odd hair fibre or something easy to talk your way out of, no, it's his blood. Explain that if you can. Because he can't for sure. He denies going anywhere near them! Ever!'

'Quite,' Elaine Bell added. 'It would be a complete waste of everybody's time to spend another minute on her. She won't help him and she certainly won't help us.'

'Yep,' Simon Oakley said, unwrapping a Crunchie and looking at it fondly, 'The woman's a liar, Alice, on her own admission. Best leave it, eh?'

They stood, side by side, outside the front door of the tenement in Jerez Place while the forensic team searched the priest's flat for anything to connect him to the killings. Alice glanced longingly at her companion's hat, a broad-brimmed leather Stetson, before shaking her head to get rid of its layer of accumulated snow.

'It'd be too big,' he said, as if reading her mind, and she smiled, impressed again by his perspicacity.

'Think they'll find the knife?' he added, staring listlessly down the street, his eyes alighting on a woman wrestling with a buggy, her upended toddler bawling beside her.

'Nope,' Alice replied, unwilling to re-open the argument and risk a further bruising for the doubts that she continued to harbour. She knew only too well that they were irrational anyway; she did not have any alternative explanation for the blood traces. Best change the subject.

'Got anything planned for tonight, Simon?'

'No. You?'

'Nothing much. Ian's going to an exhibition in Dundas Street. A friend of his. I might join him if I get off in time. You could come too, if you want?'

'No thanks. I'm staying in. Broke up with my girlfriend a couple of weeks ago, and I keep hoping she'll phone. Maybe even come and collect her stuff. She's still got a key, but I don't want to miss her.'

A waddling figure, head down against the blowing snow, approached them from the Fort Street direction, bags of shopping swinging and banging alternately against each leg. It was Mrs Donnelly, and she looked aggrieved at the very sight of them.

'Can I not get back in yet?' she demanded in a cross tone.

DS Oakley shook his head, edging to his left to allow her to share the little shelter that they had found below a stone lintel. For a few minutes they stood together in disharmonious silence until Alice's phone went, and she fumbled in her pockets for it, fingers rigid with cold. It was the crime-scene manager to inform her that they had found a woman's blue scarf in a cupboard in the priest's bedroom, and to ask if was to be accorded priority at the lab.

'What does it look like?' she asked.

'As I said, blue – baby blue – and it's got pink tassel-like things hanging off it.'

'Hang on a sec.' Alice passed on the description of the scarf to the housekeeper, who answered excitedly, 'It's mine – my scarf! But I gave it to him. He kept borrowing it, so I gave it to him.'

'Jim,' Alice said 'don't worry. No priority with the scarf. Are you lot nearly ready? We're freezing out here.'

'Almost finished. At worst, another five minutes.'

'Any photos of the priest up there?'

'Aha, loads. There's pictures taken at Nunraw, some of his first –' Mrs Donnelly began, thinking the question was directed to her, her face falling when Alice raised a hand to silence her, trying to make out the crime-scene manager's words against the din.

'Plenty. I'll bring down a selection for you.'

'Why do you need photos anyway?' Mrs Donnelly said bitterly. 'You've got Father after all? Probably took a mug-shot, or whatever you call it, too.'

Simon's eyes met Alice's, but neither of them felt inclined to tell the housekeeper the truth. That any individual suspected of killing two women was considered capable of doing almost anything, and that time, effort and public money would now be spent in an attempt to discover if Father McPhail was responsible for other, as yet unsolved, crimes. And photographs of him at all ages, from boyhood to middle age, would be required to that end.

Alice's phone rang again, and this time the crime-scene manager's booming voice was audible to the three huddled people.

'I've just put them in a box, dear, d'you want to come and collect them?'

As Alice started to move, Mrs Donnelly threw an accusatory look at the policeman, communicating wordlessly that if he was a gentleman he would be the one to climb the many flights of stairs, and carry the heavy weight down.

'I'll go,' Simon said, acute as ever, tipping the brim of his hat to let the snow fall off and stamping his feet before entering the tenement block. Once he had gone, Mrs Donnelly shuffled towards Alice.

'Sergeant,' she whispered, heedless of the fact that they were now alone together, 'did you find that Sharp woman?'

'Yes.'

'Could she not help this time? Explain where he was, I mean?'

Alice shook her head.

'Before…' Mrs Donnelly said distractedly, looking into the middle distance, 'before, she was always the reason, *always* the reason. When I didn't know where he was, I mean. He'd be there with her. And it got them both into awful trouble. The Bishop was merciless with him. Actually, I'm quite sure it was perfectly innocent this time, but… he just couldn't keep away from her. It was as if she'd cast a spell on him. I met her once, just the once, she seemed a silly woman to me.'

———

Stacked in the cardboard box were four photographs, all of them in frames. The first one Alice picked out was of a small boy dressed in a white, long-sleeved shirt and white shorts, staring hard at the camera with unsmiling, deep-set dark eyes. A woman's hand, encased in a mauve glove, rested on the boy's shoulder. The size and uneven edge of the snap suggested that the rest of her had been cropped from it. A gawky youth clad in bell-bottoms figured in the second, his long wavy hair parted in the middle and a shy grin on his face. In the next a man was robed in priestly vestments, a solemn expression on his face, shaking hands with a cardinal, and a handwritten caption at the bottom read '10th October 2005. The Retreat.' The final image was more difficult to make out, the glass in its frame partially opaque, a star-shaped crack across it, but it showed a young man and a young woman, arms around each other's shoulders, their laughing profiles close enough to kiss. As Alice was examining the double portrait more closely, she became aware that someone was standing behind her, looking over her shoulder at it.

'Alice,' the DCI said, extending her arm to take the picture from her as if by right, 'we've just heard from the lab that one of the eliminatory samples we took in the Portobello area, on the fourteenth of January, matches the semen stain on Isobel Wilson's coat. The sample came from a man called Malcolm Starkie. He's listed at 'Bellevue' in Rosefield Place. Crown Office want him spoken to right now. Could you do it?'

———

An old fellow, muffled in a thick overcoat, held the door open for her as he was leaving and Alice found herself in a tiny hall, decorated in fine regency stripes with a minute chandelier dangling below the ceiling rose. A clumsily-constructed reception desk, painted in white gloss, divided the room in half. The woman behind it was speaking in a hushed voice down the telephone. When she saw Alice she gestured for her to approach, crooking a finger at her and putting down the phone with her other hand. No farewells were, apparently, thought necessary.

The oddness of the receptionist's looks ensured that first impressions of her would not be easily forgotten. She was wafer-thin, almost two-dimensional, with a complexion as pale as death itself, and short-cropped, blue-black hair. Unnaturally dilated pupils shone through electric blue lenses, and they contracted as soon as they focussed on Alice.

'Have you an appointment?' She demanded sharply.

'No, but I've come to speak to Mr Starkie. I'm Det –'

'Well,' she was cut off mid-word, 'without an appointment there's no hope of seeing him today, I'm sorry to say.' The woman hesitated momentarily before adding, 'unless, of course, it's an emergency?'

Alice explained her business and was escorted to the waiting room, an even more cramped space, furnished with a few cane chairs and a coffee-table. Inside an anxious-looking woman sat, and on her knee a small girl rocked contentedly back and forth. Alice nodded at the woman, collected a torn copy of *Hello* and stood by the window, looking out onto the nearby red sandstone church.

'Mrs Rice?' a man's face peeped round the door, his mouth open in a wide smile as if to allay any misplaced fears, but looking nervous all the same. The mother immediately rose, pulling her surprised child by the wrist towards the fellow and made to follow him.

'We're your twelve o'clock appointment, Mr Starkie, and my meter's going to run out.'

'I'll be very quick with... ah... Mrs Rice,' the dentist said in a placatory tone, recognising the genuine patient and withdrawing immediately into the hallway.

The air in the surgery was sweet with the scent of oil of cloves, and a female hygienist scurried out of it as soon as they walked in. Alice perched herself uneasily on the edge of the reclining dental chair, but Malcolm Starkie remained standing, arms crossed defiantly on his chest, long legs wide apart. As he listened to her, the reason for her visit slowly dawning on him, he closed his eyes, putting one hand on his forehead, but said nothing.

Waiting for him to respond, she took in the surgery, noting a mantelpiece covered with family photographs, pride of place going to an oval portrait of a smiling middle-aged woman dressed in a cherry coloured cardigan. Adorning each wall was a blown-up photograph of an owl, their huge eyes staring at the patients as if at prey. Seeing her gaze on the birds, the man began to speak. 'I took them. That one...' he pointed, 'is a snowy owl. A female. This one's a barn owl...' Then, stopping mid-sentence, he ran his fingers through his hair.

'I didn't even know her name,' he said slowly, 'until I read it in the papers. Isobel Wilson. We never say much, converse... I was at home when those girls were killed. I'm almost always at home. When I'm away I wish I was back. Printing my photos, watching the television or whatever.'

'Could anyone else confirm that you were at home those evenings, those nights? Your wife, maybe, even a neighbour, someone like that?'

'My wife died last January. A neighbour possibly, but I wouldn't bet on it. I hardly know either of them.'

'So when did you last... er... see Isobel Wilson?'

'I can tell you exactly, officer, on Saturday. On Saturday the sixth of January, to my eternal shame...'

'Sir?'

'Our twenty-fifth wedding anniversary.'

II

A full moon does no-one any favours, Lena Stirling thought sourly, slipping into the shadow of the warehouse, finding herself now exposed to a harsh wind which swept along the corridor of Seafield Road, slicing through her thin clothes and leaving litter dancing merrily in its wake. She cupped her hands together and blew into them, fingertips bloodless and painful, her eyes still wide for any passing traffic. For the second time that evening a silver Mercedes glided past, the driver's gaze never leaving hers, but it continued its stately progress, red tail lights receding into pinpricks as it reached the horizon. Yet another man, she thought, out window shopping, but unable to pluck up the courage to make an actual purchase. Of these soiled goods, at least.

Stepping back again from the pavement edge she heard a crack as the ice on a large puddle broke under her weight, cold water immediately flooding into her left shoe. And on her thirtieth birthday, for fuck's sake! She shook her foot, and as she was doing so another car began to approach, moving slowly like a stalking cat, coming to a halt directly opposite her. As the window was being rolled down she ambled closer, relieved finally to have secured a punter, and crouched down to speak to the driver.

Suddenly, something scalding landed on her face, making her recoil instantly. Screaming in pain, she pawed her eye sockets in a desperate attempt to rid them of the burning liquid. Frantically, she wiped hot slime from her cheeks with her coat sleeves, then put her hand to her head, finding her hair matted with the same gunk. It was dribbling down her jacket too, and the smell was entirely familiar. The bastard had flung his carry-out at her; sweet and sour pork, the weapon of choice. As she looked at the Fiesta it tore off, horn parp-parping in triumph.

Sunk in uncharacteristic despair, she slowly closed her eyes, blocking out the world and everyone in it. For many years she had not allowed herself time to think. In her first weeks on the street she had occasionally done so, until one awful morning something had struck her, something blindingly obvious but which, nonetheless, she had not figured out before. And it was that there was *no way back*. But now, feeling suddenly more miserable than she could bear, her brain started to work overtime, unconstrained, uncensored, careless where her thoughts might take her or what damage they might do. Opening old wounds and picking at old sores.

How had she failed to realise that that first, hurried transaction would change everything? Stupid, stupid bitch. Thanks to it, she had become a whore and could never unbecome one. It was not like being a junkie, you could be 'cured' of that habit, cleaned up, your reputation restored. But this had less to do with what the world now thought of her, more to do with what she now thought of herself. Knew, in fact. That she was worthless. Since that revelation the most ordinary acts of human kindness had seemed unexpected, each one a bonus; and disdain, if not disgust, had become the price of truth. Whoring was not like any other job, any other profession. The lying involved destroyed your past and your present, and there was no future. As if in a daze, she had chosen it and burnt her boats. Three whole days after leaving school.

—

A stout man was ambling along the pavement towards her, and despite her dejection and bedraggled state, she automatically looked up into his face, intending to smile her willingness, needing a fix whatever the cost. But the sight of his balaclava-covered head startled her, frightening her sick, until she reminded herself of the jubilant newspaper headlines, felt the freezing weather and calmed down. Perhaps he was simply a Leith resident worried that he might be recognised? Or maybe the boot would be on the other foot and he would be put off by her unclean appearance? It had never happened before, mind. Looking her in the face, he gave a slight nod, and then began to speak, and as soon as he did so she relaxed, certain that she recognised his voice. Good, it must a regular, or perhaps someone she had been with just the once before – so much the better on a night like this. No time wasted haggling, talking or anything much else. With luck she would be home within the next forty minutes, out of the cold, back with the kit to share with Archie.

—

While Lena Stirling was shaking the water from her shoe, cursing the world and its inhabitants roundly, Bill Keane was giving his front door an almighty slam. Let Audrey hear it! Let the whole bloody lot of them hear it! Another precious evening wasted on tart patrol, and if it was his turn, 'if' being the operative word, it seemed to be coming round mighty quickly. Someone, somewhere, was not pulling his weight. And, worst of all, he would miss

Glamour Night at the photography club, a bi-monthly treat he had arranged for the delectation of the members, or at least most of them. He kicked a tin can out of the gutter, watching unconcerned as it flew up to land directly in a cyclist's path, finding himself equally unmoved by the V-sign flashed at him by the irate rider.

Anyway, this whole thing was becoming a complete waste of time, a sodding fiasco, no less. Thanks to the 'Leith Killer', as the papers unimaginatively insisted on labelling the fellow, heedless of the effect such a title might have on house prices in the area, the hussies had become increasingly scarce. Like house buyers, in fact. The downside of his capture being, obviously, that the rest of the coneys would now re-emerge from their burrows and resume their traditional pastime. But not yet surely? They were brazen but not actually barmy.

Thinking about things, perhaps if he raced at full pelt to Carron Place, a highly favoured venue, he could forget about the other places, Ma Aitken's and so on. Then he could nip home and catch the last fifty minutes of Sharon's exposure, or was it Bridget tonight? It was a tempting thought, particularly as the wind-chill factor must be in minus figures and his knee was playing up. Then, to his fury, he heard the 'Greensleeves' ringtone emerging from his pocket.

Snatching the phone from his anorak impatiently, recognising the number and rueing his own efficiency in remembering the damn thing, he demanded, bad-temperedly, 'What d' you want, Adam?'

'Whereabouts are you at the moment?' What a nerve! To be checked up on by a runty little IT creep. A man who would not have been allowed within spitting distance of his boardroom.

'Never you mind, Adam. I'm out doing the patrol, aren't I? Is there anything else you want? It's brass monkeys out here, so please don't waste my time with stupid questions.'

'I'm sorry, Bill,' the voice sounded gratifyingly apologetic, respectful even, 'it's just that I've had a report. Todd's been out in the Merc and he's pretty sure that one of them set up stall at General George's. Are you anywhere near there now?'

Red in the face and about to explode and release frothing expletives, Bill Keane suddenly had a bright idea, one designed to maximise his brownie points within the group and allow him to ogle Sharon, Bridget or whoever, too. He looked at his watch. Half an hour to go before the disrobing at eight or thereabouts.

'Well,' he began, 'unfortunately, I'm on Fox Place at the mo – right at the far end away from Ma's – but I'll turn around right away. Don't worry, I'll see the baggage off PDQ. Over and out, Adam.'

So saying, he dropped the mobile back into his anorak pocket and continued, whistling merrily now, along Seafield Place, Ma Aitken's pub already in sight. No need any longer to check out the West End. The group believed it had been done, and quite enough of their quarry located for the evening. Glamour Night might just be back on the menu.

◆

As he bowled briskly round the warehouse corner, his mind on shutter speeds and apertures, he noticed two figures lurking together in the shadows, the man's bulky form almost obscuring the woman's markedly slighter one. Maybe he could tiptoe up to them, give the dirty

157

bugger the fright of his life by tapping him on the shoulder and barking, 'OK son… you're under arrest!' or some other such nonsense. Mind you, the chap was built like a tank, and, on closer inspection, perhaps they had not yet begun to fornicate. Also, the fact that he was not a well man should not be forgotten. In the circumstances, discretion might be the better part of valour. The desired result could be achieved simply by, say, the loud clapping of hands or some other sudden noise.

While he was standing still, contemplating the best strategy, a shrill scream pierced the silence, terrifying him and making his heart pound in his chest. But when he realised where the sound was coming from, he found himself instinctively running towards its source. The small woman. At the sound of his footsteps clattering on the tarmac, the stranger whirled round to face him and ran straight at him, colliding deliberately and shouldering him to the ground. Stamping on his hand for good measure, he hared off in the direction of Leith.

From his new vantage-point on the tarmac Bill Keane looked up at the stars, breathless, shocked by the violence he had felt, still bewildered by the speed of events. Groaning slightly, he rolled onto his side, trying to rise. But as he put his weight on his right knee it gave way below him and he thudded down again, cracking his elbow against his ribs and yelping in pain like a startled puppy.

His high-pitched cry penetrated the woman's numb brain, rousing her from her stupor. With the return of full consciousness came an overpowering sense of dread. She had opened her eyes and seen moonlight reflected on the blade of the punter's knife, seconds before its point had been pressed hard into her ribcage. She looked round the desolate scene, her eyes finally resting on the injured man, still collapsed and moaning gently to himself.

Immediately she stepped towards him. Dropping onto her knees beside him, she put an arm under each of his armpits and began to try to haul him up. He did not protest and she continued pulling until he lay with his back propped up against her, both of them gasping with the effort, neither sure what to do next. As they waited together for her to gain a second wind, hailstones appeared from nowhere, striking their faces and bouncing off the ground. Nature herself seemed unmoved by them, showed no pity at their plight.

'Best get help, dear,' Bill Keane said. 'I don't think we'll manage...'

'Aha. Nae dosh in ma phone, but I'll gae tae Ma Aitken's, eh? I'll get us an ambulance frae there. You be a'right?'

'Fine... maybe sense to get the police, too?'

'Aye.'

She eased herself away from him, and then lowered his head gently back onto the ground. Shivering, she removed her thin jacket, intending to make a pillow for him from it, but ashamed of its squalid state she turned it inside-out before rolling it up, raising the old man's head and carefully placing it underneath.

⸺

At half past eight the next morning, Alice pushed open the door of the Ladies and was momentarily disconcerted to find herself confronted by her old adversary, the cleaner, Mrs McClaren. The woman was polishing the mirror in large circular strokes, crooning 'Little Bubbles' tunelessly to her own reflection as she did so. Never mind, Alice thought, nothing to fear nowadays. She was no longer a man-free zone, an easy target.

'Still got yer boyfriend, eh, dear?'

Alice nodded. Speech might result in her accidentally entering the joust again, and she was unwilling to risk that, even if she did now have some armour.

'Ah says, still got yer boyfriend, eh?' the cleaner repeated at increased volume, as if the policewoman might be deaf.

'Yes, thanks.' Safer to scotch that rumour, too.

'How long hae ye managed tae keep this wan then?' The cheek of it.

'I'm not sure exactly. We've been together about nine months, something like that.'

'Ye'll need tae get a move on, mind, hen.'

'Sorry? I'm not with you.'

'Kiddies. Or ye'll miss the bus, man or nae man,' she laughed croakily, 'otherwise ye'll need one of thae… eh… donor kebabs.'

Determined to avoid any further chat, Alice nodded again, squeezing past the woman and her trolley contraption to get to the nearest cubicle.

'An' ah had five by the time ah wis thirty!' Complacent cow.

'If ye lose yer man, right, dinnae touch that Oakley boy, mind, eh?'

Alice's curiosity was momentarily aroused and she waited, the door still ajar.

'Why not?'

''Cause he's crackers, ken. Want to watch yersel' wi' him, even if yer desperate. I'd no' trust him further than I could throw him. Telt me I'd lost ma job, a new company hud got the contract. I nearly got the sack fer no' turning up the next day, thanks to him. Laughed hisself silly when I gave him a piece o' my mind, but he'll no' dae that again.' She smiled wickedly. 'I spat on his hob-nobs, an' I'll tell him once he's scoffed the lot.'

A cautionary tale, Alice decided, finally finding sanctuary in the cubicle. Mrs McClaren should not be crossed.

With the cleaner now clanging about outside, careless of her presence and pressing need, Alice sat down, praying for her speedy exit. Eventually, Mrs McClaren departed in her own good time, 'Little Bubbles' still tripping from her lips. Alone at last, Alice looked at her appointment letter, an anodyne missive simply requesting her presence at the Infirmary for a blood check. No more than a formality, of course.

The lady at the main reception desk in Little France was deep in conversation with her neighbour, something about her son's infatuation with a female parasite and him blowing all his college money on pieces of hair, hair extensions if you please, for her. And for his birthday all the girl had managed had been a bottle of cheap aftershave and a packet of Maltesers. Unwilling to interrupt, but conscious that she might appear to be eavesdropping as she was, Alice managed to catch the speaker's eye and was directed wordlessly to a seating area in close proximity to the chattering staff. Before she had reached the middle pages of a vintage *Heat* magazine, a female doctor called her name and she traipsed after her through a labyrinth of corridors to a small, unassuming office.

As her flesh was being swabbed she felt the need to talk, conscious of the incongruity of being manhandled by a complete stranger in silence, so she said, 'I was much relieved that the victim proved clean – so this should be just a formality, eh?'

'Assuming the needle belonged to the victim, aye.'

Seven words, stating the obvious, but until they had been said it had not seemed so to her. Of course, the woman had been a junkie, and needles were often shared.

'I could have caught something from someone else's blood on the needle?'

Now concentrating on the task of siphoning blood from her arm, the medic said, ' Aye, but it's unlikely. She'd been dead for days, after all, and she'll have got the thing before she died. The virus itself dies quite quickly. It's a tiny risk, but we can't take that chance, eh?'

No. We certainly can't, Alice thought, praying that Isobel Wilson used the needle exchange, and telling herself that worrying would alter nothing, other than to add a few more grey hairs to her scalp. Oh, but ignorance had been bliss.

As she passed the cafeteria the scent of coffee tickled her nose and she followed it, having had no breakfast and determined to remedy the omission before returning to the hurly-burly of St Leonard's. She took a seat by the window looking out onto a sky so dark it seemed undecided whether or not morning had broken. Earlier it had not seemed so bleak, but gathering above the new horizon were lead-coloured snow clouds, filled with the promise of blizzards to come.

'Alice!'

She glanced up, surprised to see Professor McConnachie slipping his large frame into the seat opposite her, clear-eyed and without a trace of the mortuary pallor for which he was renowned.

'Didn't expect to see you here!' he continued, beaming widely with all his gap-toothed charm and putting his tray onto her table.

'No, I'm just here for a test… a blood test.'

'Of course,' he replied brightly. 'In connection with that needle-stick injury, I suppose?'

She did not want to talk to him about it, she was still trying to reconcile herself to the news she had received and its implications. Best, she decided, to try to shift the conversation onto him and his recent spell as an in-patient.

'How are you, Prof? Jock told me you lost a lot of blood. Have you been discharged now?'

'Mmm,' he replied, sipping his coffee and immediately spilling some of it into his saucer. As he poured the slops back into his cup he continued. 'I've been for a check-up today, restored with the blood of others. They pumped five pints into me, I gather. I wonder who is circulating in me now?'

'Sorry?' Her mind was still somewhere else.

'Blood donors, Alice. Are you one? You know, tinker, tailor, soldier, spy, policewoman… all or any of them could be circulating in me now.' Having re-filled his cup, he took a noisy slurp and then spoke again. 'Mind you, just as well it wasn't an organ I suppose,' his voice tailing off in thought.

'Why?'

'Something I read not so long ago. Apparently, if you have a bone marrow transplant, and your own marrow is irradiated, then your blood will contain cells bearing the donor's DNA indefinitely. Maybe kidney transplants have the same effect, for all I know.'

She nodded her head, trying to concentrate on what

he had said and succeeding until her phone rang. Its strident tone made her jump.

'Alice, where the hell are you?' It was Elaine Bell, direct as ever and with real urgency in her voice.

' Er… fairly close by. Little France, so I could be back in the station by, say –'

'Set off right now. Something's happened, and either we've got the wrong man inside or a copycat's been spawned and is on the rampage in Leith. I need you now. We're short-handed, Tom's on a course and Simon's been laid low by a stomach bug. I want you here to help Eric with Lena Stirling, to talk to some of the Leith residents again – that Keane man for a start. By the way, did you have any joy with Guy Bayley?'

'Not much. He only seems to have seen the Russian prostitute we've spoken to already, no punters.'

'He was at the bloody locus on both nights, he must have seen something. You'll need to chase him up, too

12

Glancing through the glass window into the interview room, Alice saw Eric Manson and he appeared uncharacteristically relaxed, leaning back on his chair, his hands linked on his belly, favouring Lena Stirling with a charming smile. The prostitute, in contrast, sat hunched, evidently tense, biting the fingernails on her right hand. As the policewoman came into the room their heads turned simultaneously to look at her, but, immediately, they turned back, their conversation continuing as if no interruption had taken place.

'He was called… eh, Billy, no, Robbie – I'm right, eh?' the DCI said, still beaming at the girl.

'Aye. He's called Robbie,' she assented quickly.

'And he'd have been in the year above me, so that makes him about fifty-two or so, that right?'

'Aha. He's fifty-two this April.'

'What does he do, what's his job?'

'The now?' she enquired.

'Aye. The now.'

'Em… he's a plumber. He wis in social work… worked wi' the Council fer years 'n' years. Then he decided he needed a change, took up plumbing.'

'Does he know about you,' the DI pursed his lips, 'about your job, I mean?'

'Naw,' she shook her head dolefully, '…thinks I work for BT, in sales, ken.'

Alice pulled out a chair, its legs screeching on the bare floor as she did so, the girl wincing at the sound.

'And your father, Robbie,' the inspector continued, his curiosity not yet sated. 'He used to go out with a lassie in my class. Susan... Susan... Susan... Susan something or other. Went out together since they were, must have been... fourteen, fifteen. Did they stay together?'

'Aha... Burn. Susan Burn. She's ma mum.'

'And what does she do the now?'

'Her job, like? Eh, she's a classroom assistant – remedial teaching, ken, oot Dumbiedykes way.'

'Isn't it amazing!' Eric Manson said, turning to face his sergeant. 'I know both of Lena's parents. We were at school together, secondary school. I think that's incredible!' Lena Stirling looked singularly unimpressed, despite his exclamations. It seemed neither remarkable nor unbelievable to her that a policeman should, once, have known either of her parents. Why shouldn't he?

'When you next see them, eh, tell them I was asking after them, eh?' Eric Manson said warmly.

'How'd I dae that then,' the prostitute said, sarcastically. 'Mum, ken, the last time I wis in the polis station, well, this Inspector telt me... somethin' like that, dae ye think?'

'No. No, of course, I'm sorry. I see the difficulty,' Manson replied, deflated and embarrassed, his naivety exposed.

'Now, Lena,' Alice interjected, keen to start the interview, 'we need a description of the man that attacked you last night?'

'Yeah,' the girl said dully.

'So, what did he look like? Could you tell us that?'

'Am I allowed tae hae a fag in this place?' the prostitute

166

asked, cigarette packet already open in her hand, ready to take one out and light up.

'Sorry. No can do,' Eric Manson said. 'One puff and all the alarms in the station would go off. But if you're desperate we could go outside to the car park, there's a smoking area out there. I'll have one with you an'…'

'Nah… I'll nae bother then,' Lena Stirling replied, putting her Silk Cut back into her anorak pocket.

'So,' Alice began again, 'the man who attacked you. What did he look like?'

'Big. He was big. Fat an' a'.'

'How big? How tall would you say he was?'

'Gey tall.'

'Taller than me?' Alice asked, standing up.

'Naw. Yer height – mebbe a couple o' inches bigger. Nae much though.'

'And was he actually fat, obese or just well-made, heavily built or what exactly?'

'Eh… he was solid, like. No' blubbery, just solid.'

'And what colour was his hair?' Eric Manson asked, confidence returning.

'Em…' she thought, 'he'd fair hair, plenty of fair hair.'

'His eye colour?'

'Aha.'

'What colour were his eyes?' Alice Rice tried again.

'I wis thinkin'!' Lena scowled, 'I dae ken. Hardly seen his face. I only did at the end when he took his balaclava hat oaf…' and sensing their growing curiosity at her words she added, 'and afore yous ask, it was woollen. Grey wool kind of stuff.'

'What did he sound like?' Alice asked.

'How d'you mean?' The girl looked perplexed, her forehead now corrugated in consternation.

'His voice, his accent?' Alice explained. 'Did he sound local or foreign or English or what?'

'He's local, I think. But he hardly said nothin'. Jist the odd wurd, ken... like he didnae want tae speak. He wis pointin', mind, tae show us where tae go an' all.' She pointed with her index finger, imitating her attacker's gesture.

'I recognised him,' she added, as if providing some inconsequential detail.

'His face?' Alice enquired immediately.

'Aye, but I cannae mind where I seen him before. I recognised his voice an' a'... but I cannae think how I kent him.'

'Maybe he was a regular, er... been with you before?' Eric Manson asked delicately.

'Naw, I dinnae think so. But I ken him frae somewhere... I seen and heard him before. Mebbe he wis wi' me before.'

'Lena, have you come across a man called Guy Bayley, he's the leader of –' Alice began, but was interrupted immediately.

'Oh, aye. Snowflake, we cry him. It wisnae him, though.'

'Snowflake?'

'Ken, wi' all that skin flyin' aroond. Whit aboot him?'

'Did you see him out and about on the night that either Belle or Annie was killed?'

'Want tae ken something really funny?' Lena said, her question directed at Eric Manson.

'Aye, on you go,' the inspector said indulgently.

'A couple of years before a' the residents got tegither, like, tae get us, Snowflake wanted a turn wi' me, but I couldnae face it cause I wisnae feelin' richt, been throwin' up an' everythin', so I says naw. He went mad, ravin' mad, bawlin' at me in his plummy voice, "It's not catching, you know!". Ever since I wished I had done it, keep him oaf all oor backs. I telt the wumman frae the *Record* an a', but she didnae believe me, never put it in, like.'

'But did you see him out on either of the nights?' Alice asked again.

'Em... I might hae seen him oan the nicht that Belle an me fell oot wi' each other, aye. He wis in his green vest. I waited in Carron Place till he'd gone, moved oan.'

'And on the night Annie was killed?'

'Naw, I dinnae mind, hen. Could've been there, he's aye on the prowl.'

'Does that get us any further, Sergeant?' Eric Manson said, covering his eyes with his right hand and then stroking his eyelids 'Lena's already said that he was not the one who attacked her.'

DC Lindsay popped her head round the door, noted the temporary silence, and announced, 'That's the photofit team here now, sir.'

'Like on the telly?' Lena enquired eagerly of the stranger, excited at the prospect.

'And Sergeant Rice is to go down to Leith and collect the CCTV tapes,' the DC continued, as if the woman had said nothing. And Lena felt invisible as well as worthless.

—

At ten o'clock that morning Salamander Street was quiet, few cars using the coast road, and even they seemed to be enjoying the sea breeze, driving at a leisurely pace, showing neither urgency nor impatience. The sound of seagulls filled the air, crying forlornly as they flew over the sunless road to wheel around the docks or perch on familiar, whitened roofs to preen themselves before heading back out to the open sea. Uncertain of the exact location of the Third Training Company, Alice was able, without fear of flashing lights or hooting horns from the drivers behind her, to crawl along examining the buildings on her right hand side, until at last she spotted a sign with the company's name on it.

Leaving the car she walked towards the entrance of the pebble-dashed building and found its double doors locked, with a notice hanging from one of the handles. In large handwritten capitals, it said 'CLOSED FOR TRAINING PURPOSES'. Puzzled in the light of the instructions she had received from Elaine Bell after the interview, she wandered around the side of the building, periodically raising herself onto her tiptoes to look through the windows. All the offices seemed to be empty, although lights remained on in some, doors were left open and in one a telephone was ringing endlessly. As she approached the last unchecked window, the sound of Dolly Parton's voice, with accompanying clapping beating out the rhythm, assaulted her ears.

Within the hall area, all the office staff were assembled, tapping their feet energetically and nodding their heads, apparently engaged in a bout of line-dancing. In the middle of the room a bearded man stood on top of a chair beating his thigh in time to the music and issuing instructions in a broad American accent. Beside him, a bony woman in overalls controlled a CD player, occasionally adjusting the volume to ensure that the man's commands could be heard above Dolly's plaintive tones. Alice watched, captivated, as a scrawny teenage boy, clearly broadcasting his reluctance to participate, was manhandled by numerous of his female co-workers to ensure that he completed the correct steps, in the correct way, at the correct time. Having finally done so, he looked around the room, pleased with his own efforts, and accepted with blushing grace a couple of pats on his shoulder from a big bosomed matron on his left.

As soon as Dolly's song ended, Alice knocked gently on the window, watching as the bearded man almost toppled from his chair in surprise, before he sprang from his makeshift podium and gestured for her to meet him at the main entrance. After turning over the 'staff training' notice to reveal a timetable of office hours, he held out his hand to her, saying in his natural Highland accent, 'I'm Ian McRae, Sergeant. We expected you a little later, I must confess. I'll just tell Michael to get the CCTV tapes for you.'

'Staff training, eh?' Alice smiled wryly. 'I thought you Government departments taught young people how to prepare their CV's, job applications and so on?'

'Aye,' Ian McRae answered, 'but Tuesday mornings are always quiet. The young people just don't seem to turn up.'

As they waited together in the manager's office in an uncomfortable silence, all their small talk used up, the scrawny boy entered empty-handed and looked anxiously at his boss.

'Did you say you needed the tapes, last night's tapes Mr McRae?'

'Aye. From all the cameras, not just those on the east side.'

'Well,' the boy shook his head sorrowfully, 'there's been a bit of a… mess, you could say. No-one's changed them, the tapes I mean. So there's nothing – nothing since the middle of last week actually.'

At her final destination, the next-door warehouse, the supervisor insisted on taking Alice personally to visit their CCTV equipment, as if she might otherwise doubt what he had told her. Crossing the car park he chattered nervously, twice bumping her shoulder, apparently having no normal concept of personal space. Suddenly, he stopped and pointed upwards to a severed stalk, the only remaining part of Camera Point One. He explained angrily that some 'wee bastards' from Portobello had decapitated it with the aid of a chainsaw and a set of steps. 'And that one,' he said, waving at the side of the building, 'has been done over an' a'.' She looked up and saw that the remaining camera had been deliberately re-positioned so that its lens pointed downwards, towards the ground, where someone had painted in white letters, 'Welcome to Wankerland.'

—

Had he forgotten or, perhaps, begun to take for granted, the lovely sound of Audrey's voice, Bill Keane wondered, relaxing in bed and listening as she read *David Copperfield* out loud to him. A low, mellow tone, so she would be classified as a contralto and none the worse for that; think Kathleen Ferrier, think… whoever. And it warmed his heart, moved him, the effort that she was putting into the story; deepening her voice to reproduce the cold, unfriendly tones of Mr Murdstone, and attempting a rural Suffolk accent in order to become Peggoty, or was it Ham? No matter, he thought, they should do this sort of thing more often together, instead of squabbling about what to watch on the box, cookery or gardening, gardening or cookery.

And it was not as if they had all the time in the world left, or even enough, to waste the precious stuff bickering over the ordinary, domestic trivialities which coloured their life together. His prostate had seen to that, and it would not be fair to keep her in the dark about things forever. But the 'right' time had not yet arrived. Something must be said soon though, or later, after he had gone, she would reproach herself needlessly over any impatient words uttered, any unloving looks bestowed. They would not now grow old together, irritating each other to the end. And from this new, lonely perspective, such a fate seemed, suddenly, blessed, something to be most earnestly desired. Dear, dear Audrey.

He looked tenderly into his wife's face as she read on, unaware of his scrutiny, noticing the split veins over one cheekbone and that her neck now had a strange, dry texture with two prominent tendons running its length. Once she had been flawless, perfect, like a peach ripe for the picking, and her hair, a torrent of unruly gold. At least she was lucky enough to have her locks left, he thought almost enviously, unconsciously stroking his few remaining strands several times as if in disbelief. Life was unfair – men losing their hair due to their virile hormones, although, thankfully, the stuff should also ward off the development of man boobs. And that TV programme had shown that it was all connected, in some mysterious way, with battery chickens, the contraceptive pill and the water supply. They were responsible for the feminisation of men, fish, polar bears and so on. But it was no longer his problem. Unlike his father, he would not go to the grave as bald as a coot. And, oddly, that thought gave him some satisfaction.

As the doorbell chimed Audrey Keane closed her book with a nervous snap, gave her husband's cheek a stroke, straightened his bedcovers and then bustled away to greet the stranger. In less than a minute the sound of her heavy footsteps padding back up the carpeted stair, a lighter pair in tow, could be heard. The duo stopped outside the bedroom door and he could just make out their whispered conversation.

'You are not, I repeat not, to tire him out, is that understood, Sergeant?'

'Of course, Mrs Keane. I'll be as quick as…'

'I mean it. He's got a broken elbow, cracked ribs and some kind of crucified ligament.'

'Honestly, I'll be as quick as I possibly can, Mrs Keane. Just signal when you want me to go. I appreciate being allowed to see him at all.'

Having obtained a suitable undertaking from the policewoman, Mrs Keane led the her into the bedroom, settled herself on the edge of her husband's bed and gestured for Alice to sit on its twin. Seeing the Sergeant, Bill Keane attempted to do up his pyjama top with his one good hand, and failing, found the job completed for him by his wife. Looking at the policewoman he felt sure that he recognised her, and pleasingly quickly it came to him. She had come to their house before, and hers was not an easily forgotten face.

'We need a description, sir, only if you can manage it, of course,' and the policewoman threw a wary glance at Audrey Keane, 'of the man who knocked you over in the car park last night?'

'The only man ever to knock me over, Sergeant, I'll have you know,' he replied sharply, 'in a car park or anywhere else!'

'Yes, sir.'

'He was huge, burly, built like a house in fact. And over six foot tall, I'd say.'

'Did you manage to see his face at all, sir?'

'Not that I can remember. The second he turned towards me, he charged – like a mad bull elephant. That was how he knocked me off my feet.'

'You didn't see if he had dark hair, fair hair, any of that sort of thing?'

'No. But what I can say, using your police jargon, is that he was male, Caucasian and maybe thirty-five or a little bit older. Is that any help? I'm afraid I'm not narrowing things down much for you.' He smiled wanly at the Sergeant, wishing that he could have assisted her more.

'And his clothes?'

'Oh… a big grey waterproof, I think. Something like that. It was so quick and at the best of times I never take in what people are wearing, do I, Audrey?' His wife nodded stiffly in response.

Alice took one of the photographs of Francis McPhail as an adult from a large envelope and passed it to the invalid.

'Have you seen this man on your patrols in the area, where the women hang out or anywhere else in Leith?'

'No,' Bill Keane replied emphatically. 'Not him. An odd-looking bugger for sure. I've seen all sorts but not that one. I've a good memory for faces too. I remember seeing you, Sergeant. Even before you came here the first time, I mean.' He beamed at her again.

'Oh?' Alice answered guardedly, watching as Mrs Keane ostentatiously brushed a non-existent speck from her husband's shoulder, clearly scent-marking her property.

'Yes,' he went on, still gazing at her. 'You were in the rammy in Carron Place, too. You spoke to that Barbour woman. Remember?'

175

Only too well, she thought, particularly the sinister drumming noise you orchestrated. But seeing Mrs Keane's eyes on her signalling frantically that her time was up, she rose, only to sit down again immediately, having remembered Lena's photofit. His head sunk now uncomfortably low on the pillows, the man looked closely at the composite picture held in front of him, but eventually shook his head, pushing her hand away with a disappointed expression.

'One other thing, Sergeant, before you go,' Bill Keane said, grimacing with pain as he altered his position in the bed, 'how is the girl, the one who helped me?'

'The prostitute, he means the prostitute,' his wife added unnecessarily. And as if he had not heard her words, Bill Keane repeated, 'The girl, Sergeant. Lena. How is she?'

'She's fine, sir.'

Going round to the end of her husband's bed, Audrey Keane lifted a full carrier-bag off his silken eiderdown and handed it over to the policewoman.

'It's… Lena's. You'll have her address, I expect,' the woman said shyly, and Alice looked inside to find a newly-washed, newly-ironed jacket, together with two boxes of Crabtree and Evelyn soap. Both Lily of the Valley.

'It was Audrey's idea, you know,' Bill Keane said, holding his wife's hand in his own.

—

Walking down Broughton Street that evening, Alice stopped outside the newsagent's, her eye caught by an *Evening News* billboard which stated in large, black capitals, 'LEITH KILLER STRIKES AGAIN BUT VICTIM ESCAPES WITH HER LIFE'. Who had told the press, she wondered, thankful that she would not have to perform on the high wire that Elaine Bell would now find herself balancing on. The DCI's performance at the next press conference would require an unusual degree of skill, with each member of the press corps secretly praying that she would splat onto the ground in front of them, and the Chief Constable watching unseen, through the flap of the circus tent. A timid ringmaster, indeed, one afraid of his own whip.

And no wonder, with their suspect charged and behind bars, and a killer apparently still on the loose, busy attempting to notch up further victims. But if the priest was not guilty, she wondered, then who the hell was the murderer? Such forensic evidence as they had pointed fairly and squarely in his direction. And he had provided no explanation for the presence of his DNA on the two bodies, whether or not the alibi provided for him by June Sharpe was accepted. Thinking idly of her conversation with the professor, it occurred to Alice that, perhaps, McPhail had donated bone marrow to somebody? After all, the only other traces were those left by herself, Simon Oakley and the dentist. Starkie seemed the next most likely suspect, so she decided, first thing tomorrow, she would revisit Rosefield Place. And she should check out Ellen's front-runner again, Guy Bayley.

Strolling past the window of the Raj Restaurant, she looked in longingly, picturing the packet of old sausages and the tin of beans that would probably constitute their meal in the flat. There was no time to shop during a murder enquiry and it was her turn, rather than Ian's, to produce supper. The next thing she knew she was sitting on a red banquette inside the place, queuing for a carryout, one hand full of Bombay Mix and the other holding a Tiger beer. She looked up to see if any of the waiters were being vigilant, alert for her order, and was amazed to spot Ian sitting opposite her, glass already in his paint-spattered hand, reading the newspaper open on his knee.

'What are you doing here?' she asked. He looked up immediately, and seeing her, smiled.

'A little treat for us,' he replied, meeting her eyes. 'On your night, too. Today I sold three paintings, so I think nothing less than a banquet is in order.'

While they were Inspecting the menu together, their heads almost touching, a moustachioed waiter appeared between them, saying, 'Ooklee… one chicken jalfrezi, one lamb kurma, one pulao rice, one garlic nan and one kulfi…', and then he looked round expectantly for Mr or Mrs Ooklee to collect the meal. Having just entered the restaurant, Simon Oakley approached the man, hand outstretched, and wordlessly took the bulging carrier-bag from him before favouring Alice with an almost imperceptible wave.

As they hurriedly ascended the cold, stone tenement stair in Broughton Place, both hungry, thinking about nothing other than starting their food as soon as possible, Alice heard the usual racket created by Miss Spinnell's attempts to liberate herself from her fortress. Since the unlocking, unbolting and unsnibbing process usually took minutes, rather than seconds, she was tempted to continue upwards as if unaware of what the old lady was doing. But it was too mean. Who else would Miss Spinnell wish to waylay on the stair? So she handed the greasy brown paper carrier to Ian, mimed 'Miss Spinnell' and pointed upwards to signal that he should carry on without her. She stood waiting until the old lady emerged from her lair, blinking hard, clad in a turquoise, silk kimono worn over her flannelette nightgown. Immediately her eyes lit on her neighbour leaning against the banister, and she sidled up to her.

'Well?' she demanded, looking up expectantly into Alice's face.

'Well… er, good evening,' Alice replied, momentarily at a loss as to what was expected of her.

'Your missing person enquiry… misper… you can call it off,' Miss Spinnell declared, pulling the kimono tight around herself and grinning.

'The missing person has –'

'Yes,' she was interrupted. 'Call it off, dear. I was at the Lodge today and she spoke to me quite clearly, but this time it was from the other side.'

'No,' Alice cut in. 'No… no, your sister's in Milnatho –'

As if she had said nothing, Miss Spinnell continued speaking, sounding oddly triumphant.

'Of course, it was to be expected at her age. No-one goes on forever, and she's a good five, no, eight years older than me. I always knew I'd outlast her!' And she beamed delightedly, eyes twinkling brightly until, noting the shocked look on Alice's face and readjusting her own expression accordingly, she added, 'Much, much, much, older than me, dear, you see. So I had prepared myself. Now at least, we'll be in regular communication through the Lodge, you understand… probably once a week or so. More than if she was alive!'

Understanding nothing, Alice climbed the last few steps to her flat, arguing with herself, wondering whether or not she had made the right decision. Mrs Foscetti wanted to thrill her sister with her unheralded appearance, but the element of surprise would be lost if Miss Spinnell learned beforehand of her twin's existence. On the other hand, seeing Mrs Foscetti in the flesh, Miss Spinnell might now die of fright, thinking it an apparition. Or, and worse again, at their advanced age either twin might now expire of natural causes before the Saturday meeting arrived, and Alice would then be responsible, solely responsible, for their failure to meet again in this life.

13

Everywhere stank, everywhere smelt. Nowhere felt clean. Wherever Francis McPhail went, his nostrils were filled with the same stale stench, a mixture of old urine, disinfectant and unwashed human flesh. Even in the prison van it was present, periodically obliterated by new smells, the tired scent of exhaust fumes, nicotine and the tang of spilt diesel. So when, finally, he climbed down the step onto the St Leonard's Street car park he stood for a moment, motionless, on the tarmac and inhaled deeply, reviving himself with the purity of the cold air, ridding his lungs of the captive atmosphere of Saughton.

The blue of the sky above him had never seemed bluer, the white of the billowing nimbus clouds scudding past more startling or sun-filled in their brightness. If only time would stand still, here and now, he thought, then he would begin to feel what happiness was once more. Not in the old way, when he had been needed, respected, revered even – that belonged to the past – but in a cleaner, simpler way. Unencumbered and unregarded. Instead, somehow, he would have to try to store enough happiness in this single instant to sustain himself for a lifetime. The absence of male bodies crowding round about him, milling aimlessly at his elbow, felt like luxury, as did the near silence of the place. No incessant, foul-mouthed chatter or music on the radio to intrude into his thoughts, muscling their dreary way into his consciousness. And without the crowding, the noise and the smells, he could achieve a state of near serenity, sufficient peace to let his mind roam freely, wander to beloved people and places.

A flock of gulls flew overhead, the thick, white plumage on their breasts catching the light as they banked together before turning eastwards towards Duddingston Loch, crying like banshees as they left. And he craned his neck to see them, noticed everything about them, savoured everything he saw, like a man whose days are numbered.

—

Seconds later he was escorted into a dark basement area, the air foetid again, and bustled past the charge bar into a room with 'Viper Suite' stencilled on its only door. It was windowless and the walls and ceilings were painted a cement-grey colour with six foot of strip lighting illuminating the sober space. The same young solicitor stood inside, chatting to a bored-looking policeman, and he looked up on Francis McPhail's entry. His shocked expression confirmed to the priest that his appearance had deteriorated since their last meeting. In less than a week he had acquired an institutional look, greasy hair crowning his ashen-hued complexion, and stained, rumpled clothes adding to the impression. And it went deeper than that; he no longer recognised himself.

Edging towards him, the lawyer attempted to explain the purpose of the procedure, referring vaguely, in a self-conscious whisper, to the fact that identification parades were on their way out and being replaced with this new video-clipping rigmarole. After his brief explanation, the young man looked at the inspector instead of his client, as if seeking an expression of approval, but got none. For a moment, the policeman met the priest's eyes, but he did not address a word to him, turning his head disdainfully as soon as the AV Operator, Janice, beckoned her prisoner towards a revolving stool in the middle of the floor.

In the simplest language she instructed him to sit down and look straight ahead at the camera. Everything was translated into monosyllables in case she was addressing an idiot. But he heard little, distracted by her curves and the strong scent she was wearing.

'His tee-shirt will not do, Janice,' the Inspector said, in a tired voice.

'Yeah,' the solicitor agreed instantly. 'It's too bright. Far too red, too eye-catching. My client wants it changed.'

Harrumphing noisily to signal her displeasure, the AV Operator bent down to extract a white plastic crate from below the camera shelf and began looking through the items of clothing in it, discarding blouses and hats, and eventually selecting a plain, white tee-shirt which she lobbed, good-naturedly, at the priest.

'Get your top off, Father, and put that one on for us, please.'

As ordered, Francis McPhail began to tug at the bottom of his tee-shirt, pulling it up his torso and exposing his plump, hairless belly to the gaze of all. As it came up over his head he blindfolded himself, finding that he preferred this eyeless state, whatever he might be exposing to the bright lights and unsympathetic company in the room. Seconds passed, but he did not emerge.

'Get a move on!' roared the Inspector, right next to his ear, and the priest clumsily peeled off the last of the garment. Obedient as a child, he put on the substitute that he had been given. It smelt strange, unfamiliar, imbued with a pungent odour from the innumerable bodies it had covered. Impregnated with their fear. Dressed, finally, in a stranger's ill-fitting clothing, his midriff uncovered like that of a teenage girl, he faced the camera again, and tried to master his face.

'Up a bit,' the AV Operator said, and he noticed that she was looking at his image on her monitor, attempting to centre his head on a cross. The Inspector then adjusted the stool until the woman, checking and re-checking the screen, signalled her approval with a thumbs up.

'OK, son,' the Inspector began, himself young enough to be his prisoner's child, 'sit back on the seat, right, then look straight ahead, then slowly turn your head to the left, centre it again, then turn it to the right. Alright? Got that?'

The priest nodded and attempted to carry out the manoeuvre described, but was interrupted mid-way.

'No. That'll not do. Slowly, OK? I said slowly, son. Look straight ahead, then *slowly* move your head to the left, then *slowly* back to the centre then *slowly* to your right.' As he was speaking he performed the required movements in a dumb show. Then he glanced at his watch, implying that his time was valuable and that he should have been elsewhere long ago. Mortified by his failure, Francis McPhail tried, once more, to obey the man's commands, this time following them to the letter, and after a further thirty seconds the necessary video had been obtained and the camera switched off. Sensing that the operation was now over he walked towards the door, as if he was free to leave. He wanted to vacate the room to ensure that he caused no further delay, did not hold up their next assignment. They were busy people and his ineptitude had irritated them long enough.

'Have you not forgotten something, Father?' the Inspector said.

The priest looked blank. 'Thank you?' he said quickly, feeling like a child again, desperate to avoid any more open expressions of disapproval.

'Your tee-shirt, eh? We need ours back.'

———

The floor of the cell was slippery, still wet to the touch, from being swabbed with a vinegary mop following the departure of the last occupant half an hour earlier. A metal toilet protruded from the wall, unflushed and uncleaned.

Curled up in a ball on the cement bed-shelf, the priest shivered with cold despite the prison-issue blanket he had wrapped around his body. He should try to pray, he thought, beginning to recite an 'Our Father', but found, to his distress, that he had reached the end before realising it, the familiar words now as meaningless to him as a reading of the football results. If his favourite childhood prayer had lost its power, then he no longer had any means of approaching his Saviour.

And yet his need was as great as it had ever been, all his hopes gone after reading yesterday's newspapers. If the 'Leith Killer' was still at large, as the headlines had proclaimed, then why had he not been released? Why was he still being treated as if he was the Leith Killer? But he knew the reason only too well. It was because they continued to believe that he was the girls' murderer, although someone, in his absence, had stolen his mantle. And his knowledge of his own blamelessness would not deliver him from this ordeal. No. That would only happen if he provided them with proof of his innocence. Otherwise he would grow old and end his days inside. The lab results, however misguided they were, would be more than enough for most juries. Never mind his lies.

He covered his face with his hands, clenching and unclenching his jaw until his molars ached, in torment, reminding himself that he could not afford to tell the truth however tempted he was. Not if the cost of saving himself was the destruction of June's marriage and the children's happiness. And he had not even touched her since the birth of their child, content just to look at her, be near her, although no-one would believe that after the last time.

He had cherished that little flaw of hers, her vanity, finding it appealing, endearing, recognising that without it he would never have been allowed through the door. A priest! A man sworn to chastity but unable to resist her singular charms, his vows making him a catch.

And, he castigated himself, it was not as if he was even a good priest in other ways. 'Know thyself' the oracle demanded, and he had not flinched from the task. But how could he be a good priest when celibacy was demanded, and he could not keep to it however hard he tried? Oh, but when he had someone to touch, to love, it was so much easier to be kind to the rest of mankind, to understand them. Because he did not love his fellow man, he simply tried, often unsuccessfully, to live as if he did so. And even if no-one else could see the difference, he could and was constantly aware of it: that between the naturally good man and his pale imitator, the difference between gold and fool's gold. But he had, ironically, come closest to being gold, the real thing, when sinning on a daily basis, seeing a woman and being loved by her. With her by his side he could have been a good priest.

He smiled ruefully at his own perverse, unorthodox analysis, pulling the blanket tighter, his hip now beginning to ache on the unyielding bed. In this world, he mused, some were born good, drawn instinctively to the right path, naturally kind in thought and deed, not prone to judgement and compassionate in their conclusions. And then there were the others. The vast majority, people like him, born without that grace but trying to live as if they had been blessed with it; performing generous acts, not artlessly, but as a result of a calculation to ascertain what the 'right' thing to do was. The end result, of course, was the same in terms of the act performed, but one sprang from the heart and the other from the head.

Well, he comforted himself, he had done his best. Apart from the women, anyway. But who, dying of thirst, could think of anything other than water? Whereas with that thirst sated, there was nothing that he could not have accomplished. And as a result of his weakness June had suffered once before, but it would not happen again, he would not be responsible for her unhappiness this time, never mind the children's or that husband of hers. Their son would have a father, even if it was not him. The other women had emerged relatively unscathed from their contact with him and she would too.

Anyhow, it must be faced, his days of being a priest were over whatever happened to him now, because he was no longer fit to be a servant or a leader. Even if they would let him, and they would not. He had been too frail a barque for the journey he had set himself, holed from the start. But any other life was unthinkable; he did not know himself without his dog collar.

Jim Rose, the senior turnkey, blew out the candles on his birthday cake with a single breath. A polythene cup, lager spilling from it, was passed to him, and a deep chorus of 'For he's a jolly good fellow' started up in the restroom, everyone joining in enthusiastically, fuelled by the many bevvies consumed earlier.

'Any o' yous fancy a piece of ma cake?' Jim asked, stabbing the knife into the centre of the square, extracting it and then using it to point at each of the men around him.

'Aye, I'll take a wee slice.' The voice came from an open doorway where a squat fellow leaned against one of the lintels, thick tyres of fat concertina-ed within his navy pullover, his trousers so tight they looked as if they might split if he flexed a knee.

'Naw, Sean, no' you. You're oan a diet,' Jim Rose said merrily, 'an' I promised Sheena I'd keep an eye oan you. What aboot anyone else though? It's chocolate an' –' he took a large bite out of his own slice, '…absolutely lovely.'

Another man, clad in the regulation navy blue uniform, swaggered into the room and stood, beaming, with one of his hands behind his back in front of the observation screens. The monitors revealed two empty cells and one with a cleaner at work inside it, attempting to wipe graffiti off the ceiling with swipes from her mop, droplets of dirty water falling down onto her head.

'Am I too late?' the newcomer asked.

'No, not at all, Norman,' his host replied, picking up an empty mug and readying himself to pour the contents of a can into it.

'Whoa, I'll hae nane o' that pish, Jim,' Norman said, whipping his arm from behind his back to reveal a bottle of whisky in his hand. When the spirits were finished they returned to the Tennants until, after a further forty minutes, empty tins littered the floor, screwed up and contorted, and the crisp plates were bare. The birthday cake remained largely intact on its foil-covered base, a few half-eaten slices in the wastepaper basket and one deposited in a pot plant.

'You checked the cells yet, Sean?' Rose asked, sounding uninterested and looking at his colleague benignly.

'No.' A simple statement of fact.

'How do you mean "No"?'

'No, boss. I've no' checked the cells.'

'When did you last look in on the bugger then?'

'Eh... forty, fifty minutes ago, mebbe.'

'And he was fine?'

'And he was fine.'

'You needn't hae any worries, boss,' Norman said, grinning and tipping his mug to drain it of its dregs, 'they're nae allowed tae dae awa' wi' themselves anyway. It's against their law.'

'Their religion,' Sean corrected.

'Aye,' Norman agreed, 'their religious law, ken.'

'Naw,' Jim Rose said bombastically, 'that's the Catholics. Papes cannae top themselves. Everybody else can!'

'Christ!' Norman shouted, 'he's a priest, man. A Catholic priest. What's your intelligence quotient, boss?'

'Ma whit?' Jim asked, laughing uproariously.

—

In his cell the priest was lying spreadeagled on the cement floor. He had used one of his knee-length socks as a ligature but he had miscalculated, losing consciousness before complete asphyxiation occurred, releasing his grip as he passed out.

When Norman peeked through the spy-hole he thought, at first, that an escape had succeeded, as the cell appeared completely empty. Hurriedly, and gabbling excitedly to himself, he fumbled with the key in the lock, twisting it first one way in his panic and then the other until it turned, and he was able to open the door, finding it unaccountably heavy. As the body slid over the glistening floor, he put his shoulder against the metal, forcing the door further open to reveal the prostrate figure within. The dark-red, plethoric colour of the man's face, fluid dripping from the nostrils, frightened the warder and he knelt close to the head, hearing a strange rasping sound coming from the mouth. But the bastard was alive, thank the Lord, their jobs would be safe.

———

Malcolm Starkie lived in a soot-blackened, Georgian terraced house in Sandford Gardens, a couple of minutes' walk from his dental surgery. In his sitting-room he sat bolt upright in his armchair, unsmiling, displeased that the police sergeant had tracked him down to his home, not restricted herself and her enquiries to his professional premises in Rosefield Place. On the arm of the chair rested a piece of unfinished embroidery, a needle dangling loosely from it, suspended by a thread of red wool. On top of the dusty cloth, also dust-speckled, lay a pair of gold-rimmed, ladies' spectacles.

'I would prefer, Sergeant, that from now on you restricted your visits to my workplace.'

'They told me you were here, sir. I just need to follow up one thing.' Alice hesitated, oppressed by the gloomy atmosphere in the room and the forbidding expression on the dentist's face. 'Can you tell me where you were on Friday night, the twentieth, from, say, seven p.m. onwards?'

'This Friday?'

She nodded.

'Yes. I was at the photographic club in Durham Terrace.'

'On your own, or with others?'

'It was, eh... a special night. Most of the members were there, they could... corroborate, if that's the right word, what I'm telling you, if necessary.'

She had no doubt that he was speaking the truth, Bill Keane had mentioned the club in passing in his statement, specifically referring to the number of professionals among the membership.

'By the way,' the dentist added, intruding into her thoughts, 'I think that I can prove that I wasn't anywhere near the prostitutes or their stamping grounds on the ninth.'

'Good,' she said encouragingly.

'I'd forgotten when I last saw you, in the surgery I mean. Tanya, my receptionist, insisted I go bowling with her. She told me,' he looked sheepishly at Alice, 'that I've to be "taken in hand, taken out of myself". So, every so often, she makes me... well, takes me out, you could say. We've been to a film once, went to the ice rink in Princes Street Gardens too.'

Trying to imagine the stick-thin, pale creature behind the reception desk having the strength to lift, never mind bowl, a bowling ball without being pulled, helplessly, towards the skittles herself, or pirouetting on ice in skates, risking her bird-like bones in the cold, Alice marvelled at her kindness. Books should not be judged by their covers.

'Fine. I'll nip round to the surgery right now and speak to her,' she said, rising, eager to leave.

The man looked surprised and then burst into laughter.

'Not my current receptionist – Christ Almighty! My last one, Tanya. Norma's not interested in sport... or men, for that matter.'

As she was leaving the house Alice caught a glimpse, through an open door, of the man's bedroom. A tangled mess of clothes covered the floor and the curtains were closed. But within the chaos there was an island of order; a wooden chair on which a set of women's clothes were laid out, including tights, a skirt and a cherry-red cardigan. Like a shrine.

━━

When Alice broke the news to Father McPhail's named next-of-kin of his hospitalisation, following his failed suicide attempt, Mrs Donnelly covered her mouth in shock and let out a heart-stopping wail, understanding more fully than most the depths of the man's despair. Unexpectedly, she then grabbed both of Alice's hands, clasping them tightly in her own.

'You believe, Sergeant, that he didn't do it, don't you?' she said earnestly.

Alice hesitated for a second or so before answering. As it happened, she did not feel that he was the killer, but the damning forensic evidence against him had never been satisfactorily explained away, and a hunch seemed too little to go on.

'What I think doesn't really matter, it's what the Detective Chief –' she began, non-committally.

'Stop right there!' Mrs Donnelly said, interrupting her angrily, still clutching Alice's hands and drumming them on the table as she spoke. 'Of course it matters. If you think he's guilty, you won't continue looking for those women's murderer, will you? And Father will try again, maybe succeed the next time. He must have lost all hope…'

The truthful answer would be short and simple. No. We won't. But it sounded so final, likely to make the woman's unhappy existence unhappier still, and so Alice found herself replying, 'Actually, I do still harbour some doubts…'

I knew it – I knew it!' the woman repeated, exultantly. 'You've seen what Father's really like. I've known him, been with him, for over two years, and there's not a vicious bone in his body.'

Alice nodded, disconcerted by the situation and unimpressed by the length of time on which the housekeeper's testimonial was based. If she'd known him over twenty years, maybe. Also, by admitting her doubt she might be, unintentionally, nurturing Mrs Donnelly's false hopes, raising them higher yet before they were finally dashed. In all probability, they would be dashed.

'I will keep trying,' she said out loud, although speaking more for herself than the housekeeper. Mrs Donnelly smiled, finally releasing the policewoman's captive hands, clearly embarrassed by her own reaction.

'I don't suppose,' Alice said, the longest of long shots, 'that Father was a bone-marrow donor – a kidney donor – anything like that?'

'No. He is a blood donor, though, we both are.'

14

Gusts of wind gave the arctic air a razor's edge, cutting Alice's face as she fought her way up Broughton Street and making her eyes sting. Every few hundred yards she turned her back against the blasts, finding a temporary respite from their force before, with a sensation of dread, turning to brave their full fury once more. Throughout her slow ascent she fumed inwardly, thinking about Mrs Donnelly and the burden the woman had somehow managed to put on her shoulders, all hopes and expectations now resting on her. If Father McPhail was to try and kill himself again, never mind succeed, she would feel responsible – unless she had, whatever the rest of the squad thought, turned every remaining stone.

She rubbed her eyes, aching from lack of sleep. She had spent the early hours agonising over the woman and her concerns, frightening herself with visions of the priest swinging from some makeshift noose or blood-spattered, his wrists sliced to ribbons. After all, his ingenuity was not in doubt, and nor, it would appear, was his determination. So, long before the alarm went off, she had given up the losing battle and crept out of bed, dressing hurriedly in the dark, lingering only to brush her lover's temples with her lips.

The icy silence of the tenement was broken by the sound of her footsteps on the stone stair, echoing in the lonely space as she took the steps two at a time with only her shadow to accompany her descent. Frost had silvered the cobbles on Broughton Place, shafts of white light catching them each time the clouds raced past, revealing the face of the moon.

—

Overtaking a solitary old man, busy muttering to himself and tugging an aged spaniel behind him, the dog's barrel-chest rolling from side to side as it made its bandy-legged way along the pavement, she attempted to focus on the case, hoping that the intense cold would help clear her head and sharpen her thoughts, rather than paralyse her brain.

All the evidence relating to the man must be recon-sidered and she must reach her own conclusions. But, thinking about it, other than the forensic stuff there was nothing. Among the hundreds of witnesses questioned, not a single soul had identified him or spoken of his presence in the prostitutes' territory. Of course, he had denied any involvement in either of the killings, and June Sharp had provided him with an alibi of sorts for the first one. And while he was out of circulation, twiddling his thumbs in Saughton, someone else had attacked another prostitute, and with a knife, the killer's favoured weapon. Obviously, the city's unofficial red-light district attracted a disproportionate number of its less well-intentioned citizens, creeps, perverts and pimps, but the selection of the same type of victim and the use of the same sort of weapon seemed an unlikely coincidence.

—

Her hair already flying about her face, unruly strands lash-ing her eyes and making her blink rapidly, Alice walked along North Bridge, finding herself hit by cross-winds that blew, dust-laden, from the east, their eddies making the cigarette-ends and sweet-papers in the gutter waltz. Turning her collar up, she tried to concentrate, but found that she could not, a raw ache in her ears distracting her until she clamped her hands over them, trying to stop the pain.

Start from first principles, she told herself, consider everything anew and think the unthinkable. On each occasion on which the priest's DNA had been found, it had come from blood that also contained some of Simon's too. Suppose McPhail's DNA had come, not from a mixture of two bloods but instead from a single sample containing the two types of DNA. Simon had told her that he had received multiple blood transfusions and Mrs Donnelly had said that the priest was a blood donor. Suppose Simon Oakley's blood contained Francis McPhail's DNA? It seemed a long shot, to put it mildly, but with nothing else left she would have to check it out. Another unpleasant vision of the man in his prison appeared, unbidden, before her eyes. A figure weeping and in despair, railing against the world and its works, a piece of broken glass hidden in his hand. And it would be her sodding fault this time.

Creeping past Elaine Bell's closed door she noticed light spilling under it. She had taken up residence there, pushing herself to the limit and reducing the compass of her life to the confines of the station. A sheet of lined A4, with 'Do Disturb' written on it in biro, had been attached to the door handle, as if in supplication. And it was hardly surprising that her temper, never fully in check, now ran wild and free, or that the targets of her irritation were becoming increasingly arbitrary. The squad tiptoed around her like well-intentioned Brownies humouring a cantankerous Brown Owl, desperate to avoid her attention. And while there were badges for following her instructions to the letter there were none for pursuing idiosyncratic, unauthorised lines.

———

As expected, the murder suite was empty, and Alice flopped down in front of her computer, beginning to tap its keys before she had even removed her coat or scarf. Typing in 'Blood donor and alien DNA' produced a number of possible entries. The first suggested that processed donated blood would be unlikely to yield any of the donor's DNA, as very few of the donors' white blood cells would remain in it post-transfusion, and only white blood cells contained nuclei from which the DNA could be extracted. Neither red blood cells nor platelets, the other constituent parts of blood, had nuclei. Any white blood cells remaining in the blood, after processing, would be destroyed either by the standard storage temperature used or, post-transfusion, by the recipient's immune system.

The next hit initially gave her some hope, suggesting that if the recipient of donated blood left their blood at a crime-scene or wherever, it would contain 'mixed' DNA. However, the information was so poorly written and disorganised that any reliance on it seemed foolish. The last but one link led to a paragraph contributed by the National DNA Database of Canada, and it showed a markedly more sophisticated approach. It distinguished between types of fluid transfused, contrasting whole blood, containing red blood cells, platelets and white blood cells, and other fluids which included some but not all of the mix. The author of the article asserted that if the donee received either white blood cells or platelets, or both, then the mixed blood would reveal, on analysis, two separate types of DNA, one attributable to the donor and the other to the donee. It also expressly stated that not only white blood cells, but also platelets, contained DNA. The final piece Alice looked at referred to two studies, one involving a woman who had received fourteen units of blood (four whole blood, ten red blood cells only) and a man transfused with thirteen units (four whole, nine red blood cells only). In both cases, neither individual had detectable levels of the donor DNA profile when tested the day after the transfusions.

⸺

As Alice was leaning back on her chair, lost in thought, and still staring at her screen, trying to reconcile the partially contradictory information, Elaine Bell swooped into the murder suite in search of her wandering coffee mug. Spotting it from afar on her sergeant's desk, she had crossed the room before her colleague had even become aware of her presence. And the gasp Alice released on seeing the DCI betrayed her guilty secret. For a second, she wondered whether her adversary, the cleaner, had planted the mug on her desk from mischievous motives, before recognising the notion for what it was, the product of paranoia and sleeplessness. As Elaine Bell snatched the mug, hissing like a snake about to strike, Alice hurriedly returned to the Google page, hoping that the DCI, still preoccupied with her mug, might not have noticed her unusual research.

'What on earth are you wasting your time on now, Sergeant? Our time, more accurately, when there are countless things which still need to be done!' the Chief Inspector thundered.

Still at a loss for words, Alice realised that her optimism had been misplaced. An exhausted, semi-addled Elaine Bell would still be sharper than a cat's tooth, and that uncanny sixth sense of hers never failed, alerting her to any of her subordinates' irregular activities.

And it was such a difficult question to answer. Alice had no idea where to start, particularly, as she had not satisfactorily resolved the matter in her own mind. In truth, she was simply dotting 'i's and crossing 't's, excluding the improbable, making it the impossible. This had to be done even if it did involve wild speculation or worse. And whatever was left would yield the answer. After all, if Father McPhail was innocent, then they should still be hunting a double murderer, not just on the lookout for some low-life who had assaulted a prostitute. But, losing all confidence in her ability to make her activity sound anything other than madness, even to a well-rested Elaine Bell, never mind the frazzled reality confronting her now, she murmured something about 'long shots' and 'intellectual curiosity', and waited for the storm to break around her. And it did, its ferocity taking her by surprise until she remembered her own earlier, intemperate reaction to Mrs Donnelly and her concerns. That burden now rested on her lighter than feathers in comparison to the one carried by her tired superior.

'That Guy Bayley man, have you spoken to him again?' the Inspector demanded.

'Not yet, Ma'am.'

'Well, get a move on, for Christ's sake!'

After her extended and apparently cathartic outburst, Elaine Bell patted the back of her unbrushed hair, disconcerted to feel a pair of upstanding tufts, exhaled heavily and marched out of the murder suite with a spring in her step, empty-handed. Inspector Manson almost collided with her in the corridor, flattening himself against the wall to let her past. Still striding forwards, she said over her shoulder, 'Have you checked up McNeice's alibi, Eric?' Getting no immediate response, she added, 'Well, shift your arse then.'

———

The minute she was alone again, Alice made a quick call to the forensic science lab, praying to herself that someone would be in at such an unearthly hour and that the DCI would not return for the forgotten mug. To her delight the phone was picked up after only four rings, and, better yet, she recognised the voice at the other end.

'Dave… would you do me a favour?' Fear of discovery was making her succinct, if not actually terse.

'Ms Rice, I presume. What can I help you with this time?' Was there an edge in his voice? One too many favours sought?

She must be clear, get her enquiry across without delay and hope that her near pathological brevity did not cause him terminal offence.

'Dave, I need to know whether or not it's possible for X to leave Y's DNA, as well as his own, if X leaves a sample of his blood at a crime scene or wherever. Assume X received a blood transfusion with Y's blood at some point before X left the blood.'

It did not sound as lucid as she had hoped it would, but there was no time for rewording the query and he was a bright man. She would have to trust in that.

'And why do you want to know that, pray?'

'Because,' she hesitated momentarily, thinking she heard the tell-tale clump of Elaine Bell's heavy tread, 'because if such a thing could happen, it might explain the presence of someone's DNA at a crime scene – when, if they're to be believed, they were never there.'

'OK, Alice. It sounds a bit off the wall, but I'll check it out for you during my lunch hour. How are you? How are things at St –'

'Dave. I'm really sorry but I've got to go,' she interrupted him, alert to the sound of the door handle turning, vowing to herself to make it up to him as soon as she could, to explain everything properly. 'I'll phone you in the early afternoon. Thanks a million for your help.'

Just as she put the receiver down the DCI re-entered the murder suite and removed the blue and white mug from Alice's desk, a slightly sheepish smile on her face, hair now brushed flat, ready to face the world.

❦

'Has your stomach recovered yet?' Alice asked, the words slipping out before she realised the unintentional barb contained in them. Simon Oakley's mouth was wide open, about to take another bite out of a cheese pasty. They were waiting in the Astra at Brighton Place for the lights to change, sitting behind a white van that belched exhaust fumes and had 'I love you' written on the dirt on its back door.

'Yeah,' Oakley replied, reddening as if remembering the fiasco at the Raj.

'Tanya seems to have got Mr Starkie off the hook, eh?' A quick change of subject would show that the ostensible dig was not deliberate.

'Yeah.'

'Did you notice her amazing coloured lenses?'

'Nope.'

Being electric blue they were impossible to miss even by the dullest observer, never mind someone as keen-eyed as Simon, Alice thought. She wondered whether her companion had retreated into his habitual near-speechlessness and had no desire to talk. On the other hand, perhaps, he had taken offence at her opening gambit and she should try to coax him round, reassure him that she had meant nothing untoward? As she was racking her brain, as seemed to be happening all too often, for some other uncontentious subject, her phone went.

'What was that about?' he asked, as she put it back into her pocket.

'A cleaning up exercise, I'm afraid. The boss thinks that the DI and I didn't get enough information from Lena Stirling about the assailant's voice, so we're to go to her flat in Harbour Street, see her there and ask about it and about the bloke's looks again. Another witness has turned up, someone from Cadiz Street, who saw a dark-haired man running in the area at about the right time.'

'What about "snowflakes" or whatever he's called? I thought we were to go there?'

'Lena first, apparently.'

To her amazement, when they reached the Portobello roundabout, Simon Oakley continued over it, heading back into Leith instead of turning right towards the sea.

'Simon, it's Harbour Street – back there. We need to turn round.'

'Sorry, Alice, I can't. It's my tummy, it's started playing up again. I've got to get home quickly. I think I'm going to be sick.' He swallowed hard, his Adam's apple bobbing up and down in his pale throat.

She glanced at him, annoyed not to have been con-
sulted, and he immediately caught her eye, returning her
look sheepishly, as if asking for forgiveness. But he looked
blooming, in the pink, and he had recently finished one
and a half pasties. Maybe that was the trouble.

'OK. But a minute ago you were fine. Couldn't we just
do this first? It's all hands to the pump now and we're
right next to the woman's house, practically. I'm sure
she'd let you use her loo and it won't take long, I'd be
as quick as quick can be. You could even stay in the car,
if you like, and I'll go there by myself. I'll be in and out
before you know it,' Alice said, looking back at their turn-
off as it disappeared into the distance.

The man shook his head, then, Alice noted, extended
his hand apparently towards the unfinished pasty on the
dashboard, before redirecting it in the nick of time to the
gear-stick and performing a gear change. Then, to her
surprise, he winked at her.

'Have you finished that packet of hob-nobs in your
desk drawer?' she asked him, a sudden thought striking
her.

'Yes. Why?'

'Nothing.'

⟞

Back in the murder suite, having spoken to Lena Stirling
and learnt nothing, Alice reached for the receiver. She
would have to phone Simon to tell him that he had left his
jacket in the car, but first another call, and the luxury of
having her curiosity finally assuaged. She stirred her cup
of milky tea with her left hand, about to take a sip when,
unexpectedly, the burst teabag bobbed to the surface, a
trail of tea dust surrounding it.

'Dave, I'm sorry I was so short, so uncommunicative, this morning. I was worried the boss might come in, put a stop to what I've been trying to find out about. Anyway, I didn't mean to be unfriendly. Have you had a chance to find out anything about the blood donation/DNA stuff, yet?'

She took a quick swig, dust and all.

'Yup. And it's very interesting too. I think you have described a phenomena known as "transfusion-associated microchimerism".'

'Something about a tiny monster?'

'No. Nothing like that. It's a biological term, and I'll explain it to you, if you'll just let me get a word in, OK? What happens is that in some individuals, if they get a massive transfusion of fairly fresh blood, the transfused blood obviously having come from multiple donors, a population of one of the donors' white blood cells persists and replicates in the recipient's blood...'

'Just one of the donors?'

'Yes, just one of the donors usually, at most two, but usually only one. Apparently, the injury resulting in the need for the blood transfusion sometimes causes an immuno-suppressive reaction, which helps naturally, and the proportion of donor white blood cells among the recipient's white blood cells can reach as high as 4.9%.'

'How long does the effect persist for?'

'Can last for... ta, da...' he sang, 'two years or more. Is that of any help to you?'

'As good a start as I could wish, Dave, you genius. One other thing, though, in the McPhail case – you got the less-good profile from his DNA, didn't you?'

'Mmm. There was only just enough of the stuff to make a match. Most of the DNA was your pal's. How the hell did he manage to bleed all over the bodies anyway, hasn't he had any training?'

'Yes, course he has, but with the first body he –'. She stopped, unable to think how he had managed to get any blood on to the corpse, picturing him swaddled tight against the snowy weather. But something must be said in his defence, so she skipped to the second victim.

'Just before we found Annie Wright he fell, got a huge cut on his thumb,' she continued. 'He was bleeding like a stuck pig before he got anywhere near her, I saw it myself.'

But the question had been a good one. How the hell had he managed to bleed onto Isobel Wilson? She racked her brain, trying to remember the conversation in the office, with Elaine Bell laying into them and his ready reply, 'Brambles'. And she had been so appalled by her own carelessness, and her boss's reaction to it, that she had hardly considered his excuse, feeling solidarity with him when both of them were under attack. But recreating the scene in her mind's eye now, she saw snow and dying undergrowth, felt again the pain in her shins from her falls in the freezing weather, but recalled neither prickles nor thorns.

———

Guy Bayley looked disappointed when he opened his front door in Disraeli Place to find the police sergeant standing on his doorstep, but, recovering quickly, he waved for her to come in. As she wandered down the dark corridor leading to his sitting room she tripped over a vast basset hound which had unexpectedly lumbered across the passageway right in front of her. As she hit the ground with a thud, Bayley let out a cry of distress: 'Oh, Pippin!'

Then, stepping over her as she half-lay on the floor, he rushed to the dog and patted it, saying angrily, 'Can't you see – he's blind, for goodness sake. He might well have been hurt!'

Seeing the hound's cataract-filled eyes, apparently looking up at her reproachfully, Alice managed to say nothing, despite an almost overpowering urge to do so.

The lawyer's sitting room was bland, with magnolia walls and an oatmeal carpet, a blank canvas which its owner had decided, for some reason, should remain blank. Virtually the only colour in the room came from a black leather suite, and propped up against the leg of an armchair was a parcel with gold wrapping paper and a broad red ribbon tied around it in a bow. The place was bereft of pictures and ornaments, and the only photo in it was a small one on the TV set, depicting Pippin in his salad days. However, parts of the floor were covered in papers and files, including the entire space between the curtains. A laptop sat on an occasional table, the screensaver also featuring a portrait of the basset hound, but this time in puppyhood. Haydn's cello concerto was playing at low volume on an expensive CD player, and the lawyer made no move to switch it off.

'Well, Ms Rice, what can I do for you? I am supposed to be working at home today, and I'm expecting someone to lunch very soon.'

'It's about the nights you were out on patrol…'

'I've already admitted,' his voice sounded impatient, 'that I was present at the locus at the relevant time, although with an innocent explanation. The rest is surely up to you.'

'Quite, sir. I simply wondered, if you cast your mind back to those nights, if you could consider again whether you might have seen anyone else apart from the Russian lady?'

'Have you followed "the lady" up?'

'Yes, and to no avail. There is a possibility, you see, that you, and possibly only you, did actually see the killer.'

'Mmm.' The man hesitated, seemingly mollified by her placatory approach, and silently tried to conjure up, once more, the night of the murder. After about a minute, he said slowly, 'Maybe there was someone, late on, a man, a big fellow. I can see, in my mind's eye, a big fellow with a hat on… but he may be no more than a figment of my imagination. I didn't mention him before because, frankly, I hadn't remembered him. And at this distance in time, I can't be sure of anything. Except the Russian and the choice mouthful she gave me.'

'Anything else you can tell me about the man, sir?'

'Such as?' the irritable rejoinder shot back.

The question had seemed quite reasonable to Alice when she posed it, but now she found herself racking her brain for a sensible follow-up. ' Er… his gait, his clothing… Was he carrying anything, a stick, an umbrella – anything at all that comes back to you?'

'No. All I can see… all I can remember, I hope, is that the chap was big, broader than me. Nothing else,' the lawyer said, looking thoughtful again, as if trying to summon up every recalcitrant detail.

The sharp smell of burning milk hit Alice's nostrils and she waited, looking at Bayley, for him to react to it, but he said nothing, did nothing as it got stronger every second. Eventually she said, 'Have you got something on the stove, sir?'

He stared at her and then leapt to his feet and ran out of the room. A couple of seconds later, his canine shadow bumbled after him, bumping into the doorframe with its fat body.

As Alice was about to leave, an elfin woman, with hair cut as short as a boy's, put her head and shoulders around the door, her face falling on seeing the visitor. She was dressed demurely in a brown jacket and thick calf-length skirt with heavy leather shoes on her feet.

'Oh, I was expecting Guy,' she said, entering and looking at Alice anxiously. As she finished speaking Bayley walked in. Seeing her, his entire face lit up, smiling with his eyes and his mouth, his pleasure in seeing her unrestrained, impossible to hide. She, too, beamed; they met in the middle of the room and, for an instant only, held hands. In their absorption in each other Alice seemed to have become invisible, and they remembered her only when, as she rose from her chair, the leather squeaked below her.

'Er... this is Sandra Pollock, sergeant, a friend of mine,' Guy Bayley said uneasily. The woman added, her eyes never leaving the lawyer's face, 'Sister Sandra, usually. I'm a nun as well as a friend of his.'

—

He watched her, amused, as she stamped her feet on the promenade, then paced to and fro, evidently feeling the cold, desperate to do the business and go home. Let her wait, catch a chill, catch her bloody death for all he cared. She was already his, that much had been agreed and, for more cash, she would hang about in the freezing air until he decided that the time was right. Auspicious. And all he needed to do, to keep her quiet, was to open his wallet like a flasher's raincoat, and her high-pitched complaints would cease. That sulky expression would fade, she might even manage a smile until the meter ran out again.

The sea, in the faint, orange lamplight, looked like liquid mud, thin filth, churning and re-churning itself before receding into blackness, and instead of the fresh smell of ozone there was the stink of sewage, an outlet-pipe nearby discharging its foul effluent on to the beach below. Not really a place to die, but few had the luxury of choosing the spot, and there were worse ways to go out. Decaying, slowly and inexorably, in an old folk's home, for a start.

Sometime soon he might be caught, must be caught, so tonight's entertainment could be his last. It should be savoured to the full, relished, enjoyed, drained of pleasure to the last drop. Noticing the prostitute throwing a malevolent glance in his direction, he walked across to her and handed over a fiver, watching as she folded it and put it into her skirt pocket, pulled her jacket more tightly around herself and began her restless pacing again, like a caged beast. But he was the beast here, he thought, a nice reversal, and had selected his prey with care. Huge pupils were the giveaway, too much smack or vodka and coke in the bloodstream. Those undiscriminating dark pools welcomed everyone, levelling mankind and tricking nature. Black holes sucking everybody in.

'Look, pal,' the prostitute said, through chattering teeth, 'it's f… f… fuckin' freezin' here, eh? Let's… just get it ove… eh, oan wi' it, eh?'

'Get it over with,' you mean, he thought, blinking at her but saying nothing. Unpleasant experiences had to be got over, teeth-pulling, injections, that kind of thing, but he was not that kind of thing and she would not get over him.

'What's your name?' he asked.

'Eh… Muriel.' Her hesitation betrayed her lie.

'Well… Muriel. What I'd like is for you to stand over there…' he pointed to the wall, 'and close your eyes. Tight shut, mind. Then we'll d… d… do it, eh? Get it over with, eh?'

'Naw.' She drew on her cigarette, firing the smoke at him, imagining that she was in control of the situation.

'Naw? it's not so much to ask is it?' he said holding another fiver in front of her face and pointing again at the same area of wall. 'There's a good girl. Just stand there, close your eyes… and there's extra money in it for you.'

Looking heavenwards to let him know she was humouring him, she strolled across, whirled round to face him, eyes tight shut with her cigarette still between her lips, a reminder that kissing was off-limits. In a second, he had the knife out of his jacket and stood with it poised opposite her heart.

'You ready yet, pal?' she said, lashes still down, conscious from the sound of his breathing that he had moved closer to her, smelling his breath.

'Oh, aye… ready.'

She did not scream or thrash about as the last one had, instead she collapsed on the spot, her legs no longer supporting her, and lay, face upwards, as her heart continued its task, pumping blood onto the cement of the promenade, some spurting heavenwards into the sewage-scented air. For a second he thought he saw himself reflected in her pupils and then, slowly, she closed them, embracing the darkness. Bending over her, he put his face close to hers as if they were lovers, feeling for the warmth of her breath on his skin and inhaling her perfume as he did so. He could kiss her now if he wanted.

Suddenly, something gave a little peck or claw to his cheek, and he hit it away as you might a fly or wasp. Then, practical as ever, he turned his waterproof jacket inside out and lifted the slumped body away from the jet-coloured pool surrounding it, carrying his burden to an area of scrubland bordered by the sea and the promenade. He dropped her a couple of feet onto the wiry grass below, then climbed over the railings and began to roll her onto her back, positioning her arms across her breasts as if in prayer. Just as he had seen in a forensic science text book, a long time ago. He would have to clean her up, he thought, check her over, then remove any tell-tale signs.

'Diesel! Diesel!' a dog-walker's voice rang out, an irate baritone and only a few hundred yards away. He peered up, over the end of the promenade, and saw a collie prancing about, skittering in all directions, with its tail held aloft and a ball in its mouth, but always advancing forwards, in his direction. Getting closer by the second. He must go.

15

The bus looked empty and the prostitute climbed aboard it, relieved to be returning to the safety of her home and that the night's labours were over. As Julie Neilson lowered herself into the seat her right hand touched something warm, soft and sticky. She recoiled instantly as if burnt, examining her palm and finding it scented with the sweet, sickly aroma of spearmint. Recently-chewed chewing gum. Taking her hankie from her pocket, she spat on to it and began to wipe her palm clean, noticing as she did so that the back of her hand had a couple of liver spots on it and that the veins were clearly visible, flowing like frozen rivers towards her knuckles.

'Hen, hen… whit ye oan this bus fer?' demanded an unfamiliar voice, one which swooped from treble to bass and back again. She raised her head from her cleaning task and watched as a couple of youths bundled each other into the seat directly in front of hers, one of them upending a bottle of Buckfast into his mouth and the other grinning at her, his face now unnaturally close to her own. They were both young enough to be her children, and she had no desire to talk to them, but they were an unknown quantity. They were likely to be unpredictable, and ignoring their question would be seen as rude.

'Fer a ride…'she said, adding quickly, but not quickly enough, '…hame.'

Immediately, they burst into raucous laughter, one nudging the other with his elbow, repeating together, 'Fer a ride, eh? Fer a ride! You'll be lucky!'

She lowered her eyes, looking down at her knees, hoping that if she seemed withdrawn and uncommunicative they would become bored, find something else to attract their attention and allow her to continue her journey in peace. Let her think about other more pressing things.

'Like fags, hen?' the dark-haired one asked, taking another draught from his bottle and waving an open cigarette packet under her nose.

'Naw,' she said quietly. 'Thanks, though.'

'Naw – you like real men, eh, men like us!' the youth guffawed, puffing out his thin chest and beating it before rising from his seat to sit next to her. She edged herself towards the window, sliding away from him, but he followed, cramming himself alongside her until their hips touched and she was crushed against the side of the bus. He turned to face her and his breath stank of alcohol and tobacco. But, close up, he was no more than a boy.

'Ye no' fancy me then, hen?'

Exhausted as she was, she prodded her brain into action. If she said that she did fancy him, then God alone knew what he would be up to next. On the other hand, if she said that she did not, then he might take offence, get angry, become more abusive or whatever. And she had not enough energy left to administer the tongue-lashing he deserved. So, in a voice that sounded as weary as she felt, she said softly, 'You're just fine, son. But ah'm auld enough tae be yer maw.'

Her companion pretended to look angry and the other youth, now hunkered down on the seat in front but facing her, grinned and started to wag a finger at his friend. The

dark-haired boy looked at the woman again, experimenting with another furious expression, his teeth clenched
and his jaw jutting out aggressively.

'D'ye think ah fancied ye or somethin', ye auld dug!'
he shouted in her face.

Something else would have to be said, something to
calm him down and end this exchange, otherwise she
would have to leave the bus to escape their attentions,
with three stops still to go and a mile or more to walk.

'Naw, son,' she replied soothingly, 'naw, I ken fine ye
dinnae.' And no wonder, she thought to herself, catching
a glimpse of her reflection in the dark glass. She looked
haggard, more like her mother than herself.

The vehicle's brakes screeched noisily as it drew to a
halt, and the dark-haired boy stood up and swung himself
back into his original seat, slumping down beside his companion. Julie Neilson sighed and rubbed her tired eyes,
then looked hard in the driver's direction in the hope that
someone else would get on the bus, and she would not
be alone with the two youths for any longer. Her prayers
were answered, and a teenage girl, with dirty blonde hair
scraped tight into a ponytail and thick black mascara
under her eyes, stepped aboard and then sashayed up
the aisle to lounge across the back seat. As soon as she
was seated she lit up ostentatiously, looking around her
neighbours and daring anyone to object.

'Whit ye oan the bus fer?' the fair-haired boy enquired
of her, a salacious grin on his face and his eyes resting on
her long bare legs.

'Nae fer a ride wi' either o' yous, ye wee tossers,' she
spat back, flicking her cigarette-ash towards him contemp-
tuously as she spoke. And watching them blush, reduced to
children again, Julie Neilson felt almost sorry for them.

Once inside her flat she opened the door to her daughters' room and tiptoed inside, picking up a primary school skirt and blouse from the floor and hanging them over the back of the chair, for use the next day. Two pairs of miniscule tights had been discarded, one draped over the toy-box and the other suspended from a mobile. She folded them up and put them in the dirty washing box, removing a doll from it at the same time.

In the light falling from the hallway the girls' faces could be clearly seen; one pale with long upturned lashes, her unruly auburn hair spread behind her on the pillow like a lion's mane, and the other a redhead too, but with short, curly locks. Julie Neilson knelt between her children's beds, listening with pleasure for a few seconds as they breathed in and out, before, tenderly, brushing a ringlet from the younger one's brow with her fingers. Gazing at their perfection she felt at peace, blessed even, their presence reminding her that, whatever had gone wrong in her life, something had gone right, something good had come out of it all.

How lucky she had been, how lucky she still was! And might be for a couple of years longer, because ignorance was bliss, and their innocence protected her from herself as well as from the rest of the world. One day they might be ashamed of her, even wish that she was not their mother, but not today or tomorrow. And perhaps, by then, everything would have changed and she would change too, find a job as a shelf-stacker or something. In the meantime they had enough money for school trips, dancing lessons and everything else. Man or no man.

She crept out of their room and into the kitchenette,

starting to brew a cup of hot chocolate, trying Muriel's phone number again while waiting for the milk to boil. As before, she got a ring tone but no answer and, glancing at her watch anxiously, saw that it was past half eleven. If Muriel did not get in contact within the next hour then she would have to call the police, that was the arrangement. No doubt all would be well, her lateness being down to some minor accident or oversight, but with things as they were, or had been, she could take no chances. Not with a life at stake.

Her legs folded beneath her, she nestled into the settee to watch the TV, burning her lips on the boiling cocoa and nearly tipping it onto her lap. Her eyes rested on the screen, but she knew she was taking in nothing, preoccupied, unable to follow the simplest plot. In her head she was busy rehearsing what she should say on the phone, the exact words she would use in describing the punter, and trying her best to remember everything about the man. Screwing up her eyes with the effort, she attempted to create a picture of him, visualise the figure she had seen, but little came. He was big, bulky even, wearing some kind of flapping waterproof with a broad brimmed hat on his head. That was all there was, no name, nothing to identify him or distinguish him from half a million other Johns.

Eventually she stopped trying, convincing herself that she was being melodramatic, overreacting, manufacturing a crisis and enjoying the drama and her own starring part in it. But every few seconds, an insistent voice in her head repeated a single, unanswered question: why has Muriel not called? And, on the stroke of midnight, she found herself talking to a policeman, blurting out all that she knew, sobbing uncontrollably and being comforted by the enemy.

At eight a.m. on the dot, Elaine Bell arrived in her office and triumphantly extracted her mug from its new hiding place behind a pot of African violets. Their sad, dust-encrusted leaves proclaimed that the spot was unvisited by the meddler with her tickling stick. Detective work at its best. She dipped a teaspoon into her yogurt and then sucked it, distractedly, her mind on the complaint made against her and the meeting at two p.m. with the DCC to discuss the outcome of the investigation. Surely, nothing would come of it, at least not if the expression 'free speech' retained any meaning and progress up the greasy pole did not involve the surgical removal of any sense of humour.

And, please God, no counselling this time! The prospect of facing another bright-eyed innocent dispensing the blindingly obvious in the guise of a unique and rare insight was too much to bear. When would they grasp that the problem lay not in an inability to distinguish between an 'appropriate' comment and an 'inappropriate' one, but rather in the challenge of withstanding provocation?

Of course, the sensitivities of the public had to be accorded due regard, but how many of them, she wondered, could have kept silent in the face of the self-righteous spectacle that had confronted her? Looking out of the window, spoon-handle sticking out of her mouth, she visualised the 'complainant', his portly figure now standing before her, hands on his hips and on the edge of apoplexy. A man who had no difficulty finding his way in his simple, black-and-white world and who knew whose side the angels were on. Invariably, his own. And that harmless quip had escaped her lips before her brain had an opportunity to censor it.

Worse still, she thought, it had been the truth. This was rarely, in her experience, a mitigating factor, and not one that she would be sharing with the rest of the force. Chance would, indeed, be a fine thing if a used condom were to be found in her hall or anywhere else within her house. The average octogenarian, if the magazines were to be believed, had a richer, fuller sex life than she did nowadays. And the future seemed every bit as bleak, promising a cuddle-less existence, unpunctuated by kisses, ending in a cold and lonely grave.

She shook her head, trying to ward off the mood of self-pity that was threatening to overwhelm her, and turned her thoughts to practicalities. Obviously, an apology would have to be made and, thinking about it again, she did genuinely regret any offence caused to the man by her 'inappropriate levity', as he had described it in his letter of complaint. Having couples copulating in the common stair and posting their prophylactics through the letter-box would be unpleasant. Yes, saying sorry would be 'appropriate' and, she breathed out loud, she would be prepared to concede the 'inappropriateness' of her crack. Although, when all was said and done, that was all it had been. A crack, a joke, a wry observation, not a very funny one, but at her expense not his. What had happened to 'Laughter, The Best Medicine', she wondered?

As she was about to lick the layer of thick yogurt off the pot's lid, the telephone rang and she dropped it, watching in horror as it landed sticky side down on her letter from the Conduct Department.

After getting the news of the day, in particular that another prostitute was missing, she sat motionless at her desk, her left hand covering her eyes, breathing slowly in and out. Her hour had come. She must summon up all her strength or, all that remained of it, as the race had just changed from a sprint to a marathon. If Muriel McQueen was dead, as now seemed more than likely, then everything had altered, and the eyes of the world would be upon them. And they would all be under the spotlight, its unforgiving radiance revealing every flaw and shortcoming, with nothing to protect them from its heat. Now orders must be given and there was no time to waste, disciplinary meeting or no meeting. She threw the yoghurt pot into the bin, licked the spoon clean and strode out of her room.

Having been sent to Julie Neilson's home by her tight-lipped boss, the first thing that struck Alice on entering it was how unnaturally neat and tidy it all was. The common stair leading up to it was dark and dismal, with two light bulbs broken and the other in a terminal state, flickering uncertainly and making a strange clicking sound. Graffiti adorned the hallway's chocolate-coloured walls, and flakes of peeling paint hung off them like bark on a dying tree. The landings had been sticky, never a good sign, and the stairs leading to them were as unswept as her own.

In contrast to the communal squalor, the flat at number 35 shone like a beacon of domestic pride. All the furniture inside it gleamed as if newly polished, and a spotless cream carpet covered every inch of floor space. Three pairs of shoes, two of them tiny, lay neatly beside the door, and on noticing Julie Neilson's unshod feet, Alice removed her own. The woman herself looked exhausted, drawn and pale, with long features and a down-turned mouth. As soon as Alice sat down, she rose from her chair and, apparently unaware of what she was doing, started plumping up the cushions that she had just crumpled.

'I know you've already spoken to the Sergeant on the telephone,' Alice began, uncomfortable to find herself seated and her hostess standing, 'but we need, if possible, the best description you can give of the man that Muriel went off with last night.'

Julie Neilson nodded, her attention now turned to the curtains, which, although they would have appeared perfect to most onlookers, evidently required some kind of fine adjustment.

'Aha. Ah cannae say much, hen, though. Ah'd some-wan wi' me, so Ah wisnae payin' that much attention tae her fella. Aw Ah can say wis that he wis big, ken, a big strappin' lad.'

'Over six foot?'

'Aye, a wee bit.'

'And his figure?'

'Aha… well built, ken.'

A huge plasma screen in the corner of the room evidently needed to be polished again and Julie Neilson had begun to rub it with a duster, becoming completely absorbed in the task. As she worked, her sleeves fell away from her forearms exposing their underside, and revealing strange textured skin like that of some kind of reptile. The whole area from wrist to elbow was covered in horizontal scars, each touching the other without a millimetre of undamaged flesh between them.

'And his face, his clothes – can you tell me anything about either of those?' Alice asked, unable to take her eyes off the pitiful spectacle.

'Never seen his face… tae far awa' fer that, an' his claithes were normal, like, a big waterproof jacket, grey mebbe, an' he wis wearin' a hat an' a'.'

'What kind of hat?'

'Eh… wan like what the cowboys wear. A… a… a…'
She hesitated, trying to think of the word.

'Stetson?'

'Aye, a Stetson… wi' a broad brim.'

For a few seconds, the woman sat down again next to Alice, indicating with her hands the width of the brim, until her attention was caught by a small pile of magazines on a low table which, plainly, she considered disordered. Instantly, she rose again to remedy the imperfection.

'Did you hear the fellow's voice at all?'

'No, he wis tae far awa'… an' the wind wis roarin' an everythin'.'

Having tidied the offending magazines, the woman returned to Alice and stood in front of her, looking down anxiously into her face. She asked, 'D'ye think she'll be a' right?'

No, Alice thought, but said, 'She may well be fine, and we'll find her. Has this ever happened before, Muriel failing to call you, I mean? You know, having forgotten to phone or something like that?'

'Naw,' the woman shook her head. 'She's like clockwork, ken, that's why Ah paired up wi' her. She's completely reliable – she aye calls.'

‒

Tam McNeice looked up from his drink, saw the policeman marching towards him, put his hand into his crisp packet and took out some crisps. The heads of a couple of drinkers turned towards him, curious, aware that some kind of scene might ensue and unwilling to miss it. One of them raised a glass to him and gave him a cheery wink.

'That was a pack of lies you told me, McNeice,' Inspector Manson said, now standing opposite the man, out of breath and red in the face from recent exertion. 'I've spoken to your neighbours, and they all say they never saw you on the twelfth, that there was no party at your flat.'

'Naw… Ye dinnae say,' McNeice replied, putting a couple of crisps into his mouth.

'Yes, I do fucking say. So where the hell were you?'

'I thought ye might be back. Been wasting yer time, eh, ploddin' up an' doon the stairs an' all, jist when ye'd hae better things tae dae?'

'Aha. But I'll not be wasting any more of it here, I'll just take you off to the station this minute, you wee bastard.'

Coolly taking a sip of his beer, McNeice replied, 'Then ye'll get promotion, eh? Takin' in the Leith Killer…' and he raised his hands and clawed them like a grizzly bear, a big smirk on his face, 'all by yersel', an' a'.'

Conscious suddenly that everyone in the pub now seemed to be listening to their exchange, some of them gathering round for ringside seats, Eric Manson asked, in a slightly more conciliatory tone, 'Just tell me where you were on the night of the twelfth, eh?'

'Well, big fellow… luckily, it's a' comin' back tae me the noo. I wis havin' ma time wasted by yous people. The twelfth is ma birthday, like I says, an' I wis to be havin' a pairty in ma hoose, but I got merry that little bit early, in the morn, an' you know what? Some soddin' polisman took me down tae the cells in Portobello. So there was no pairty like what I had planned, an' I wasted ma time in the pokey. Sorry aboot that, ma memory's nae whit it wis. If ye've any puff left, go tae the polis office doon the street and they'll tell ye that. Spent a' day an' a' night there. And whit's mair, ye can believe them, eh?'

Driving to the Seafield cemetery to assist DC Littlewood in searching the place, Alice cursed her own carelessness. In her haste to leave the flat, following the DCI's call, she had forgotten to pick up her coat and could see it, in her mind's eye, still hanging on its hook in the hall. She turned, briefly, to check the back seat in case she had made a mistake and saw on it Simon Oakley's oversized anorak. It would have to do, she thought, and it would be considerably warmer than her own coat. He would not mind.

As she pushed open the car door, a shower of hail appeared from nowhere, and after waiting a couple of minutes in the hope that it would stop, she put on the large padded jacket. She quickly zipped it up before taking the plunge into the cold, hostile air. In the far distance she could just make out her colleague, looking methodically from side to side as he patrolled, shoulders hunched against the cold, hailstones ricocheting off his head and shoulders. She set off, trudging between the first row of gravestones, alert to anything and everything, and followed the line of stones towards the boundary wall. After five minutes she reached the path at the northern end and turned back, into the wind, to march down a parallel row. Half way along the second corridor, one of the memorials caught her eye.

The stone had been carved from black granite, gold lettering naming the deceased, and in its shadow was a strange little shrine. Within a glass case were two teddy bears, each leaning against an arm of a crucified Christ, their paws clasping a miniature bottle of scotch to their fat little bellies. While she was standing in front of them, wondering at their oddity and curious about the individual commemorated, she noticed a collecting box with

'Alcoholics Anonymous' printed on it. Without thought she put her hand into her coat pocket in search of any loose change, her fingers scrabbling around to find any coins, but found, instead, a small, irregular-shaped item together with something circular. Head bowed to protect her face from the hailstones, she examined the objects in the dull morning light. One was a yellow smiley badge with an oversized pin as a catch, and the other was a small gold crucifix. The sight of it frightened her.

As the cross still rested in her palm, DC Littlewood's voice rang out from near the crematorium, carrying faintly over the noise of the gale now rising around them.

'I've finished my area, Sarge, and there's nothing here. Have you found anything yet?'

'No,' she bellowed back, still thinking, twiddling the cross between her fingers and finding it hard to tear her attention from it. Eventually she made up her mind, and added, 'I've got one other thing to check over, Tom, then I'll come and join you.'

⟡

The exact spot where Isobel Wilson's body had been discovered was not hard to locate. Countless feet had trodden a path to it, and a couple of bunches of roses, their blooms now brown and shrivelled and the wrapping paper in tatters, lay where the woman had rested. Without a covering of snow to simplify everything, the large, burial ground looked shabbier and smaller than before, but the overgrown bed in which the body had been hidden remained distinctive, a bedraggled, wind-lashed mess in amongst the stillness of the manicured lawns. Instinctively, Alice began to walk through it, hurrying in the cold and feeling the rough grass brushing against her legs again, receiving an occasional jab from some wood-stemmed weed or dying nettle, but seeing and feeling no brambles. Twice more she forced herself to walk through the bed, vigilant for their looped barbs or any other prickly vegetation, but found nothing capable of inflicting a cut or scratch on anyone. And she was not wearing trousers.

'Alice… Alice!' It was DC Littlewood again, his voice louder than before, desperate to be heard above the roar of the wind.

'Yes? Hang on a sec, I'm just coming.'

'That was the boss on the phone. They've found her. A uniform's with the body. It's past the turn-off to Fillyside Road, on waste ground at the end of the prom. We're to set off there this minute.'

———

The young constable's lips were blue, his arms clasped tightly around himself, hugging his torso in an attempt to stop his spasmodic shivering and warm himself up. His head was bare, a sudden gust from the North Sea having whipped his cap off, and he had watched helplessly from his position by the corpse as his headgear bowled its way along the cliff edge before dropping into the turbid waters below. Each successive wave had then carried it a little further out until, finally, he had lost sight of the little black speck and, reluctantly, turned his attention back to the woman lying at his feet.

The job in the force was not turning out to be quite as he had visualised it. He had seen himself as the centre of attention, the first to find the corpse, stolen goods or whatever, but he had overlooked other matters. Important matters, like the weather, the inadequate, ill-fitting gear and the general discomfort that seemed to be part and parcel of his new profession. Still, he would have cracking stories to tell in the pub one day, but, first, he would have to steel himself to take a good shufty, impress upon his memory all the gory details for the delectation of others in days to come. And, this time, the sight of blood would not make him faint and he could stare at her as much as he pleased, no offence being taken by the dead.

Looking hard at the woman's face, he was struck by the thought that, in life, she must have been pretty with such large eyes and high cheekbones. Gradually, he allowed his gaze to slide down from her chin to her neck, then, slowly, to descend to her breasts. Taking things bit by bit would be the answer, and this time there would be no element of surprise. But the sight once more of the unnatural cleft on her chest, clotted blood fringing its edges, made his gorge rise, and he bent over, convulsed, to vomit onto the ground beside her. Swallowing hard, and deliberately inhaling the icy air deep in his lungs to purify himself, he straightened up and stood erect, shocked by his own weakness and alarmed at the trembling that had begun in his legs. Feeling another upsurge of bile into his mouth, he tried to shift his mind and distract himself, fixing his eyes on the horizon and following its perfect line past the Cockenzie Power Station and onwards towards Aberlady Point. Never letting his gaze fall. When the CID arrived he was still standing with his head erect, looking seawards like an old salt unable to tear himself away from the sight.

Suited and booted in her paper overalls and overshoes, Alice knelt beside the body to examine it, noticing immediately the wound to the breast and the crossed arms, both

226

trademarks with which she was sickeningly familiar. One of the fingers of the right hand had blood at its tip and she stretched over the torso to examine it more closely, finding dried blood on its sharp, uneven nail. Perhaps, in death, the woman had scratched her attacker, taking a minute piece of him with her and leaving him marred for a day or two at least.

Alice closed her eyes and breathed out slowly, a sinking feeling now in her stomach, increasingly unnerved by the conclusion to which she seemed to be being driven. No journalist had been told about the attitude of prayer in which the victims were invariably found, so no paper had reported the detail and it remained a secret known to two parties only, the police and the murderer. Whoever had killed Muriel McQueen had also killed Isobel Wilson and Annie Wright, and it was not Father Francis McPhail.

And the conclusion that was forming in her mind was one that she was loath to reach, disliked herself for even considering. But it was also one which could not be ignored, however much she might wish that she had never reached it. The pieces of the puzzle were slowly fitting together, but the picture that they were forming scared her, making her doubt her own judgement.

Simon Oakley's blood was on both bodies, and its presence on the first, she now knew, could not be satisfactorily explained by contamination. There had been no brambles near the body so some alternative explanation for it must be sought. Furthermore, he appeared to fit the descriptions given by the majority of the witnesses and twice had pled illness, his absence each time bringing about a particular result. It meant that Lena Stirling, the only victim to survive an attack and therefore able to describe her attacker, had not seen him since. She had never had the opportunity either to recognise or identify him. Had he really been sick, or was it simply a ruse to avoid the prostitute's scrutiny? On both occasions on which he had used his health as an excuse to absent himself he had not seemed even remotely off-colour, and his order at the Raj suggested an unimpaired constitution.

And if he was the murderer, then Lena Stirling had been right when she had said that she had met her assailant before, because they had sat together in a police car the day after the first murder, never mind any earlier meetings. And here she was touching a gold crucifix, found in his pocket, and bearing a remarkable resemblance to the one she had seen around Annie Wright's neck throughout McNiece's trial. But the idea that she was, even to herself, accusing one of her colleagues, filled her with dread. Immediately she began to try to unpick her own case.

To be sure, she reassured herself, it was based on little or no evidence and much speculation. It could probably be explained away, and would probably not even have been reached by a less tired mind. Please God, an innocent answer would be forthcoming for everything. After all, lots of people owned crucifixes, brambles could be cut down and she, herself, had seen his blood dripping in the scrappie's yard. And Ian had a tummy bug this very morning.

Kneeling down again, she studied the body beside her, her attention drawn once more by the bloodstained fingernail on the right hand. Whoever had killed Muriel McQueen might have a small reminder of their encounter on his face. Conscious that her paper suit was beginning to get soggy at the knees, she rose to go and walked slowly towards the car, unzipping the garment as she went until the wind found its way inside and made it billow in all directions, transforming her into a Tellytubby. Still deep in thought, she dropped the crumpled mess into the boot and hesitated, leaning against the driver's door, trying to work out what to do next. The blood on the woman's nail, if that was what it was, might provide samples of the murderer's DNA, but the extraction process, never mind the subsequent matching, would take time. And meanwhile the guilty man, whoever he was, remained at liberty, able to kill once more, his escape possible. As every second ticked past, his trail would be getting colder.

But the accusation she was making was so awful that she could tell no-one of her suspicions, not while that was all they were, all they might ever be. It was shameful to harbour such thoughts about another member of the squad, the DCI's team, her own team. She was not sure that she would ever forgive anyone who considered that she could be guilty of such acts. On reflection, she knew she would not.

Shifting her weight from foot to foot, she looked out to sea and found herself calmed by its immensity, reassured by the sight of the endless breaking waves with their crests of white foam colliding with each other before running to the shore, all anger spent. Of course, thoughts in themselves neither harmed nor defamed anybody, and could be quickly forgotten by the thinker. But, she reminded herself, this one, however hare-brained, would have to be translated into deeds, because in the unlikely event of it turning out to be correct and nothing being done, then another woman might be attacked, might be killed. There was no easy option, and even the least bad alternative, alienation from one or more of her colleagues, required action.

And, fortunately, she had a pretext to take a look at Simon Oakley. His jacket was lying on the back seat of the Astra, folded neatly, ready to be returned to him. She would go to his flat, hand it over to him, and while doing so, take a good look at his face. If it remained smooth and uninjured as before, then her flight of fancy would be over, and he need never know the unworthy doubts that she had entertained. Within a day or so the results of the DNA would come in and he would, presumably, be exculpated. And for as long as they continued to work together, he would be mystified by her thoughtfulness, her solicitousness on his behalf. Because, come what may, she would find a way of making it up to him somehow.

But, standing outside the bright purple front door of Simon Oakley's flat in McDonald Road she could feel her stomach starting to churn, the urge to return to the car almost getting the better of her. If she left, then no-one need ever know her dirty little secret. She turned to go but managed to stop herself, facing the door again and forcing herself to knock, deliberately losing control of the situation. Seconds crawled past, and feeling giddy with relief she was just about to leave when she heard the sound of heavy footsteps approaching and the door swung open. To her surprise, an elderly woman stood in front of her wearing a pinny over her skirt, and evidently having just peeled off one of her rubber gloves before turning the door handle.

'Are you lookin' for Simon?' the stranger enquired in a cockney accent, pulling the other glove over her thick wrist to reveal a reddened hand.

'Yes,' Alice replied, 'I'm one of his colleagues.'

'He's out at the moment, but he'll be back shortly. You could wait here if you like?'

'How shortly is shortly?'

The woman looked at her watch. 'Oh, within the next five minutes or so, I expect. I haven't seen him this morning, he wasn't here when I arrived, but he's bound to be back before one o'clock. He knows that I have a hair appointment at half past, and he left a note saying he'd gone to the bank to get my money. I'm Sue by the way…' she held out her damp hand, 'and I clean for him once a fortnight.'

Sitting at the kitchen table, exchanging occasional words with the cleaner, Alice felt ill at ease, apprehensive about what was to come. In the meanwhile, the situation seemed more than slightly surreal, absurd. Here she was being offered tea while the cleaner busied herself sorting the underpants of a putative murderer into piles of coloureds and non-coloureds. On the other hand, Alice also felt reassured by her homely presence, the smell of washing powder and the ordinariness of her domestic routines. As long as Sue was present then she was surely safe, whatever she was going to see, and whatever Oakley observed in her.

At the sound of the front door opening Alice rose, but found herself waved back to her seat by Sue and thought better of her initial movement, maybe it would not be him anyway. Two voices in conversation could be heard from the hallway, the woman's tone rising as if in surprise, followed by sympathetic clucking noises, then Simon's voice and, finally, the ominous click of a key being turned in a lock. And at that final noise her heart began to hammer frantically in her chest, as if trying to beat its way out of her body through her rib cage. Now she was on her own with him and, for some reason, he had blocked her escape. As he walked through the doorway he looked her straight in the eyes, watching her watching him.

On his cheek there was a small, almost invisible scratch, dried blood still on it.

Holding out his jacket for him, she asked, as casually as she was able, 'How d'you get the cut, Simon?'

His hand went up to it and, still feeling its texture, he replied, 'Shaving, this morning.'

She looked at his face. Evidently, he had not had a razor anywhere near it since the previous day, dark stubble still covering his cheeks and chin, and the cut was at least an inch above the highest point of any beard growth. For an instant, he shielded the injury, hiding it playfully with his palm before letting his arm drop, and smiling.

'Your jacket, Simon,' she said, thrusting it towards him, praying that her hand would not tremble and betray the fear that she felt weakening her. But, ignoring her wishes, it shook violently, and as it did so his eyes remained on hers, until, eventually, he took the garment from her The first thing he did was to search the pockets, and from the right one he extracted the smiley badge.

'And the cross?' he said slowly.

'What do you mean?' she asked.

'Come, come, Alice. You know there should be a crucifix in there. But, I have to say, you're slipping up.'

'I'm still not with you.'

'Well, I'll explain shall I? You've given me back the badge – the very thing I cut myself on when I was getting rid of Ms Wilson. Obviously, I took it away with me… you would wouldn't you? But, unfortunately, I'd left a little calling card on her jacket. Still, we explained it away didn't we? And you can imagine how pleased I was with that cut at the scrappie's. I knew it would cover a multitude of sins, if I had slipped up again, I mean.'

Alice said nothing, and her silence seemed to annoy him.

'Are you afraid of something, Alice?' he asked in a mocking tone. 'Me, perhaps? You and me together, by ourselves, in my house?'

'No,' she lied, 'but I am cold. I've been out in freezing weather searching around Leith and Portobello for…'

'Muriel. That's her name, apparently, if you can believe a thing they say. And you found her, I suppose – at the end of the prom? I somehow thought I would have a little longer, a day at least. But, then, you're sharp, eh? And now you're scared of me, too.'

From her chair she glanced up at him, still at loss for words, unsure how his mind was working.

'Yes, Alice,' he said, again looking her straight in the eyes. 'You are right. I did do it.'

'Why?' Her voice sounded weak, exhausted and old. And she knew she had wandered out of her depth, into realms far beyond her understanding.

'You would like there to be a reason, wouldn't you? You want… you need… the universe to be well-ordered and logical, and everything in it, too. But, suppose it isn't like that? Maybe it's completely unpredictable, uncontrollable whether by you or anyone else. And monsters don't always look monstrous, do they? Myra's image… quite ordinary when divorced from her history, I expect. You, of all people, should appreciate that, being in the force I mean.'

She nodded, her mind having shifted onto other things, concerned to conceal the fact that she was raking the room with her eyes, searching it for anything she could use as a weapon. After all, it made no sense for him to confess and then let her go. Her gaze alighted on a meat tenderiser resting on a chopping board and, transfixed by it, she did not hear his last few words.

'Alice!' he said sharply.

She looked up at him again, and seeing that he had her attention, he continued. 'It is a possibility – complete disorder, I mean. But people like you have to make connections, false connections of course, but ones that provide you with comfort and an illusion of order. Otherwise you couldn't cope, eh? But that's not how life really is. Think about it, if I'd stopped at two, an innocent man would have borne the blame, wouldn't he? Cruelty regularly rewards kindness and evil often blooms from good roots, doesn't it? Look at me, eh? You liked me, maybe considered me a friend even? But I'm a bad, bad man.'

She shook her head, unable fully to comprehend what he was saying, but desperate to keep him talking while she tried to calm herself, make some kind of plan. 'Maybe, or maybe there's no such thing. Some people are born blind, eyeless, without retinas or optic nerves. Perhaps others arrive in this world without normal consciences, souls or whatever. Without pity…'

He laughed uproariously, confident, at ease with himself and everything under his control. No stammer troubling him now. 'So, no-one's to blame, eh? That's lucky for me. No one should be punished either, just treated perhaps, an odd view from a policeman. Good news, I'm sure. And, presumably, the more heinous the crime…'

'The more abnormal the perpetrator,' she interrupted him, catching his drift, 'the less their culpability. Because then they are clearly sick, not bad.'

'And this line, Alice, between normal badness and abnormal badness, where is it drawn? Where do you draw it?' he asked, walking to a knife-block on the kitchen unit and coolly, in front of her unblinking eyes, drawing out a black-handled knife.

'A little biff to the wife and you're responsible, but gouge her eyes out and you're not?' he continued, beaming at her and waving his weapon about. Then suddenly he stopped, stood still, and felt the point of the blade with his fingers.

'Anyway, you said you'd like to know the truth Alice? Why I did it, I mean? Are you quite sure you want to know?'

'No, I don't want to know,' she said quietly, and she meant it. She no longer wanted to know the truth, even if he was privy to it and prepared to share it with her, and neither seemed probable. If she was about to die, such knowledge would do her no good, and survival with it would be no boon. Too much reality for anyone. But it was a rhetorical question. He was not interested in her wishes, had rehearsed his justification far too often for there to be no performance.

'I did it because if the whores are not there, then no one will be tempted by them. No-one will fall from grace, descend to their level. Like McPhail did, for a start, he must have been all over them whatever he told us. I cross their arms so that when they meet their maker, they appear penitent. And killing them is a kindness, really, for them, I mean. What kind of life do they lead, eh? If they were animals the RSPCA would have something to say about it... doped, drunken and dirty. They're like a controlled drug, only they're not controlled and the substance itself has feelings – well, of some sort. And they're just as destructive as smack or whatever. Breaking up families, my own dad...'

He went on and on, justifying himself, attempting to provide a rational explanation and then realising that he had contradicted an earlier argument, starting all over again. And although his speech was entirely intelligible, its coherence could not disguise the underlying chaos of his thoughts.

Still speaking, he moved towards her. Seeing the blade now so close, she felt her whole body tense, her mind alert to everything, ready to respond to his slightest movement. And time no longer mattered, no longer governed anything, its passage an irrelevance. As he lunged at her, she sprang towards the chopping board and seized the tenderiser, swinging it at his hand and bringing it crashing down onto his knuckles. Roaring with pain, he dropped the knife and turned to face her squarely, his features suffused with anger. She swung the mallet again, but as she brought it down, aiming now for his head, he caught her wrist in mid-movement. With his free hand he grabbed her neck, kicking away one of her legs with his own.

Immediately, she felt herself falling, crashing to the ground, her skull catching the edge of the chair and his whole weight crunching on top of her. It's over, she thought, pinned down by his body, breathless and winded, and feeling his hands as they tried to link with each other around her throat, preparing to throttle her.

Somewhere at the back of her mind she heard a distant clicking sound, then footsteps, and sensed that someone else had entered the room, but the effort involved in staying conscious was becoming too much for her. The air seemed to be alive with shouting, but when she tried to scream, to draw attention to herself, all she heard was a dry moaning noise coming from her throat, more like a death-rattle than anything else.

Suddenly, a loud crack vibrated in the air, and Simon Oakley's head fell forwards, lolling onto hers. She squirmed, desperate to rid herself of him and his clammy face. His skin was sticking to hers, and revolted at the very thought she closed her eyes and held her breath. A serpent's scales touching her cheek would have been more welcome.

A few seconds later she became aware that someone was rolling the dead weight of his body off her, and looking up she saw a young woman, a wine bottle still in her hand, peering down at her with a look of intense anxiety on her face.

'Are you all right?' the stranger asked.

'I think so,' Alice said, slowly heaving the rest of herself out from under her attacker's leaden limbs and fingering her neck, hardly able to believe that it had not been broken or squeezed out of shape.

'Who are you?' she added, her voice sounding hoarse and unfamiliar.

'Fiona Shenton. I used to be his girlfriend,' the stranger replied. And so saying, she dropped the bottle onto the floor and collapsed onto the sofa, covering her pale face with both of her hands.

'Well, Fiona, thank you very much. You saved my life.'

—

With the engine of the ambulance revving outside and a paramedic attending to the concussed figure of Simon Oakley in the back, DC Littlewood was pressganged into escorting him to the Royal Infirmary. He grumbled loudly that he had been up all night and that a replacement should be found. Anyone could do the job, he said crossly, climbing into the ambulance and continuing to complain to the crew as the vehicle indicated right and then pulled out into the sluggish traffic on Leith Walk, heading for Little France.

In the lull before the DCI and the SOCOS arrived Alice sat down again. Everything had begun to hurt and the base of her skull seemed to have tightened around her brain. One side of her throat was throbbing, a painful pulse shooting through it every millisecond. Her rescuer leant against the arm of the sofa, drained of all colour and apprehensive, unable to leave until a statement had been taken from her. Her nails had already been bitten to the quick but she continued to worry at them, in search of any loose skin.

Conscious of her anxiety and keen to soothe it, Alice tried to think what to say to calm her and help her pass the time until they were free to go.

'You were very resourceful with the wine bottle...' she began.

'I just grabbed whatever I could see, lucky that it came to hand. I've never hit anyone before, you know, never mind knocked them out. At first I tried to pull him off you, but he knocked me backwards...' The woman rubbed her shoulder-blade, then patted it as if it had taken the impact from a fall.

'How did you manage to get into the flat?'

'Keys. I've still got my own key. I came to collect my stuff, I thought that the coast would be clear, that he'd be out at work.' She bit her lip, chin now trembling.

'We don't need to talk,' Alice said gently. 'Maybe you'd prefer not to?'

'No, I'd rather we did. Somehow it makes things seem more normal.'

'Of course. Do you mind me asking what Simon was like?'

'I don't really know. It was all lovely to begin with…
But after I moved in, after a couple of months I mean, he
changed. It ended, well, when he hit me. It was so unexpected. Up until then he'd been so gentle. He's always
so kind to his mum, and I thought he'd be like that with
me…'

'But she's dead – and he didn't get on with her!' Alice
interrupted, startled by the final remark.

'Yes, she's dead,' Fiona Shenton nodded, clearly surprised by the sergeant's reaction, 'but only very recently.
And he adored her to the end, visited her every day at the
home until she died. And she loved him to bits, too.'

'That's not what he told me,' Alice replied, remembering vividly one of their earliest conversations.

'No?' The woman chewed on her fingernails again.
'You don't surprise me. You see, he played games with
people, manipulated them… enjoyed seeing what he
could get them to do. Told one person one thing, and
another, another. But in amongst the lies, he usually
threw in an occasional, unexpected truth… dared them
to be able to tell the difference. He thought it was funny,
and he didn't mind what he risked by disclosing it. An
intimate truth disguised as a joke or a throwaway line. No
one would ever know.'

With her hand massaging her neck, Alice asked, 'When
did you break up with him, leave him?'

'Er…' Fiona hesitated, clearly thinking. 'It would have
been about the sixth of January or so.'

With a couple of photographers now bustling around
them, and feeling too wan to think or speak, Alice headed
towards the front door, intending to walk the short distance home to Broughton Place. Mobile clamped firmly
to her ear, Elaine Bell signalled for her to wait, then held

something out in her hand for Alice's inspection. It was a polythene bag containing a wedding ring, like that normally worn by the second murder victim. Alice tried to smile, recognising the grotesque memento immediately and fully aware of its likely significance at the man's trial. Instead, against her will, she felt tears forming in her eyes and quickly brushed them away, unwilling to let the DCI witness her weakness. Then, remembering the gold crucifix that she had found in her colleague's jacket, she took it from her pocket, handing it mutely to her superior in the sure knowledge that she, too, would recognise its importance. Immediately, Elaine Bell ended her telephone call and put an arm around her sergeant's shoulder.

'It's a red letter day, Alice' she said smiling broadly.

'I know…'

'Really? You heard that the complaint against me had been dismissed, too?'

—

Mrs Foscetti twirled a small handbag by her side as she dithered along the pavement in fits and starts like a little bird. She was dressed in a navy skirt with lemon piping around the cuffs and collar, and had an amber brooch pinned to her breast. Once inside Alice's car she settled down in the seat, inspecting her face in the passenger's mirror and smoothing her skirt over her bony knees.

As they were driving out of Milnathort the old lady pointed to various places, intent upon interesting Alice and keen to find out a little about her sister's friend. A church they passed was immediately written off as 'an impostor'. Mystified, Alice enquired why she regarded it in that light. In reply her companion simply said, 'Their services, dear

– no foot washing on Thursdays, you understand,' as if that provided sufficient explanation. After that short speech she flashed a bright grin, and nodded her head vigorously several times. As Loch Leven came into view, she bent down and took her knitting from her bag and started to click her needles with great speed and dexterity. The knitwear she was making was a sweet pink in colour and appeared to be some kind of bootee, so Alice asked her if it was destined for a grandchild.

'No,' Mrs Foscetti replied, her tongue flicking in and out with concentration. 'I have none. No children either. Charlie and me… well, very quickly we were rather more like babes in the wood than Anthony and Cleopatra, if you get my drift. It's for my friend's new granddaughter.'

'Yes, I see,' said Alice, non-committally. 'And what did you and Charlie do, your jobs, I mean, if you don't mind me asking?'

'Not at all, dear.' She was frowning, concentrating hard on not dropping a stitch. 'We opened a dragonfly museum in Didsbury. He came from Manchester, you know, and he was a real enthusiast, loved the Scarlet Darter particularly. After hours, he used to dance about the place singing like a big lark, unable to believe his own good fortune. Entrance to it would've been free if he'd had his way, but,' she added, fingers still engaged in fevered activity, 'of course, we had to eat.'

'How did you meet him?'

'Morag brought him home with her, like you would a stray dog. Actually, she's always preferred dogs to people,' she laughed. 'But as it turned out, I was the retriever. I retrieved him from her – you could say I whippet him away from her! She drowned her sorrows in a Great Dane called Whisky and his companion, Brandy. It was a *ménage a trois…*' She burbled on, amusing herself and giggling all the while.

Once they entered the tenement, the old lady's spare frame made light work of the stairs, an emaciated claw sliding up the banisters as her highly polished shoes clacked their staccato way on the stone steps. Following the instructions given by Alice in the course of their journey, she waited patiently on the landing directly below her sister's flat as her escort went to knock on Miss Spinnell's door. After the usual cacophony of clicks and thuds, Miss Spinnell's small face peeped from behind her fortress door, eyes wary and a slight scowl turning down her mouth. Seeing Alice, she straightened herself up to her full five feet and stepped out on to the landing to greet her.

'So, Ali… dear, what do you want?'

Despite the note through her letterbox, dropped by Alice earlier that morning to warn her of an impending visit by a VIP, the ensemble sported by her was as eccentric as ever. She wore an oversized mauve beret, a canary yellow cardigan, elasticated slacks and carpet slippers.

'Well,' Alice began, pleased to be the bearer of good news at last. 'You know I told you about your sister…'

'Of course, I've not lost my wits you know,' Miss Spinnell said, impatiently.

'Well…' Alice tried again, 'I'm delighted to be able to tell you that she's alive, not dead as you thought. No, she's very much alive and…'

'Nonsense!' Miss Spinnell cut in. 'I've spoken to her on the other side. And she came across, clear as a bell!'

'Morag… Morag!' A piercing voice could be heard coming from the stairwell.

'In fact,' Miss Spinnell said, completely unperturbed, a complacent smile transforming her face, 'I can hear her this very minute.'

'Yes,' Alice answered, 'so can I. She's here, you see, in this building. Waiting for you –'. But before she had finished her sentence the sound of Mrs Foscetti's sharp little heels could be heard tapping their way up the stairs and within seconds she had bobbed up onto her sister's landing. There she stood, clapping her hands and grinning merrily. Then she extended her arms as if expecting an embrace, face proffered, and waited patiently for her sister to react.

'Annabelle,' Miss Spinnell said in a stand-offish tone, arms tight to her sides, 'how lovely to see you.'

Giving Alice a large wink, Mrs Foscetti clasped her twin in a huge hug, ignoring her very obvious distaste and planting several kisses on her papery cheek. Then, beaming in delight at the success of the reunion, she blew Alice a kiss as well. Miss Spinnell, with an expression that said that Alice was really *her* friend, stiffly followed suit. A real red letter day.